THE HERO

ROBYN CARR

THE HERO

HARLEQUIN® MIRA®

ISBN-13: 978-1-62490-703-6

THE HERO

Printed in U.S.A.

It's with pride and gratitude that I dedicate this book to Terri and Dave Miller, forever heroes in my eyes and to countless other people.

One

Devon McAllister walked down a tree-lined back road, not really sure where she was but certain that she was far away from the family compound. She felt safe enough that she no longer took cover when she heard a vehicle approach. She'd been walking for at least eight hours and saw the first rays of light coming over the mountains behind her. This reassured her that she was traveling west, toward the coast. She carried her three-year-old daughter, Mercy, and a backpack stuffed with a few items of clothing and forty dollars that had been given to her by the kindhearted stranger who had given her a ride.

She was exhausted but would not stop to rest until she reached Highway 101. Every so often she would put Mercy down and hold her hand, but that made the walking unbearably slow. When she heard a vehicle, she just kept her head down, staring at the ground.

It was a truck—it drove past them, but then it stopped up ahead. It was cranberry-red and old, but in mint condition. A man got out and yelled to her. "Miss? Need a ride?"

She walked toward the vehicle. "Am I close to Highway 101?" she asked.

"I'm going that way. I'm on my way to work," he said. "I can give you a lift."

He was an older guy. He wore a red, white and blue ball cap and his cheeks and chin were stubbled in places that he'd missed with his razor. Though it was June, he wore a jacket. The early morning was misty, which told her she must be in a valley near the Pacific. "Where are you headed?" Devon asked.

"Thunder Point," he said. "It's a very small town on the coast in Coos County. I work at a beach bar and I open the place in time for breakfast. Been there a few years now. It's mostly fishing towns around there."

Well, she'd gotten out of Douglas County, but she wasn't sure where Coos County was. She didn't know where anything was—she rarely left the compound and had never been to any of the small coastal towns. Still, she knew that Highway 101 stretched as far north and south as she needed to get. Highway 5 was bigger and closer to the compound and if anyone was looking for a couple of runaways hitching rides, they'd probably start there. "How close to 101 is your town?"

"Plenty close. Want me to drop you there?"

She walked toward the truck. "Thanks," she said. "You're sure?"

"No trouble," he said.

She put her backpack in the truck bed. Holding Mercy on her lap, she buckled them in together. She kept her head down, her hands tucked between her knees.

"Name's Rawley Goode," he said. She said nothing. "You got a name?"

"Devon," Devon said. She shouldn't use her real name. What if someone came poking around, asking if anyone had seen a woman named Devon? But she was almost too tired to lie. Not to mention nervous. At least she hadn't said Sister Devon.

"Well, you're not an escaped convict, are you, Devon?" he asked.

She looked at him. "Is there a prison around here?"

He smiled. "Just kidding," he said. "Where you headed?"

For lack of a better answer she said, "Seattle. Eventually."

He whistled. "You're a long ways from there. What brings you to this old back road?"

She shrugged. "It's where I was dropped off, but I'm heading for 101."

"You hitchin' rides?"

She nodded. Her ride over the mountain had been planned, but was kept secret. "Yes, 101 will have more traffic," she said.

"Unless the police see you. Then it could get complicated."

"I'll watch."

Devon wasn't really headed to Seattle, but she just said that because that was where she came from originally. She thought there might be a shelter or charity of some kind in one of the bigger towns on the coast. "I don't know this area very well. Is there a town or city near Highway 101 that's pretty big? Big enough that it might have a shelter or maybe a hostel?" she asked him.

"Couple," Rawley replied. "Listen, I have an idea. You decide exactly where you need to go and I'll fix you up with transportation. How's that?"

"Why?" she asked suspiciously. "Why would you do that?"

"I been in your spot, hitchin' rides, lookin' for the easiest way to get from here to there, takin' a little help sometimes. I normally went to the VA when I needed a little assistance." He paused. "You got room for a little breakfast? 'Cause that's my job in the morning—perking the coffee, warming up egg sandwiches, watching the sun come over the mountains. It's not far from the highway, neither. I could show you a map while you and the little one eat something."

"No, thank you. I have a couple of apples for later."

"I know that look of no money," he said. "Been wearin' it and seein' it for forty years now. No charge for the map. Or the breakfast. Then I'll give you a ride to wherever you need to go to catch your next ride. It ain't no gamble. I admit, I ain't always been the best person in the world, but I ain't yet done nobody harm. You can hang on to those apples."

Rawley didn't know for certain, but he was pretty sure the young woman was from The Fellowship—a small religious compound along the river in Douglas County. She was wearing their "uniform" or "habit" of overalls, sturdy shoes, long-sleeved T-shirt with one button at the neck and a long, thick, single braid down her back. He'd donated to the group a couple of times himself and had noticed that the women were all attired the same while the few men in evidence all wore their own combinations of jeans, plaid or chambray shirts, hats and down vests. A few months back, when Cooper had been renovating the old bait shop and turning it into a first-rate bar and café, Rawley had taken the used industrial-size washers and dryers, along with a lot of kitchen wares they couldn't use, over to The Fellowship compound.

They were a private bunch, but he knew they had a roadside stand near their compound where they sold produce, quilts and woven goods. He'd only stopped once and had seen a group of them gathered around the stall, the women doing the business and the men helping with the heavy work, but mainly just presiding over everything. And he'd seen a few of them wandering around the Farmers' Market in Myrtle Creek where they sometimes had a stand, again the women together in a tight knot and the men following along or standing behind them, watching.

He had never given the group a second thought until this morning when he found the young woman and her child walking down the deserted road at dawn. Now he wondered what that group was all about. Beautiful, young, smiling, soft-spoken women apparently watched over by big, silent men who were clearly in charge.

The girl seemed skittish, so Rawley played his cards close to his vest. As they drove the twenty minutes to the beach at Thunder Point he kept the conversation light, only saying things like *Gonna be a right fine day* and *Fog'll burn off the water early today* and *Should get up around seventy degrees, and that's a heat wave on the ocean.*

She kept very quiet, offering the occasional *Mmm-hmm* but nothing more. Her little girl rested her head on her mother's shoulder and a couple of times they whispered quietly to each other. As they drove down the hill toward the bar she saw, for the first time, the beach sheltered by the rocky coastline, the bay studded with giant rocks and the fog at the mouth of the bay just lifting. All she said was, "Wow."

"Pretty, ain't she?" Rawley replied.

Moments later they arrived at the bar. Rawley parked out back behind the building and used his key to open the place up. It was 6:00 a.m.

"Come on inside, sit up at the bar and I'll put on the coffee and heat up some eggs. Got some fruit, too. And Cooper, the owner, he likes his Tony Tigers—you or the little one like Frosted Flakes?"

"Anything is very generous," she said. "And appreciated."

"Like I said, I passed your way plenty of times. I got a lot to pay back."

As he turned to get things started, Rawley noticed the coffee was already brewing. He looked out the window and saw a lone man out on the still bay on a paddleboard. That would be Cooper, getting in a little early morning exercise. And as he watched, a Razor ATV came across the beach with a big black-and-white Great Dane riding shotgun—Sarah, Cooper's woman, must have a day off from the Coast Guard.

Good, he thought. Cooper and Sarah would be out on the water for a while. That would give him enough time to figure out what to do with Devon. Because obviously something needed to be done. A woman and a small child with a single backpack out walking the back roads at dawn with no money and no plan… It didn't take a genius…

He wet a cloth with warm water and handed it to Devon in case she wanted to wipe the grime of the road from her hands and face, and she did so. Then wiped off her daughter's hands and face, muttering a very soft "thank you" as she put down the cloth.

Rawley got started with the food. He put out a fruit plate, a box of Frosted Flakes, two bowls, utensils, a carton of milk, a couple of small glasses. Then he pulled two egg sandwiches out of the cooler and popped them in the microwave.

Devon served her little girl, sharing everything. When the egg sandwiches arrived she gave voice to her thoughts—"So much food."

"Traveling makes a person hungry," Rawley said. And then he poured himself a cup of coffee. While they tucked into their breakfast he wandered out to the deck to think. He wanted to see where Cooper and Sarah were, and give Devon and her little girl time to get some food in their stomachs. If he watched them eat, they'd try not to eat too much—a man who'd been hungry and had taken charity knew this.

Hamlet, the Great Dane, was tied to the dock while Sarah paddled out to join Cooper on the bay. Rawley propped open the doors to the deck so Cooper would know he was on duty and that the place was open for business. A few moments later as he stood on the deck with his cup of coffee, Cooper waved. Rawley lifted a hand back. Then he watched them glide over the calm water, chasing the fog out of the bay.

By the time he went back inside, Devon and her little girl had put away a good deal of food and that made him smile. He went back behind the bar with his coffee. "Fill you up?"

"Oh, yes, sir," she said, giving her mouth a pat. "If you'll write down your name and address for me, I'll try to repay the kindness when I'm able."

"I'd rather you pass it on, Devon," he said. "That's what I try to do when I can."

"Of course. I'll do that, too."

"So. Looking for a larger town? One with a shelter?"

"That seems a good place for me to start," she said.

"Mind if I ask? What put you in these straits?"

She took a breath and stroked her daughter's back. "It's not complicated. I lost my job and couldn't find another. I got some benefits and food stamps, but it wasn't enough to pay the rent and I didn't have family to take me in. So, here I am."

"What kind of work you lookin' for?" Rawley asked.

Devon laughed a little bit. "I've been working since I was fifteen, I can do a lot of things. Office work, waitress work, worked in a nursing home for a while. I even worked on a farm. I cleaned, cooked, worked in child care a lot—once I was a teaching assistant in a preschool. I went to college. But none of those things paid enough to keep me and Mercy comfortable. I had a boyfriend, but he left. See?" she finished, tilting her head to one side. "Pretty simple. Just rotten timing. Bad luck."

Rawley leaned on the bar. "You know, there's this place on the river. Some kind of religious group. They call themselves The Fellowship. I could drive you out there, see if they'd take you in for a while, fix you up with some—"

"No!" she said hotly. "Please, no! If you could just give me a lift to the highway."

He held up a callused hand. "Shh," he said. "Devon, I know you're from there. I don't know why and you don't have to tell me, but it's pretty clear you needed to be out of the place if you'd drag your kid out in the dark of night and walk over a mountain." He frowned. "She is your kid, ain't she?"

"Of course!" She looked down. "I got a ride over the mountain. I should just get going...."

The child looked like her mother. Rawley was just checking. "Just sit. I can help you out here. You and the little one would be safe while you figure things out. You don't have to be out on the highway, takin' your chances."

She just looked at him with those big blue eyes, her peachy lips parted. Her daughter continued to move Frosted Flakes around in her bowl, apparently oblivious to the conversation. "Why?" she whispered.

"I told you why. You need details? There was this war you're too young to even know about and I came home a mess and no one wanted any part of me, of any of us. A lot of us wandered, just trying to forget or get the noise in our heads to stop. We had the VA but folks didn't even know how to help Vietnam vets. Like I said, I took a lot of charity. I worked some here and there, slept on the street some, helped out at the VA some. Now—I got a house and a job. That's my story. You keep yours till you feel safe. But, girl—we're gonna have to make some changes 'cause I knew where you came from the second I seen you walkin' down the road."

Her eyes got pretty round at that, but she remained mute.

"The overalls, the braid... Once Cooper—the

boss—gets in here and decides to start work for the day, I'll take you somewhere to get clothes that don't just holler commune-for-Christ or whatever that is you come from."

"The Fellowship," she reminded him quietly.

"And, if you are trying to keep a low profile around here it wouldn't hurt to cut off that braid or something. You think that's a good idea?"

She chewed her lip a little bit, thinking this over. When she did speak she said, "I know about Vietnam."

"Be glad you don't remember it."

Thinking again she said, "Maybe I'm not far enough away. From the compound."

"You think some of them might come lookin' for you?"

She shook her head. "I don't know. I don't think so, not really. They're not bad people. But..."

Rawley let that hang a minute. "But?" he prompted.

"They didn't want me to leave. And I did anyway. And we're not going back," she added vehemently.

He cleared his throat. "Then we play it safe. If you see any of 'em snoopin' around, you better sound the alarm. I've been in this town almost every day for over four years and no one from that place ever came here. My house is in Elmore, a thirty-minute drive from here and I ain't never seen any of 'em there, either. I guess there's a chance some folks from around here have been to that produce stand, or what you call the compound, so I reckon getting yourself a new look makes sense. There's just one thing you're gonna have to do to make it work."

"What's that, Mr. Goode?"

She remembered his name. Sharp for someone who'd been up all night and was probably worn to a nub.

"Gonna have to trust a stranger, miss. That's what."

Again she dropped her gaze. "Last time I did that..."

"I can figure that much out without the whole story," he said. "I thought that place was safe. A refuge. Bent on charity and good works. But if it was a good and decent place, you'd have left in daylight with money in your pocket. I'm old and I'm jaded but I ain't stupid."

"For a while, it was a refuge and it saved me. For a while."

"Here's what we do, miss. We get you some Walmart clothes and I'll take you and the little miss here to my house. You'll have a safe and warm place to lay your head. There's food in the fridge. You might wanna pretend to be kin—like my second cousin's daughter. I didn't have no direct family."

Devon actually smiled at that. "Neither did I, Mr. Goode."

"Might wanna call me Rawley for good measure."

"Rawley," she said. "I'm not sure…"

"Devon, you're stuck with trusting strangers right now. It ain't safer thumbing rides on the highway, I guaran-damn-tee. This'll at least give you time to think and be safe while you're doing it."

Spencer Lawson was new to Thunder Point. He'd taken the job of Athletic Director and coach at the local high school and he and his ten-year-old son were living in Cooper's fifth wheel while looking around for a place to rent. He had to admit, while it was a little tight on space, especially in the bathroom, it was not only convenient but it was a pleasure to wake up every day and see the bay. He didn't have much of a kitchen in the RV, but then he wasn't much of a cook. Besides, right next door, Cooper had the equivalent of two kitchens and a nice big outdoor gas grill.

Spencer had been up for a while. With coffee still in his cup he decided to wander next door to Cooper's place. He left Austin, sprawled crossways, asleep in the big bed. They'd been sharing a bedroom since moving into Cooper's RV but sleeping with Austin was like sleeping with the entire fourth grade. Most nights Spencer escaped to the sofa in the living room. As he walked across the deck toward the open doors of the bar, he heard voices…a woman's voice as she said, "No! Please, no!"

And he stopped. He heard Rawley shush her and say, "Devon, I know where you're from. You don't have to give me details and I don't have to know why…"

Spencer saw Cooper and Sarah out on their boards, skimming across the bay smoothly, the movement of their paddles synchronized. Quietly he took a chair outside the opened doors, shamelessly eavesdropping on the conversation. In five minutes, he had the story—this was a young woman with a child who had run away from some kind of commune or religious order. And Rawley was not only going to help her, but he would help her keep it secret. While he was dying to walk into the bar and get a look at this young runaway, he didn't want them to stop talking.

A few minutes later, Sarah and Cooper were coming in off the water. They stowed their boards against the dock and untied the dog from it. Hamlet made a beeline for the deck. This was Spencer's cue. He stood and waited for them. First he greeted Hamlet and gave him a vigorous head and ear massage. "Hey, old boy! How's it going, Ham?" Sarah and Cooper strolled leisurely up the stairs to the deck.

"What's going on?" Cooper asked Spencer.

Spencer lifted his cup. "I'm out of coffee."

"You're always out of something," Cooper said. "Come on in, Rawley can hook you up. I'm just guessing, but I bet you want breakfast, too."

"I might, yeah."

"Where's the kid?"

"Sprawled across the bed. Snoring."

Cooper chuckled.

Ham was waiting anxiously, tail wagging like mad, hoping he'd get a treat. The three of them—and Ham—all walked into the bar together. Right away they noticed the young woman with a long braid and a small child sitting at the counter. Rawley looked up from behind the bar and the little girl broke into a huge grin, pointed and said, "Mama! Pony in the house!"

The woman laughed, putting a hand up to her mouth. Her blue eyes twinkled.

Ham went to the child immediately. He was excellent with kids.

"Just a dog, kiddo," Cooper said. "Want to give him his cookie? Look out, though. He's got a real slobbery mouth but he never nips." He fished a huge dog biscuit out of the jar on the bar and let the little girl hold it out toward Ham. She held it in a flat hand, as if feeding a horse. Then Cooper looked at the young woman and said, "Hi. I'm

Cooper. This is my fiancée, Sarah. And this is my friend, Spencer."

"This here's my cousin's daughter, Coop," Rawley said. "Well, second cousin, maybe even removed. Devon. Visiting."

Cooper tilted his head and queried with his eyes. "Devon...?"

But Rawley didn't answer. He didn't answer because he didn't know Devon's last name. Finally Devon said, "McAllister. And this is my daughter, Mercy."

"Pleasure. Rawley, you should've mentioned you had company coming. You could have taken the day off."

"It was a last-minute thing but, if you can spare me, I'd like to show her around a little bit. They might be tired from traveling, too, and I can leave 'em at home and come back..."

"Take the day off if you want it, Rawley. I can handle the shop. Landon will show up to help out when he gets his lazy butt out of bed. And I've always got Spencer..."

"You okay with that?" Rawley asked.

Spencer looked at this duo—mother and child. She was plain as a pancake, and yet she was beautiful. She looked very young—early twenties? She was vulnerable, that was instantly obvious. He immediately wondered how she'd gotten trapped in a commune that wouldn't let her leave. He had this sudden urge to step in, to offer advice or shelter or something.

"Sure," Cooper said. "If you need more time, just let me know so I can make arrangements. How long are you staying?"

Again, the young woman didn't respond but Rawley said, "That's up in the air. I told her she can stay for a few days or weeks—it ain't like she'll be in my way. If you're sure you don't mind, we'll hit the road, then. You ready?" Rawley asked her.

"Thanks. Nice meeting you all."

And the three of them moved slowly out the back door, climbed into Rawley's truck and the engine roared to life. It was two minutes before the truck was traveling up the road to the highway.

Then Cooper looked at Sarah and Spencer. "Rawley doesn't have any family."

"Well, second cousin, removed..." Sarah said.

"With no warning they're coming?" Spencer asked. "Nah, they're not family. I'd bet my last dollar on that." For some reason he couldn't quite explain, Spencer didn't tell them about the conversation he had overheard between Rawley and Devon.

"It does seem strange," Cooper agreed. "Rawley's a little odd, but he's not, you know...?"

"A kidnapper? A serial killer?" Sarah offered.

"More likely he found 'em hitching or panhandling. People don't know this about Rawley, but he's generous. Softhearted. He doesn't like to let on that he has a helpful nature. He's on the gruff and silent side, but he'd give anyone the shirt off his back. When we went through all Ben's things after he died, Rawley took the old clothes to the VA, but he washed 'em first. Bags full of 'em. He has a generous nature—he gives a lot. I'm not so much worried about that woman and her little girl as I am about Rawley. I hope they don't fleece him."

"Maybe you should talk to him," Spencer suggested. "What if that's what happened? What if she's desperate and takes advantage of him?"

"Well, I could try," Cooper said. "But it might be hard getting anything out of him. That Rawley...he takes pride in saying as little as possible."

"That girl looks about fifteen," Spencer said, frowning. "He must've found them in trouble somewhere." He glanced toward the dishes on the bar. "He fed them."

Two

Rawley drove Devon to the Walmart nearest his home. He parked in the big lot and looked at her. "Your people ever go to the Walmart?" he asked.

"Not that I know of," she said. "And I never did while I was there. But I have some clothes." The clothes were in the backpack left outside the fence for her. She hadn't looked at them closely and didn't know if they'd fit, but the backpack was stuffed with things for her escape.

He reached up to the sun visor overhead and pulled out a ball cap. "Tuck that braid up in this," he said. "Get yourself a few things, grab some stuff for Mercy. Get yourself any other lady things you might need. Things no sixty-three-year-old bachelor would ever have laying around. I'll get us some groceries. We'll try to be quick and not make a stir—don't want you to give yourself away. Can we do that?"

She nodded, tucking up her braid. "I have forty dollars," she said.

"Look," Rawley said. "I know you're worried. I know you're suspicious of me and of everybody, and rightly so. But you're not a prisoner, and even if you decide you can't stick around you'll want to stay clear of that camp. You shouldn't look like you came from there. And you don't have to run off in the night, all you have to do is say you need a ride somewhere and I'll take you. Hang on to your forty dollars. You'll need it, I figure."

"I was there by choice," she revealed. Until she wasn't.

"Well, it's your choice not to be there now. Let's just get 'er done. Then you can relax and get a little rest."

As for not making a stir, the second they walked in the door, little Mercy used her loudest voice to look around and say, "*Mama!* What *is* this place?"

It took Devon a second to recover, but recover she did. She pulled Mercy's little hand and said, "Just a very big store, honey. Now please use your very quiet voice and come with me." At least Mercy hadn't called her Sister Devon. That was the way Jacob liked it; no one was a mother or a father, a husband or a wife—they were all brothers and sisters. Which made his behavior seem pretty damned incestuous.

Of course Devon remembered visiting a Walmart—it's not as though she'd forgotten her life before the family. She grabbed her daughter's hand and a cart and sped through the women's and children's clothes. Two pairs of jeans, a pair of shorts, two shirts, socks, underwear, tennis shoes. She bought the exact same items for Mercy. She added two hoodies, in case they had to flee in the night, and then a few incidentals including brushes, combs and toothbrushes. And—because he was right—she bought a pair of scissors. She had to stop looking like one of them.

She met Rawley by the checkout. Her heart was racing. So, here she was with a scruffy old guy who had given her a ride and now wanted to help her even more and just by the look of him alone she should be worried. But the tall, handsome, soft-spoken Jacob with the ready, welcoming smile, who had so much to offer when she was in need, had never worried her for a moment. And he was the one she should have been worried about!

In his cart Rawley had groceries and… She looked closely. He had a safety seat for Mercy for the truck. It was an old truck and the cab was small, but it had seat belts. She was touched beyond words. That safety seat meant so much more to her than all Jacob's promises.

The new seat had to be strapped in by the door and there were no seat belts for the middle seat. She had to sit next to Rawley without belts while

Mercy rode in the passenger seat. Still, it was better than walking or hitching.

Had it been possible, she would have held her breath all the way to Rawley Goode's house. She kept telling herself she was safer in this old man's truck, or in his home, than she would've been had she stayed with the family at the compound. She kept telling herself this was safer than hitching rides. Despite her racing imagination there was something she had not been prepared for. When they pulled into the driveway of a small brick home in a neat little neighborhood, she felt a wave of nostalgia wash over her. It was like the house she'd grown up in. When they went inside, she stopped right inside the door, right in the little living room, and almost collapsed in relief and emotion. This could be Aunt Mary's place! The furniture was different but probably just as old, complete with those familiar doilies on the tabletops and arms of the Queen Anne chairs and sofa. It was small, the rug over the hardwood floor threadbare, the wood furniture distressed but polished. "Oh, my God," she whispered. "Oh, my God."

She put Mercy on her feet. "Mama, where's the kids?"

Devon got down on one knee. She put the bags she carried along with her backpack against the wall. "We're having a vacation. And I think you need a nap."

"I don't want a bacation," Mercy whined.

"We don't have a choice. We have to."

"I don't want to has to!"

"Stop," Devon said firmly. "Stop right now." Then she hugged her close.

Rawley took the groceries straight to the kitchen and began putting things away. Devon just waited by the door, holding Mercy's hand, afraid to invade the house. Momentarily he was back, handing her a slip of paper. "There's two bedrooms upstairs and you'll know which one is mine—it's lookin' mighty lived in. There's food in the kitchen and I ain't savin' nothing for later—it's all open season for you and Mercy. I eat at the bar and clean up dishes before coming home so you won't see me till eight or so. This here's a number for my phone." Then he grinned. "You're the first person to get it. I mean, Cooper has it, but only because he bought me the phone in the first place—he got tired of me never checkin' in. You just call if you need something, or if something changes with you, or if… I don't expect anyone will bother you here."

"You're leaving?" she asked.

He gave a shrug. "I could stay, Cooper wouldn't mind. But if I was you, I'd still be nervous and me gone will give you a chance to think. Check over the place. Rest. Eat. Get comfortable. Pull the tags off your clothes. Nap. Whatever you need to do." He opened the door. "There's another room up there. It's where I keep the TV. Extra blankets in the hall closet. Towels and that stuff, too."

"I guess we should wash off the road," she said.

He looked at his watch. "You got hours to do whatever you want."

"Thank you, Mr. Goode."

"It's just Rawley," he said. And then he was gone.

Overwhelmed, Devon sat on his worn old couch, pulling Mercy beside her. Mercy. She had wanted to name her Mary in the first place, after her aunt. Mary had been failing fast the last time she'd seen her alive. Five years ago.

Tears started to just run out of her blue eyes.

"We're free," she whispered to Mercy.

"Mama, where's the kids?"

It was Sister Laine who had helped Devon find a way out of The Fellowship. Laine hadn't been with the family long, not even six months. And, unlike some of the women, she was very independent and didn't seem to get sucked into group thinking, nor did she vie for Jacob's favors. She was careful, though. Disciplined and obedient. Around Jacob she seemed skittish, maybe frightened, but there were other times when she threw Devon a secret grin and wink, or maybe a startled look. She didn't talk about her past, other than to say she'd come from a bad place and that Jacob had promised her peace and safety. It was implied she had been abused by a man. Laine's story reminded Devon that they weren't all the same no matter how much Jacob wished it so.

Laine learned that Devon wanted to leave the compound and that Jacob wouldn't let her take Mercy. It was hardly secret—Devon had been making noises about leaving once she first learned she was pregnant. But Jacob said no, absolutely no, because Mercy was his child. So, for several years Devon and Mercy made the compound their home.

They were gathering eggs one morning when Laine whispered, "I know you want to leave."

"No," Devon said, hiding surprise, cautious in case of betrayal. "I'm very happy."

"I know you want to go and if you do, I can help. If you turn on me, it will be bad, very bad. If you don't want to go, just ignore me."

But Devon said, "Help how?"

"Listen carefully. On June 9 there will be a hole in the fence behind the henhouse, right over there. There will be a backpack with some clothes, bottled water, a couple of apples and granola bars— look for it outside the fence behind a tree. At midnight there will be a truck down the road— the lights will be off. The driver will take you over the mountain. He won't wait long. Go to the coast. You shouldn't travel Highway 5, it's too close to the compound and you'll be found right away if anyone decides to look for you. If they look, they'll only look as far as you can walk. Hitching a ride on Highway 101 is safer. If anything goes wrong, try to find a women's shelter and tell your story. As a last resort, if you have no other way to get help, tell the police."

"Why a last resort?"

"Because, Devon, once you tell, they might make a move on this place and everyone could be in danger. Jacob will fight back. So, only tell the police if that's the only way you can be safe."

"Why would you do this?"

She shrugged and said, "I fixed it up at the Farmers' Market. I was planning to do it myself, but I think you should go first. I'll figure out something."

"Maybe we could both go," Devon said, wondering if she'd lost her mind.

But Laine shook her head. "Two of us and Mercy traveling together would be too easy to track. If you get in a fix, tell someone what's going on here. The moods, the threats, the little rages and the gardens. If you have to tell, tell to keep yourself safe. It is not safe here."

"It was once. Or it seemed to be," Devon said.

"It's not safe now, I can tell. It's time to get the children out. I think you know that. Now let's find some eggs. And laugh at my jokes, for

God's sake!" Then she smiled. "You have this one chance. Do it."

It's time to get the children out. Those words struck fear in Devon's heart and she knew she had to act. She had to take the chance that was being given to her. She had to trust Laine. But, once she had made her decision, Devon nearly counted her heartbeats until she and Mercy could escape.

Just as Laine had promised, everything was ready. And, before she knew it, she'd done it.

Rawley got back to the beach bar around two in the afternoon. He walked in on one of the most unlikely friendships he'd ever known about, and he'd known of some odd ones since Vietnam. Cooper was behind his bar and Spencer Lawson was sitting on a stool facing him. This was a fairly new friendship. As Rawley heard the story, Spencer had been married to an old fiancée of Cooper's and the poor lady died. She had cancer or something, Rawley recalled. And several months before her death, blood work had been done and revealed that their ten-year-old son, Austin, was actually not Spencer's biological son, but Cooper's.

Well, now, Rawley thought. That'll make or break a man.

But the men had worked it out. In fact, Spencer had just agreed to take a job in Thunder Point so both dads could live in the same town and be parents to one little boy. And ten-year-old Austin had the potential to be spoiled rotten.

"Hey, Rawley," Cooper said. "How's your cousin?"

"Huh? Oh, she's okay. I left her to get a nap, relax or whatever."

"How long you think she'll stay?"

Rawley just shrugged. "Can't say. Might be she doesn't find an old Vet much fun to live with and just moves on."

"Well, what brought her here?" Cooper asked.

"You are sure the nosiest som-bitch I know. I don't have the details, don't really need the details, but I gather it was a bad situation or something and she needs a place to roost a bit. Don't matter. I'm happy to give her a bed. She's got a kid—you don't just ignore a kid. I don't want them staying in some damn run-down hotel all alone just because I'm an old coot set in my ways." He craned his neck and looked out the windows to the beach. "Speaking of kids..."

"Austin's fishing off the dock with Landon," Spencer said. "I have to go look at a house in town, even though Austin wants to live in that RV next door for the rest of his life."

"Ain't a bad place, as places go," Rawley said. Cooper's toy hauler had been operating as a guest house ever since he had finished off the upstairs of the bar into his apartment.

"I'm looking for something a little bigger in the bathroom and kitchen department." Spencer laughed. "Not to mention less sandy."

"If you could train someone to wipe his great big ten-year-old feet, you could beat that problem. Have you noticed how big his feet are? Is that normal?" Cooper asked.

"Well, it's normal on St. Bernard puppies," Spencer said.

Leaving the men to talk, Rawley went to the kitchen. There was always work to be done—cleaning, stocking, organizing. Now that Cooper had an apartment and a fiancée, he stayed out of there. Cooper could clean his own house, do his own laundry. Cooper liked taking care of the beach, raking up, hauling trash, making sure there was no detritus that could harm people or wildlife. He said it gave him an idea of who used the beach and what they used it for. He maintained his stock of paddleboards and kayaks. And he spent a lot of time visiting with folks in town, on the beach, on the dock, in the bar. Cooper was a natural people person. Rawley had never been much for visiting.

Rawley kept himself busy working around the bar and in the kitchen till about seven-thirty. With the longer days there was plenty of sunlight left; Cooper and Landon could handle the place without him until sunset when folks tended to quit for the day, except those who liked the beach at night and enjoyed their fires.

His phone hadn't rung all day. He wondered what he'd find when he got home. He had absolutely no idea. She was skittish; she might be gone. The place could be upended, valuables stolen... not that he had much in the way of valuables. But nothing prepared him for what he found when he got there. He could hear the TV upstairs and didn't want to startle her, so he called from the bottom of the stairs.

She came to the top of the stairs and looked down at him. Her hair was cut right up to the nape, kind of messy-cute, falling over her forehead haphazardly. Gone was that thick mane that hit her butt. "Up here, Mr. Goode," she said. "Oh, my God, I haven't seen TV in so long. We had popcorn—I hope that's okay. You said anything. We didn't eat much. There's plenty left. But the TV— my daughter is in a trance. She's never seen TV." Then she laughed and her whole face lit up. "Well, she was in a trance and now she's asleep right on the floor and I'm watching baseball. I *love* baseball. I haven't seen a game in years!"

He chuckled and remained at the bottom of the stairs. "No TV at the camp, I take it," he said.

"No TV, no newspapers, no internet access, no phones. No distractions, no commercialism, no propaganda. At least for us." There was that grin again. "Oh, how I missed it!"

"Did you find something for Mercy to watch?" he asked.

"Evil cartoons. She was in heaven."

"Have you eaten anything besides popcorn?" Rawley asked.

She nodded. "I scrambled some eggs and made some toast for Mercy. I had a sandwich, chips, soda..." She rolled her eyes. "Soda! It was so good! And then the popcorn. Should I turn off the TV now? So you can have peace and quiet?"

Rawley smiled. She looked lit up from the inside. He couldn't remember being quite this pleased with himself. He shook his head. "I'm gonna get my newspaper and a cola. I like sports. I used to watch with my dad before he died— that's why there's two recliners up there. And you can watch the TV all night if you want to. It don't bother me. Half the time I fall asleep in front of the TV."

"Newspaper!" she said in a breath.

"I'll share it with you."

Mercy rarely asked about the other kids or the other sisters from the family once she was introduced to television and the undivided attention of one mother rather than six. They hardly ever left the house except to walk to the end of the street where there was a tiny park with swings and a slide, and that was just for a little exercise and fresh air. Every day Rawley brought them something new. First, a couple of toys for Mercy—a baby doll with a diaper bag filled with miniature supplies—this small child from a family compound didn't know about diaper bags. Then he brought some crayons and coloring books and bubbles. Next, some library books—a few picture books for a three-year-old, a few novels he had asked a librarian to recommend for a thirty-year-old woman.

"Close enough," she said with a smile. "I'm twenty-eight."

Then he brought home a laptop computer. He said, "I thought maybe you might want to use this. It's an old one Cooper let me have. Do you know how to use it?"

"I know how to use a computer, certainly. We just didn't use the evil internet, which has probably grown to amazing heights in the last several years. And I can't tell you how much I want to have a look!"

"I ain't got no hookup. Cooper said to tell you to jump on some neighbor's or store's wireless—and I ain't got the first idea how you do that."

But Devon smiled. She'd have no trouble figuring it out.

For Devon, this time away from the compound

was like sensory overload—there were so many
new ideas to talk about, and programs to watch
and articles to read. She was in ecstasy.

Then came several days of rain in a row, which
conspired with Devon's need to be immersed in
the books, TV and computer. Rawley didn't spend
quite as many hours at work but Devon and Mercy
were so happily occupied it seemed he'd barely left
before he returned. She made a couple of dinners
for the three of them and while Rawley wasn't exactly talkative, he was companionable.

"How's 'at computer working out?"

"It's a revelation—you can find out anything."
Out of curiosity she checked out "communes in
Oregon" online and found several references, but
nothing really interesting. Compounds could mean
a host of families, religious sects, cults and organi-
zations ranging from non-certified health retreats
and rehab facilities to known sovereign commu-
nities and anti-government separatists. She was
fascinated and kept reading.

Then she found something that explained so
much: a familiar name and story—Jacob Glover.
Glover? They didn't use last names—they claimed
there was no need. But there was a picture, and it
was definitely the Jacob she had known. He was
well-known—he'd been convicted of fraud in the
past. He was known as the leader of a cult who
had recently been investigated for fraud, tax fraud,

conspiracy and kidnapping. Huh? she thought. Well, taxes…yes, that was an issue. She remembered that very well indeed. It was one of his favorite rants, taken right from his manifesto. *What am I but a poor farmer? We eat what we grow; we own our land; we don't use any government resources—we educate our own and we pay our good money for supplies we can't grow or breed or make. The only argument government has for our paltry income is our rare use of their roads! Property tax? For living? For paying our own way? I'll die first!*

She remembered thinking that was a compelling argument, but it was one that would never work. As for paltry income for little supplies—she was well aware that The Fellowship not only owned expensive farming equipment, but they also owned three black Lincoln SUVs with darkened windows that only the men drove. This could hardly be considered paltry by any stretch of the imagination. It was also hard to believe that the meager sale of apples, peaches, pears and vegetables brought in enough income for The Fellowship to purchase the equipment and the mammoth SUVs.

But kidnapping? There was not a chance The Fellowship could be accused of that! No one had ever come into the family unwillingly and if they ran away, Jacob looked the other way. At least he used to. When Greg had slipped away after just a few months, there was only sad disappointment. But when Caleb, who had been with the group for three years, left suddenly, Jacob's anger roared. All three SUVs tore out of the compound and went in search, a search lasting days. But when he wasn't found, the search was abandoned.

Then she realized that these investigations might be the reason Jacob and some of the others seemed to have changed in the past couple of years, becoming impatient and paranoid. When she'd first become a part of the group, gentleness and ease had seemed to dominate their way of life. But over the past couple of years anger and even desperation seemed to creep in. *I'll die first!* The amount of time he spent writing—some of the women called his writings a diary, some a manifesto, others claimed it was his new bible—had increased. There had always been weapons that were kept locked up and managed by a few men, but they were for security and hunting, not because there was fear.

She looked up "cult," though she knew well enough what one was. And she also knew that religious affiliation aside, The Fellowship was a cult. Synonyms were "gang," "craze," "sect" and "denomination dominated by extreme beliefs." Not always a bad thing, the L.A. Police Department was referred to as the biggest gang in L.A. They were but a group of like-minded people, bent on a single purpose. In fact, it was that alone that had caused the rift for Devon. She was no longer of a like mind.

In one of her last conversations with Jacob, right before Laine had offered her a way out, she'd said, "I miss my individuality, that's all. I don't want to be isolated and I don't want my daughter raised by six mothers. I want to pick my own books and music, read all the papers. I want to be a part of society again."

"Even if society is bad? Wrong? Dangerous? Greedy?" he'd asked.

"If I'm here, then I'm not doing anything to make it better," she'd offered.

He'd sighed deeply. Painfully. "This breaks my heart, but maybe it's for the best, Devon. You've never really wanted to be a part of this, one of us."

"I always did my share! I taught the children, helped with farming and ranching, tended animals—I did everything everyone else did, too."

"Not everything," he reminded her.

She bit her lip and looked down, astonished that he could make her feel guilty over a purely righteous act. Once she'd realized she had conceived Mercy and that Jacob had children with other women in The Fellowship, that other women in their group visited his bed frequently, she didn't want to be a part of that group. She wanted a partner, not a never-ending family. When she'd made love to him, she had foolishly believed he loved only her, that he held the other women as sisters, family members, not lovers. He *led* her to believe that. "There were too many women. It wasn't for me."

"There were a few, and we were all of one family, one mind," he said.

"No," she said. "I was of a different mind. I will only have one intimate partner."

"It's not our way," he said.

"It's probably best that I separate now," she said. "I gave my promised two years. In fact I gave more than two. I was committed and loyal even if I didn't agree with everything."

"Fine, then. You really don't fit anymore. You hold yourself slightly above the rest of us, as if you're better."

Shocked and hurt, she'd blurted, "You're the only one here who holds yourself above the rest of us!"

And he'd slapped her. He glared at her and was so angry. When she'd first come to this family, he was so gentle, so tolerant. But lately he'd become so short-tempered and his controlling nature was skyrocketing. "I think as the man who founded this Fellowship and works every day to hold it together and protect it, I can be afforded some respect!"

It was a black day that burned in her memory. That had been a year before she'd finally left.

She read on about Jacob. *Investigated and inter-viewed for allegations of kidnapping and human trafficking.*

She thought she knew what human trafficking was, but looked it up just the same. *The recruit-ment of human beings by means of kidnapping, coercion or purchase for the purpose of exploita-tion, usually for labor or commercial sex trade....*

And she knew. She just had never thought of women over twenty-one who went willingly being the victims of human trafficking—she'd always assumed underage prostitutes or child laborers in dingy, dangerous factories were the kinds of people who would be the victims of human traf-ficking.

Jacob had picked her up outside a shelter in Se-attle, Washington. He'd invested an hour in con-versation with her learning that she was alone, that she longed for a family and was needy, afraid and desperate. She also fit his profile of wanting fair-skinned and blue-eyed members for his group. He treated them all so sweetly and provided a shel-ter that was clean and had plentiful food. She was introduced to a few other women who'd joined the group for the same reason she had. They all worked hard to sustain it and to make it a suc-cess. Then they were all stripped of their identi-ties—driver's licenses, social security cards and other personal effects stored away...or perhaps destroyed.

And they all loved him. At one time, even Devon had had a deep love for him, or perhaps it was gratitude. Sometimes some of them joked behind his back in whispers: *He's penning a new bible, you know.*

Devon remembered Laine's words to her. *Tell if you have to,* Laine had said. *Tell about the gardens.*

While it was never discussed openly, they all knew that Jacob and the family financed their plentiful compound by their special gardens. No matter how well their organic gardens produced, the bounty of fresh fruit and vegetables was not enough to generate the kind of income needed to keep The Fellowship going. There were a couple of gardens that were kept concealed in a couple of warehouses. They used grow lights run on generators, going twenty-four hours a day and tended by only a few men. Devon had been a member of The Fellowship for a couple of years before she knew about their special cash crop—it was marijuana.

Jacob explained it to her by saying, "We are only growing medicinal herbs that the government wants to regulate. If they find out what we are doing they'll take it all away. Strip us of everything. But it's harmless and helpful and some states have even passed laws making it legal, which this state will eventually do, as well. Then, they'll try to tax it to the moon. We have to grow our herbs in secret. The government would love to steal from us, which is not their right."

Brother Jacob was a drug dealer. His cult, his Fellowship, was a cover. That's why he kept the members close by, and why he had children with them knowing that would keep them tied to him.

Although there was nothing in her research to indicate he was being investigated for running and operating a grow-op, Devon knew the feds must be getting closer. It would explain his behavior— Jacob was now paranoid.

Three

Lieutenant Commander Sarah Dupre hadn't worn her diamond engagement ring to work when she'd first gotten it. Rings on the flight line were a good way to lose a finger, for one thing. As well, she didn't want any of her coworkers figuring her out, for another. But the day her deadline for accepting or rejecting the orders that would ship her to a Florida Coast Guard Station expired, she wore the beautiful ring to work. She had written the two letters—one, rejecting the assignment and two, resigning her commission and leaving the Coast Guard.

Her boss, Commander Buzz Bachman, accepted the letters for his files, though Sarah would send both to the command HR department herself.

"Gonna do it, huh?" he said. "I can't say I'm all that surprised. But what's next for you?"

And that's when she thrust out her left hand, diamond glittering on the fourth finger.

"Whoa!" he said. "Throwing us over for a man? You?"

"Don't say it like that," she warned him. "It's not like it was a rash or quick decision. And I think he's a pretty good bet."

"Well, hell, I like Cooper all right, but what are you gonna *do?*"

She grinned at him and shook her head. "As soon as the Coast Guard approves my separation, I'm going to take a vacation. At least through footfall season. And until we get Landon settled on a college."

"When's the wedding?" Buzz asked.

"We haven't decided...."

"Big bash?" he asked.

"I don't think so," she said with a laugh. "I had a big bash when I married Derek, and that didn't take. I think it'll be small, quiet and private. But we're still talking about it."

"Are you saying I shouldn't stand by the mailbox, waiting for my invitation?"

"Nothing personal..."

"Well, the boys are going to want to give you a bachelor party."

She glanced down at herself. "I know it's not immediately apparent in this flight suit, but I'm actually a girl."

Buzz grinned at her. "That hasn't stopped us in the past. Now get out of here. Go tell lover-boy you put your papers in."

"That's my exact plan," she said.

Sarah drove past the turnoff to the town of Thunder Point and her house and drove the long way to Cooper's bar on the other side of the beach, parking in the rear. When she walked in, he was moving the mop around the floor, something that needed to be done frequently, given all the sand that came in on the feet of friends and customers. He stopped abruptly and just smiled at her.

"I don't see this every day," he said. He leaned the mop against the wall and grabbed her against him. He gave her a hearty kiss, holding her tightly. He shook his head and smiled. "I flew helicopters for a living for fifteen years and you're the only pilot I ever wanted to peel a flight suit off of."

"I did it, Cooper," she said. "You better not change your mind. I put in my papers."

His grin deepened. "Well, now. You do realize there's no exit date on the next deal you sign up for. Right?"

"You better not get sick of me, Cooper."

"Let me at least try," he said, going after her lips again.

A noise behind them didn't do anything to disrupt their very passionate kiss. Then seventeen-year-old Landon said, "Let's remember the rules, folks. Safety first. I hope we don't have to have another one of *those* talks."

Sarah couldn't help but laugh against Cooper's lips—Landon was echoing her constant reminder. Landon, big, strong, beautiful and in a serious relationship with a wonderful seventeen-year-old girl who happened to be the town deputy's daughter, could easily be considered high-risk by his older sister. And of course Landon constantly chided her for her mothering. "Is he too big to spank?" she asked against Cooper's lips.

"Well...by *you*," Cooper said softly.

Again she laughed, leaning her forehead against Cooper's shoulder. "At this moment, I am obscenely happy. Please don't screw this up or dump me or cheat on me or divorce me."

"All right," he said, letting go of her. He turned her toward her brother.

"Rule number two," Landon lectured, mimicking her again. "Discretion. We don't want to embarrass people with our PDA."

"We were alone, actually," she said. "So, how about giving me a beer? I won't turn you in for serving me. I'm celebrating. I did it—I put in my papers. I'm getting out."

"Holy shit, are you kidding me? I didn't think you'd do it!"

"You didn't? I told you I was going to do it."

"Yeah, but you like being the boss of things."

He pulled a bottle of beer out of the cooler and popped the top. He handed it to his sister. "Cooper, we are in trouble here. We should plan a strategy."

"Take care of yourself, kid. I like it when she bosses me around."

"You are so whipped. What are the rest of us men gonna think, you letting a woman get the upper hand like this? You should be ashamed."

Cooper grabbed his mop. "I guess Eve would never get away with that, huh?" he said, mopping.

"That's different," Landon said with a big smile. "Eve is so not my sister. And when Eve is happy, I'm happy."

"There you go," Cooper said.

Rawley came into the bar with a rack of glasses, silently sliding them under the bar.

"Hey, Rawley, how's it going?" Sarah asked. "Your cousin still around?"

Rawley stopped short as if he had to think about that. "Huh? Oh. Yeah. Still at my house."

"Not crowding you, huh?" Sarah asked. "Been a couple of weeks now, hasn't it?"

"I dunno. Maybe ten days or so," he said. "She don't bother me none. Kinda nice, to tell the truth. Remember, I had my dad full-time for years—a young woman and little child don't take half the care my dad did. She helps out around the place. I haven't done a load of dirty clothes since she's been here. Besides, she doesn't know where she wants to go yet. She said she likes it around here. Well, she likes Elmore, anyway."

"Where's she from, again?"

"Seattle. But I don't think she wants to go back there. Bad memories, I gather. She's been talking about getting work. Hard deal when you have a kid. And there ain't nothin' in Elmore."

"What kind of work?"

And suddenly Rawley seemed to light up. Shine. "She can do all kinda things. Cooking, cleaning, office work, you name it. She got herself some college degree right before she got in a relationship that didn't work out. She studied education. She was gonna be a teacher for the real little kids, or something like that. I guess that's what makes her such a good mom. She's a fine mother. That little Mercy—she's something. Real smart, real nosy."

"Well, Rawley, I think you like having them around," Sarah said.

Rawley shrugged. "It's okay. I never thought I'd know what it felt like to be a grandpa." He shrugged again. "I don't hate it." Then he turned and went back into the kitchen.

Sarah, Landon and Cooper exchanged smiles.

Rawley brought a second rack of clean glasses into the bar and Sarah said, "So—has your cousin looked for work around Thunder Point?"

"Not that I know about. You got something?"

"No. But Saturday is Dr. Grant's open house for

his new clinic. You should bring her. It's not exactly a job fair, but everyone in town will be there. She could talk to people. Find out if anyone knows of any jobs or any child care or babysitting. In fact, maybe someone *needs* child care or babysitting. Wouldn't that be convenient?"

Rawley thought about that for a minute. Then he said, "I'll tell her. But I'm not much for parties or a lot of people."

"Tell her, I'd be glad to take her," Sarah offered. "I wouldn't miss it."

Devon hadn't had a typical childhood, but it had been a safe and happy one. Devon's mother, Rhonda, was a nurse who became close to her neighbor, Mary. Mary immediately took Rhonda under her wing knowing Rhonda was pregnant and alone. And since Mary was a day care provider working out of her home, it only followed that after Devon was born, Mary watched her while Rhonda worked. And Rhonda named Mary as Devon's guardian, should anything happen.

And something did indeed happen. Poor Rhonda was struck by a drunk driver as she waited at the bus stop on her way home from work one evening. Devon had been only nine months old.

Devon knew Aunt Mary was not her real aunt, was not her mother's older sister. What she didn't know was that Mary waited tensely for years for some distant, unknown family member to appear and lay claim to Devon. She clung to that will and birth certificate with a miser's zeal, ready to do battle with anyone who might try to take the little girl away.

Mary was old enough to be Devon's grandmother, but she was a popular figure in the neighborhood, at their church and in Devon's schools. She was kind, nurturing, energetic and helpful, and Devon's friends had always loved her—especially the pizza parties and sleepovers. Mary was a great volunteer and she took responsibility as any parent would, participating in field trips and fund-raising, and when Devon was a cheerleader or on a team, Mary had never missed a game or meet. Never.

Mary had always told Devon she had pluck. And that she was tough. She was a survivor. She said the same things even when crises like Devon not making the championship girls volleyball team, or junior varsity cheerleading squad, or having to make do with a partial scholarship, instead of getting the big one. "I just won't make it," teenage Devon had wailed.

And Mary had said, "Girl, you will rise above this, and fast. You're strong. Do you have any idea how many times people have to start over and make a new path? For myself, I can't count the number of times! I buried two husbands before you were born! Lost the first in Vietnam and the second to cancer! And just when I thought my life would slide gentle into old age, who comes along but Miss Devon!" And then she would laugh and laugh. "The Lord blesses me with work and new ideas every day of my life!"

So Devon had grown up with a devoted parent and a house full of small children who were picked up by their parents by five. With the help of scholarships and part-time jobs, she'd attained a degree in early childhood education and had begun work on her Master's when Mary first fell ill. Very ill. That's when Devon had said, "I don't have enough pluck for this. I'm not that strong."

"You are if you want to be," Mary had said. Not long after her hospitalization and subsequent death came Devon's dark, frightening period when there was no work, not enough money for rent and the constant worry about how she would make it through the next day. She constantly reminded herself—I'm a smart, educated, hardworking person—how does this happen? She needed a miracle.

What do you need, sister? Tell me. Maybe I can help.

Why wouldn't she love Jacob? Why wouldn't she take to his Fellowship? She'd grown up helping to tend other peoples' children and all she'd ever really wanted was a family of her own. Perhaps this was an unusual family by normal standards, but at least she felt safe and invulnerable.

And she fell for Jacob, as did everyone else—he was not only sweet and kind but also commanding. Powerful. Charismatic. There was little doubt in her mind he was strong enough to keep all of them safe. He was just the miracle she thought she needed.

Little Mercy was quickening inside her by the time she'd been in The Fellowship for a few months. That was when she realized that Jacob was not in love with her—he was in love with everyone—or so he claimed. On reflection, Devon realized that Jacob was incapable of loving anyone but himself. As far as Devon knew, all six children in the family were biologically his and their mothers were all very special to him, all sharing his affection. Devon's heart was broken and she was suddenly disillusioned. Who would hold her up and comfort her and support her now that she was pregnant? The only people she had were her sisters in the family.

There was Charlotte, who used to act out the children's stories, making everyone scream with hysterical laughter. Lorna could bake like a demon and throw a softball like a pro. Priscilla, who they called Pilly, was prickly except on days following one of her visits with Jacob and for that the others teased her mercilessly. Reese was the oldest of them at thirty-five and though no one had elected her boss, she took on that role all the time, something for which the others were, by turns, either grateful or petulant enough to reduce her to tears. But Reese played an important role in the family—she was the one to deliver their children; she was a doula and a nurse. Mariah was the youngest, shyest, an innocent twenty years old, and all of them tried to shelter her from Jacob...and failed. And finally there was Laine, who hadn't been with them long and was the most devilish, making them all laugh at themselves and at their weird family.

They squabbled, giggled, played games, sat up late with ice cream or popcorn and told stories, cried for their lost lives, raved in happy delirium for their happiness, spied on each other, sought each other for comfort.

She missed them so. Even the ones she didn't like so much.

Mercy had been in no physical danger in the family—it was a family that loved and nurtured the children. The real danger was more subtle— having no independence, no identity, no clear choices; no view of the outside world. And then there were the men whose faces seemed to change regularly, the men who tended and moved the marijuana. The women all knew this wasn't right, that it wasn't just medicine, but as long as they were safe and happy they seemed comfortable turning a blind eye to the reality.

And then Jacob began to change. He seemed

to move from the morally superior position in his rants to being angry, desperate and paranoid. Now that she'd read the online accounts of the investigation, it seemed obvious—he must have changed as the feds encroached and threatened his authority, turning him into a frantic and anxious man. That's when the idea of leaving proved to be so much more difficult. He must have been afraid people who left The Fellowship would sell him out. Devon had actually thought about leaving for a long time. The minute her baby was born, Devon thought about leaving, trying to think of what she'd do, how she'd manage, because she didn't want Mercy growing up in that compound in a pair of soft denim overalls and a long braid. But she didn't want her to grow up hungry and afraid, either.

And now here she was, back at the beginning, living with a grandparent-type figure taking care of her in a comfortable old house in an old neighborhood.

She poured herself a cup of coffee in Rawley's kitchen. Rawley and Mercy sat at the kitchen table together, coloring on large sheets of paper he'd brought home.

"What is it?" Mercy asked, pointing to Rawley's drawing.

"You don't know what that is? That's a boat! I have to take you to town pretty soon, to the marina

and show you the boats. Those fishermen catch all
the fish and crab we eat."

"How do they catch dem?"

"One of these days I'll show you," he told her.
"And what's that?" he asked, pointing to a scribbled picture.

"You," she said. And then she giggled.

He studied the picture closely. Then he made a
whole bunch of dots on the bottom of the drawing.

"What's that?" Mercy asked.

"Whiskers," he said, and then he grinned at her.

Rawley looked up at Devon. "Remember Cooper's girl? Sarah? You met her that first morning."

"Yes, sure."

"She asked about you, asked if you was still
around. I told her you liked it here, that you were
talking about looking for work. She said you
should come to the new doctor's open house this
weekend—everyone will be there. You can visit
a little bit, ask around if anyone is hiring or looking for help. And you can get a feel for if anyone
seems to recognize you—you're going to have to
step out of hiding if you really do want work."

"I know," she said. "And that's why I left The
Fellowship—I wanted to live in the world again.
I wanted to read everything, hear everything, see
everything. I know the world is hard and scary, I
know. But, Rawley, prison is scary, too—even if
it's a fine, bountiful prison. I was a teaching as-

sistant in an elementary school for a year—the teacher asked the eight-year-olds, 'Would you rather be on a deserted island alone or with someone you hate?' And one little boy answered, 'With someone I hate so I'd have something to eat.' We laughed so hard. But that's what a pure, controlled, perfectly constructed and protected commune can be like. Everything is thought through, down to every chore, every meal, the schedules down to the minute, even what we wore so there'd be no competing or envy. Everything except what people feel. It's a deserted island stocked with your favorite foods, cozy shelters, protection and comfort. And the inhabitants eventually eat each other."

Rawley just stared at her for a long moment while Mercy scribbled on her page. Finally he said, "I gotta ask. If someone recognizes you, are you in danger?"

She shrugged. "I don't know for sure. Sometimes people left and it wasn't given any notice, like everyone just looked the other way. Sometimes they left for good, but others would stay away for a few days and then return. I didn't leave with permission. I was told I could not take my daughter away. But she's my daughter."

Rawley thought about this for a moment, then he said, "Hmm. So, you want to try the doc's open house on Saturday?"

Again the shrug. "I have to do something. Right?"

"Devon, if you need to get farther away, like way far away, I'll scrape up some money for a bus ticket."

"I'm not sure what I should do. But I ask my-self—why would they look for me here? Why would they look for me at all? They're very busy—there are the gardens just starting to yield summer produce, there's stock, there are children to tend. And they don't like spending time on the outside. Jacob believes he's being spied on by the government and by law enforcement, because they want his money and his property. I don't know how true it is but that doesn't matter—it's what he thinks."

"Jacob?" Rawley repeated.

"The founder. The leader of The Fellowship." And then she gazed briefly toward Mercy.

Rawley seemed to understand at once. "Ah," he said. "Well, you look different, Devon. You don't stand out so much. You can be my second cousin, twice removed, takin' refuge from a bad relation-ship, looking for work."

"Think that would work?" she asked.

"I ain't gonna kid you, chickadee—if someone from that camp of yours wanders into town and looks you square in the face, they'll know you. But if one of 'em comes into town lookin' for a blue-eyed blonde with a long ponytail, Thunder Point folks will say they don't know any such person. But, you could always scream if you have to."

"I can. And I used to run track in high school."

That made him smile. "You got a driver's license?"

"Had one," she said. "When I joined The Fellowship, they took all my personal things and said they'd be stored for me. When you sneak out in the dark of night, you don't get those things back."

"Hmm. Guess that means you got no birth certificate."

"Course not. But I think my driver's license is still valid. I just don't have it. And I memorized my Social Security Number. Why do you ask?"

"Because you're gonna have to get around, that's why. I been working on another truck—one left to me. Eventually it'll be as fine as that old classic red job, but for right now? It runs fine."

When Devon and Mercy arrived at the beach bar, ready to go to the job fair, she found Sarah and Spencer sitting on the deck with coffee. She didn't want to intrude, so she just said, "Hi. I'm here."

"Whoa," Spencer said, nearly jumping out of his chair. "It's a whole new you!"

"That's darling," Sarah said, smiling. "Good cut—you look like a young Meg Ryan. It must've been hard to part with that long hair."

"Nah, I was ready to let that go. It's more trouble than you can imagine." But she often found herself reaching for that long braid, running a hand down the back of her neck.

"Pull up a chair, we have time. I was just watching Cooper down on the beach."

Rawley came out onto the deck. "If you want to leave Mercy with me, I'll show her how we catch the fish. After Cooper gets done on the beach and comes up, we'll go out on the dock. I'll make sure she has a life vest."

"I don't want you to be stuck babysitting, Rawley," Devon said.

"Let her go," Spencer said. "I know how to run the bar if anyone shows up. Austin's down there already, trying to empty the bay of fish."

"And I think Landon's coming in," Sarah said. "He'll help."

"She can't swim, Rawley," Devon said nervously.

"She's not gonna swim. She's gonna fish. And she's not gonna eat worms, either. I hope." He reached for her hand and she looked up at his grizzled face and beamed. "Wanna catch some fish?" he asked her. And she nodded enthusiastically.

Sarah got up, draining her cup once she was standing. "I'm going to run upstairs and change— I've been out on the bay this morning. I'll be back in a minute. Help yourself to coffee. Then we'll make a run on Carrie's catered delights at the open house." And with that she was gone.

Neither Spencer nor Devon said anything until Rawley and Mercy were down the stairs and Sarah had closed the door to Cooper's upstairs apartment. It was Spencer who said, "Rumor has it you're thinking of sticking around awhile."

Devon looked at him sharply. "There's rumors about me already?"

He chuckled. "Not the scary kind, like that you dabble in witchcraft or eat puppies for breakfast. Rawley mentioned you were thinking about looking for work around here."

"Oh. Right. Of course. Well, it all depends. I'm unknown here. If there were jobs, I'm sure people who have lived here a long time would have them."

"You'd think so, wouldn't you? I'm from out of town. I came here for a job."

"Really? What job?" Her interest was immediately piqued.

"I'm the new Athletic Director and coach at the high school." Then he laughed. "Really, though, I'm a gym teacher in charge of gym teachers."

She sighed audibly. "A dream job," she said. "Is your wife athletic?"

He glanced away. "My wife passed away a few months ago. That's why I wanted to move. Austin and I needed a fresh start."

"I'm so sorry," she said. "My gosh, I barely meet you and I put my foot in my mouth."

"No harm done. And no, she wasn't particularly athletic. She liked boating and a little waterskiing, but that was it. And I have to give her a lot of credit—she came to all the games I coached. Not sure she had fun," he added with a laugh. "But she was there."

"You must miss her so much," she said.

"There are tough days. I try to take comfort in her relief. She fought a battle with cancer.... I'm glad that's over for her...."

Devon swallowed hard. Yet another reminder that as bad as she thought her life to be on some days, here was a brave man who had weathered the ultimate storm—parting with a loved one who had suffered.

"And why Thunder Point? Just the job?" she asked.

"Not just the job, but I'm real happy about that. It's a surprise, really. I was looking for something in Oregon because Cooper's here."

"Ah, you're good friends...."

"We're getting there. Cooper's a pretty okay guy. He's also Austin's father."

"I thought you were Austin's father."

He took a breath. "Well, it's complicated, but here goes. We were living in Texas where I taught and coached. Just before Bridget passed away we learned that Austin is actually Cooper's biological son. Cooper was engaged to Bridget way back— we honestly didn't know. So we did the right thing—contacted Cooper, explained to Austin." He gave a shrug. "So it goes. Life isn't always cut-and-dried."

"No kidding," she said. Co-dads? Just what she needed—another commune. "And it's working out?"

He gave a shrug. "So far. What about you?" he asked.

"Me?"

"Uh-huh, you. Divorced? Widowed? And why Thunder Point?"

"Never married," she said. "I was involved, that's about it, and I am no longer involved. And Thunder Point was just the town at the end of the road. And, of course, Rawley is here and he's been so kind."

"Of course," Spencer said. "And Mercy's dad?"

Jeez, she thought. She'd better get used to people coming right out and speaking their minds. "Um, not a great father figure. I'm trying to keep a low profile."

"Oh. He doesn't know you're here?"

"I hope not," she said. "But he knows Mercy is with me."

"Won't he want you to come back to him?"

"Me?" she asked. "No, he was clear about that.

We haven't been involved in over three years. And before you pass judgment, he has other women and children—a veritable tribe. Now please, can we let the subject go?"

He frowned at her and she could read his mind. He was a single father; he would have opinions about a woman stealing away his child. He wouldn't understand, wouldn't be able to give her the benefit of the doubt. Nice as he seemed, she didn't know Spencer well enough to trust him with the truth.

"All right," Sarah announced, coming suddenly from within the bar. "I'm ready. Are you?"

"You bet," Devon said, standing. "Let me wave to Mercy."

"I can help with that," Sarah said. She let go a piercing whistle and everyone on the beach, including Rawley and Mercy, turned toward the deck. They all waved at each other.

"That was awesome," Devon said.

"Thanks. Cooper taught me."

Four

When Sarah was slowly making her way up the road to Highway 101 with Devon in the passenger seat, she asked, "Does this outing make you nervous?"

"Oh, yes," she confessed.

"Just take it slow—it's not a job interview. I mean, if you hear of something promising, don't hesitate, but probably the most important thing is just getting a feel for the Thunder Point people. They're very nice. Sometimes nosy, but good, honest people."

"I'll try," Devon said.

"Of course. Listen, I was divorced after one miserable year of marriage so I'm well aware of how hard it can be. In fact, I moved here a little over a year ago, before my divorce was even final. Getting your confidence back after something like that—it's not easy."

"Landon's not your son?"

"No," she said with a laugh. "My younger brother. It's been the two of us since he was six. Ten years of being a big sister slash single mother."

"Wow. You did it on your own?"

"Our parents were killed in an accident—there weren't any choices about it. And it worked out— more due to him than to my parenting skills, I'm sure. He's a great kid."

"And now? You're engaged...."

That caused Sarah to glance at the ring. "I wasn't divorced long when I met Cooper. I wasn't going to get involved with a guy, especially one like Cooper, but he's relentless. Thank God."

"A guy like Cooper?" she couldn't help but ask.

Sarah laughed. "One look at him and I took him for a player."

"Player?" Devon asked.

"Doesn't he, though? Look like the kind of guy who could give women a real run? But he's not— he's so committed, it's almost shocking. I was the one on the run—he had trouble catching me. But I am now very, very caught. If you had told me two years ago I could be this happy, I'd say you were crazy. Out of every storm..."

Devon just listened, thinking players don't always look the way they're supposed to look. That sexy guy in the torn jeans and T-shirt who showed off his broad chest and muscled arms and shoulders is ready to settle down, but the one she fell for—so morally superior and always quoting scriptures—proved to be a bad choice.

"People don't always look like who they really are."

Sarah pulled off the highway and headed for town. "You don't have to tell me, sister. I caught my husband banging the maid of honor. A stunning moment in my romantic history. So, this doctor's office, this open house, it's a small space. I'll be close by, even if the gathering spills out onto the front sidewalk. If you do lose sight of me, I'll be waiting at the diner across the street. All you have to do is say hello, visit a little and then let me know when you've had enough. And you don't have to explain anything, even if you're asked. You're visiting your distant cousin because he offered, things are fine, you're just looking around the area, you know..."

"I know," she said, but in fact she was very grateful for this reminder. She didn't have to answer those difficult questions—the kind Spencer asked.

Sarah parked across the street from the new Family Practice. There were some streamers and balloons and the front door was propped open. And yes, the office was small. It looked like a storefront in a row of storefronts, sitting right between the sheriff's department and Carrie's Deli.

The first person Devon met was Scott Grant, the new doctor, who was greeting people at the door. And the inside of his new practice was smaller than small. She counted room for ten chairs and a coffee table right inside the door, a counter with a swinging half door leading to the back. On the other side of the counter was one desk, some shelves, a desktop computer and a room divider that opened on the right side for people to pass into the back where there must be exam rooms. Though it was crowded, there was room for a small table covered by a festive tablecloth on which sat the snacks and punch bowl. This office space could easily be used for a dress shop, a greeting cards and notions store or a travel agency.

The next people she met were Carrie, her daughter, Gina, and granddaughter, Ashley. Ashley was filling cups with punch while Gina was putting out trays of bite-size sandwiches and cookies. Devon saw Carrie pull a cooler out from under the table and withdraw a storage container filled with a variety of hors d'oeuvres, which were then placed into a cute arrangement on a large tray.

There was a little polite small talk. She met Gina's boss, Stu, who owned the diner; Gina's husband, Mac, the town deputy; and a couple of neighboring business owners. Having noticed a few people wandering around in the back of the clinic area, Devon couldn't resist. It was, after all, an open house. She walked behind the room divider and what she found was a series of cubicles and she knew what they were for. There was a treatment room with a bed, counter, sink, chair, supplies. Then another exam room. She found what must be the doctor's office—there was a desk and shelves laden with books, and the door actually closed for privacy. There was what could pass for a very small break room containing a little table and two chairs, refrigerator, microwave, cupboards and sink.

Then she heard Sarah's voice asking the doctor when he would be open for business. "Monday. I'm planning on being open Monday, Wednesday, Friday and Saturday—but I'll come in if someone needs me. I'm keeping some E.R. hours in Bandon," he said, then laughed. "I'm working in Bandon to afford this practice. I still have some equipment on the way—most of it is small and portable for now. I doubt I'll ever have an X-ray but I have a small lab and can do simple tests here. It's a very compact little setup. And I'm planning to run some specials."

"Oh?" Sarah asked him.

"Cut-rate school and sports physicals and, in the fall, ten-dollar flu shots." Devon smiled as she noticed his chest puff up a little.

It was sweet, she thought. Handsome young

doctor, brand-new practice, good ideas for bringing in new patients.

"Who's helping you?" Sarah asked.

"I'm doing everything myself, so far. I need an R.N. or, even better, a physician's assistant, but no one really wants to work for a part-time practice, and I'm afraid it'll be a while before I can give up the Bandon E.R. to keep this place open six days a week. I can cover for a good nurse, but the paperwork is going to kill me. What I really need is a top-notch office manager, one who can triage patient needs and keep the forms moving whether I'm here or not."

"Well, I'm going to be out of work by the end of the summer, but I have no idea what a person does in a doctor's office," Sarah responded.

But I do, Devon thought. It had been a long time, but she'd been a clerical worker in a small neighborhood doctor's office. She knew how to keep charts organized and up-to-date, file insurance claims, schedule appointments, all that sort of thing. She wondered if she'd find the courage to put herself out there. And just as she was considering this, she was snagged by a woman.

"So, you're the new girl. From Seattle, I hear."

Devon looked around a little nervously and the woman laughed.

"Believe me, there's only one new girl that I know of," she said. "How do you like the town?"

"I've hardly seen it," Devon said.

"I'm Lou McCain. That's my nephew, the big guy who won't leave Gina alone. Come with me, I want to know all about you."

The woman turned, clearly expecting to be followed, and Devon did so. She wasn't about to argue.

Lou sat down on one of the chairs in the small waiting room and patted the chair beside her. Devon took the chair obediently, hoping this woman didn't ask difficult questions because she would be impossible to refuse.

"Your name?"

"Oh," she said, and laughed self-consciously. "Devon. How do you do."

"Splendid, thank you. Now, tell me all about yourself. Where are you from? What brought you to Thunder Point? How long will you stay? What do you do?" Then she laughed. "I'm sorry—I'm used to dealing with middle-school kids and my nephew's kids, who I help raise. I'm an eighth grade English teacher. It's made me very direct. Kids that age live by the 'literal minimal' law— if you give them a question they can answer with one word, they will."

So will I, Devon thought.

"I grew up in Seattle. I've been kind of a... well, I was in a relationship, but I wasn't married. I was...ah...you know."

"I know," she said. "I'm still single at just a titch over sixty. Never married. However, I've had a relationship or two along the way. Just maybe more than two. Never lived with a man, however. I'm thinking about it now, though. My nephew just got married and Gina has moved in with us. It's very fun, but we are bursting at the seams. And I do have this wonderful... Oh, you don't want to know about that...."

"Sure I do," Devon said.

"But where are you staying, darling?" Lou asked.

"My very distant cousin, Mr. Rawley Goode," she said. "Just when I didn't know where to go or what to do, he offered me a place. And it gives me time to think about what to do next." Then she smiled. "I'm also a teacher, though it's been years."

"Really? What age?"

"I have a degree in early childhood development. I'd just gotten started on my master's when I was...sidetracked, I guess you could say. I became a mother."

Lou smiled. "It sounds like you made good use of your time. We could use a preschool here. Desperately so. But the town can't afford it and paying tuition would be something most people here could not afford. A couple of people have run the numbers but the bottom line wasn't good."

"But is there a day care?" Devon asked.

Right at that moment a young woman entered the office holding the hands of two preschoolers. She was welcomed warmly and Dr. Grant came from the back to greet them. He seemed very happy to see them; he picked up the little girl and ruffled the little boy's hair.

"The doctor's children," Lou explained. "Very cute. They're three and four. And yours is…?"

"My daughter is three," she said. "Right now she's fishing off the dock with Rawley."

"Day care, you asked," Lou reminded her. "There are a couple of women in town who baby-sit in their homes for working parents, but no official day care center. People tend to rely on friends, neighbors and family for that sort of thing. Will you be looking for a sitter?"

"If I manage to find a job, I will," she said. "How long have you lived here?" Devon asked Lou.

"Here? A little over four years, but I grew up not far from here in Coquille and lived there all my life until Mac took this assignment. As I'm sure you've been told, he's the law in this little town—Sheriff's deputy with a few other deputies that work for him. It's a little office, right next door. I'll be honest—I didn't want to move, but I'm glad I did. I love the school where I teach and I've made good friends."

"I don't suppose they're looking for a kindergarten teacher?"

Lou put a hand on hers. "Not that I know of, sweetheart. But there are a lot of schools in other towns not too far away."

"I'll have to call around. I've been at Rawley's house for almost two weeks. I'd better either find a job or move on."

"Where would you go?"

She shook her head. "I don't know."

"Not back to Seattle?"

"No. I don't have any family there anymore. I think it's time for a fresh start. Somewhere."

"A fresh start as a single mom," Lou said with a warm smile. "How exciting!"

Devon felt her stomach clench. "Exciting?"

"Yes, exciting!"

Devon just shook her head. "I don't know. My future looks pretty uncertain right now. And before my daughter came along, I had some pretty lean times...."

"In my life, there seemed to have been cycles— for five to ten years things were up, then followed a long struggle, then things would swing up again. Up and down. I don't think life is very consistent. But the secret is knowing there's no limit to the number of times you can reinvent yourself!"

As the little doctor's office got busier and more crowded, Devon excused herself and told Sarah she wanted to walk around the town a bit and would be back.

It wasn't a new or highly polished town, but it was pretty. Devon walked down the sidewalk in one direction then crossed the street and went the other way. She passed lots of small shops, taking note of a store that sold secondhand clothes. There were pots of geraniums hanging from lampposts, window boxes holding roses, and while some of these stores had peeling paint, others looked freshly scrubbed and painted. She peeked inside the diner, an old-fashioned establishment with booths and counter stools. All that seemed missing was a jukebox. She headed down the street toward the marina.

All she had seen from Cooper's was a marina with some boats, but it was so far across the beach she wasn't sure what kind of boats there were or how many there were. She was surprised to see big fishing boats, trawlers, sailboats, crabbers. She walked down the street that led to the boat launch and dock. There was a big restaurant at the west end of the marina.

She felt the beach pulling her. It was like seeing a movie from her former life. There was a woman jogging down the beach, reminding Devon she used to love running. She ran track in high school. She saw a volleyball net set up down the beach and a few people batting the ball around. Out on the water were a couple of people on paddleboards and one kayaker heading out toward the mouth of the bay where the frothing Pacific waited. The surrounding hills were steep and rocky and beyond this protected bay, mountains rose in the distance.

It felt like a pocket of safety. And people were living. Having fun. Being part of the real world where everything was not limited or controlled. Devon made up stories about them in her head. The woman was jogging on her day off; the paddleboarders were on a date; the volleyball players were high school or college students; the kayaker was... Wow, she realized it was Landon! He was working his arms and shoulders like a demon.

As she traversed the beach and neared the volleyball game, a runaway ball came close to her. She dashed for the ball. She flipped it into the air and served it back to the players with all her strength, sending it sailing a great distance.

"Whoa!" one of the boys shouted. "Lady, you're on *my* team!"

Devon laughed gaily and gave them a wave.

In her former life, she'd worked while attending school and she'd lived with Aunt Mary. She had belonged to a gym. She liked to run, play summer softball with friends, go to ball games and clubs. She hadn't had much of a savings account and she'd had to supplement her scholarships with loans, but that was the life of a student. It was fun and fulfilling and tense and pressured and exciting. It was *normal*.

In Jacob's world Tuesday would look like Monday had—the only variable was the weather. They worked. They were not without their own kind of fun, but it was very odd and lopsided. No one pulled on their spandex and went outside the fence and jogged down the road. They didn't load up in a car and head for the movies or the library or the coffee shop. They were all in good shape because their work was hard and physical but it was rare that they took a break from work to throw a ball around. Sometimes they'd get a little game of hide-and-seek going and let it go out of control. Most of their diversion was just a private thing between the women—popcorn, stories, a food fight in the kitchen while making cookies late at night.

But not only was there very little change, there was very little possible. Jacob's plan was simple: everyone would be safe and well cared for inside his walls and under his domination. Big Daddy. The world would end, but they would be safe together. They did not need to think as individuals or to have personal goals; they would not experience the heartbreak or the triumph of success in the mean real world.

There's no limit to the number of times you can reinvent yourself!

The volleyball came back at her and she served

it back at the players again, better than before,
and they cheered! She danced around a little for
them, arms in the air. And for the first time since
leaving the family she thought, *Maybe it's not a
choice between either yielding my free will and
identity to The Fellowship, or experiencing complete devastation and danger on my own. Maybe
there is a place in the middle.* Maybe she could
have her own life again! Why not? Not everyone
in the world lived in a commune run by a controlling, bible-beating, drug-dealing man!

She looked at Cooper's place and saw him. He
was on the deck, leaning on the rail, watching her.

It was time to go back. She turned and went
back across the beach to town. She peeked in the
diner and when she saw Sarah and Lou sitting
there with another woman, she went in. She was
introduced to Ray Anne, a small, compact blonde
about the same age as Lou but so different in appearance—bleached hair, sexy clothes and flashy,
while Lou was attractive in a much more sedate
and conservative way.

"Sarah, I want to talk with the doctor for a second before we leave. I'll be right back."

"Sure, Devon," Sarah said, looking a little be-
wildered.

Taking a couple of deep breaths as she crossed
the street, she went back into the open house. The
crowd had thinned a little. Dr. Grant was talking

to Mac, Lou's nephew. Dr. Grant held his daughter on his hip. She stood back a bit, a little nervous, until both men stopped talking and turned her way, their brows raised in question.

"Dr. Grant, I've been looking for openings, for work, and as it happens I've worked in a doctor's office. It's been a long time, just over five years, and I was only part-time, but I know how to do all the things a medical secretary does. I answered the phones, I'm up to speed on HIPAA regulation, have filed insurance claims, scheduled appointments, all that. The doctor said I did a good job, but she closed her practice. It was just less than a year of experience but it was an ob-gyn practice and there are hardly any crazier, more demanding patients, especially with a doctor who gets called out a lot for deliveries, leaving people waiting. So, if you're looking for someone... I mean, would you consider me? If there's no one else? I heard you say you didn't have anyone and..."

He smiled at her. "I'd love to talk about it," he said. "Can you come to the office Monday morning?"

She let out her breath. Even though she was well aware he might not find her qualified, she felt as though she'd just shed thirty pounds! "Yes," she said. "If you're sure..."

"I'd love to hear more about your short career

in obstetrics," he said with a laugh. "I'll be here by eight and stay till five or so. Anytime you're free."

"Thank you," she said in a breath. "I'll, ah, see you. Monday. Yes. And thanks for letting me come to your open house!"

"I'm glad you stopped in."

After better than a year of pounding the pavement looking for work in Seattle, followed by four years in a commune, Devon had a job interview. All those old feelings of vulnerability and fear rose to the surface once again.

She had worried all weekend about what to say, how to say it, how to talk about her work history with that long five-year gap and not come off looking like some freak or loser. She had learned during her struggle to find employment that many people thought the poor, jobless, homeless citizens were all drunks, addicts, lazy or lunatics. They didn't recognize how many of them were senior citizens, war veterans and other victims of the failing economy. The high rate of business closures and escalating unemployment rate made it tough for anyone to find work. Many of the jobless were well educated and hardworking, just like herself.

Though she was very nervous about her meeting with Dr. Grant, she was also determined. And it was Rawley who gave her the courage to see it through. He said, "Listen here, miss. If you find yourself a job, it's a start. And if you don't get the job, it don't matter. We'll go on the same, and you'll just try again."

"I just don't know why you're so kind to me, a perfect stranger," she said.

"Like I told you before, I been on your end of things and I have a lot to pay back. And two, you ain't hardly a stranger anymore."

She left Mercy with Rawley at the beach bar. Cooper gave her a lift across the beach to town first thing in the morning. She was waiting when Dr. Grant unlocked his office door. He was surprised and seemed pleased to see her. While he brewed some coffee in that tiny break room, they chatted about general things—how she liked the beach, the town, the people she'd met. She asked him how long he'd been in Thunder Point and was very surprised to learn he'd only been in Oregon for about a year, working in Bandon, and had found a house to rent in Thunder Point only a month ago. He had come from Vancouver.

"And I'm originally from Seattle," she said. "That's where I grew up."

When the coffee was brewed they sat down at the small table and Dr. Grant explained that he needed someone who was comfortable doing a wide variety of tasks. He was looking for someone who could manage the office; field phone calls; keep ahead of the paperwork; schedule patients;

call in prescriptions and keep the office open six days a week, even though he would only be in for four of those days.

"I have two small children, my wife is deceased and I have another part-time job in Bandon. I need someone with good management skills to help me make the best use of my time, so that I can take care of my family responsibilities. And it goes without saying I need someone who's good with people."

"The woman who brought your children to the open house—I thought she must be your wife?" Devon asked.

"My babysitter," he said with a laugh. "I'd be lost without her. Her name is Gabriella and I've known her and her family for a long time. So—this job? Is this something you think you can do?"

Devon stood and pulled a piece of paper from her back pocket.

"Resume?" he asked.

She shook her head. "I made a list of all the things I remember doing for Dr. Stadler. Imogene Stadler, if you want to try to locate her. She closed her office and joined an OB group, which left several of us out of work." Then Devon detailed for Dr. Grant her extensive list of experience—filing; transcribing; writing prescriptions for the doctor to sign; taking patient histories; processing referrals; answering phones, to name a few. "There were times I was needed in the exam room as a chaperone and I learned to hand instruments to the doctor. I also went through lab tests, put results in charts and generally made sure Dr. Stadler had what she needed. Then there were things that just happened unexpectedly—the doctor's seven-year-old threw up at school and I went to get her. We had an elderly patient suffer a stroke in the waiting room—and I swear it was nothing I did! I called more than one ambulance—a good number of OB patients want to see the doctor to ask if they're really in labor. Never a good idea. If you have to ask..." She shrugged. Then she handed him the paper. "That's everything I can remember. It's been five years."

He took the page and glanced at it. "Great. You appear to be well qualified."

"I have a degree from the University of Washington—early childhood development. I was a teacher's aide in kindergarten very briefly. It was a private school and it closed when funding ran out."

"Is that your goal? To teach again?"

"I did love it, but these days any job is a good job. And I also liked working in the doctor's office very much."

"I think you're just the person I'm looking for," he said with a smile.

"Well, maybe not," she said, bolstering herself. She sat straighter in her chair and lifted her chin.

"I have a three-year-old and no babysitter. Yet, that is—I decided to find work before I looked for a sitter."

He smiled at her. "That isn't going to be a problem. I can help you with that."

"Oh. That would be amazing. There is one thing I think you should know, though. My lifestyle before coming here wasn't...typical. I lived with a group of people for four years. I worked very hard, and was very motivated, but I was mainly a domestic and a mother. And when I left, I left with no money and the clothes on my back. Mr. Rawley Goode, a distant cousin, has given us a place to stay." Then she looked down.

Dr. Grant said nothing for a while. When she looked up, his face was gentle. "I take it you left a bad situation."

She nodded. "I left before it became worse, before my daughter paid the price."

"We'll keep this between us if you like. But a word of advice, Devon. Never feel embarrassed about taking your life back."

"Thank you."

"I'd like to hire you for a trial period. I have to protect the practice, so I'll have to do a background check, just to make sure you're not a criminal or wanted or anything that would put us in jeopardy. You'll have access to prescriptions and drugs and I have to be diligent."

She smiled at him. "I've never even had a traffic ticket. And I never have taken drugs—unless you count beer. I was a college student once, after all."

"Understood," he said, smiling back. "If you check out and if you do a good job of managing the office, we're a team. All of this could take as long as a month. I'll start you at this salary," he said, writing a figure on a notepad, sliding it toward her. Six hundred a week! Her mouth fell open and she blinked. "If all goes well and everything checks out, I'll double your pay in a month."

Her hand actually went to her heart and she fought the urge to go limp. "But…but what about work clothes…I don't… I can't…"

"I'll get you a uniform. A couple of sets of nurse's scrubs. You'll need white tennis shoes."

"I can do that."

"Do you need an advance on your pay?"

"No, but… Well, to do a background and check my employment and college transcripts, you'll have to look for the name Devon Anne McAllister. I've been concerned that someone is looking for me. I don't know that for sure, but someone… the man I lived with could come looking for me. If he were to ask people…"

Scott Grant was frowning. "Were you abused, Devon?"

Clear-eyed and calm, she answered, "He forbade me to leave. We weren't married but he said

I was free to go without my daughter. Of course I couldn't do that. I left without his approval."

Scott Grant folded his hands on the small table. "You're clear now, aren't you? That's abuse? Right?"

"It could be a lot of things, I guess."

"Should you talk to Deputy McCain about your experience?" he asked.

"No, I should try to get on with my life."

"If I understand the law, you are, as the mother, the assumed custodial parent in an unmarried situation. The biological father has rights, and he can assert those rights legally. But preventing you from removing your child from his home would be considered custodial interference. Now, if you refused to acknowledge his legal rights, you would be guilty of the same. But this is a court matter."

She shook her head. "He will never go near a lawyer or courtroom."

"I see. Well. Before we start working together, I'd like us to make an agreement. I'll help you as much as I can. I'd like you to give me your word— if you discover this man is looking for you, I want you to talk to Mac. He's a good man. You can trust him. He would know what advice to give you."

She nodded. "I can agree to that. I'd rather just put it all in the past."

"Understandable." He sipped from his cup. "So? Tomorrow at eight?"

"You weren't planning on working on Tuesdays," she reminded him.

"Tomorrow will be different. We'll call it orientation. Bring your daughter and we'll take her to my house together to meet Gabriella. I'll check with her tonight, but I have no doubt she'll be happy to take on one more three-year-old. I think the kids will like having a playmate. I think it will work for you."

"Do you know how much she'll charge?" she asked hesitantly.

"I don't know, but Gabriella is very nurturing and reasonable. We'll talk about it with her in the morning."

"Okay. Yes, that's wonderful." When Devon stood, she found her legs were weak, her knees shaky. She put out her hand. "I don't know how to thank you for giving me this chance. I promise I'll do a good job." She took a breath. She was exhausted. She smiled tremulously. "That took more energy than you can imagine."

He stood as well, taking her hand. "You've had some struggles, haven't you, Devon?"

"You have no idea," she said on a breath.

"Then I'm glad I can be the one to offer you a chance to turn things around. From this moment on, it's all up to you."

Five

As Devon walked back across the beach, her spirits rose with each step. In her previous life, things had been so *impossible!* And now, at her very first try at finding a job, she was found acceptable. In fact Dr. Grant said "highly qualified"! It was beyond her imagination. She had tears running down her cheeks before she even realized it. She wiped at them impatiently.

When she was halfway across the beach, she stopped and looked out past the big rocks to the Pacific. There was a boat out there, a mere spec on the horizon. Sarah's brother was on his paddleboard and it appeared he had a young boy along for the ride. The sun was high and bright; the air almost balmy. She passed a young mother with two small children playing on the beach, a stroller and a little cooler beside her towel. Mercy would like that—to be able to play and read and romp on the beach under a warm summer sun.

And she thought, *God, if I'm lucky enough to make a life for myself and my child in this small place, I swear I will never complain about anything again!*

She was halfway up the beach stairs when she saw him again. Spencer was just coming down. As he made to pass her on the stairs, he frowned and stopped. He reached out a hand and rested it on her shoulder. "You all right?"

He must have noticed her tears. She wiped her cheeks and smiled a little. "I got a job," she said in a faint whisper. She cleared her throat and tried that again. Louder. Stronger. "I got a job!"

He smiled at her. "Good for you. Where?"

"In the doctor's office. Full-time!"

He just laughed, silently.

She pushed past him and ran the rest of the way up the stairs and into the bar. There was just Cooper behind the bar, putting things away. She knew her smile was huge and her cheeks bright with excitement. "Where is Rawley?"

"Well, now. Looks like that job interview went well," Cooper said with a smile. "They're in the kitchen. Rawley is making bread with Mercy—a first. I hope she's taken charge. He's never done that before."

With a laugh, she darted into the kitchen. With a

stool propped up to the counter, Mercy was kneading green dough, rolling it out and making snakes. "What are you two doing?" she asked.

"Mercy said she was good at making bread and pie crust," Rawley explained. "I thought green would be fun." He wiped his hands. "How'd it go?"

"I got it," she said in a near whisper. "I start tomorrow. And unless there's some problem I don't know about, I can share Dr. Grant's babysitter. He's a single father with two little kids, so he knows it can get complicated for single parents."

"Good for you," he said. "How's 'at feel?"

"Oh, Rawley, you can't imagine." Her eyes teared up again. "All weekend I prepared myself for the inevitable—that he wouldn't find me qualified. Or even that I wouldn't look the part. You just can't imagine..."

He turned to grab his coffee. "I reckon I can imagine."

"I should...ah...look around for a place of my own," she said.

He lifted an eyebrow and gave her a half smile. "That so? Last time I looked, you didn't have no truck full o' furniture."

"Maybe there's something furnished," she said. "We don't need much."

"You do that if you want to, but it ain't necessary. I got used to the two of you. If I didn't know better, I'd think we were cousins. Family. Ain't hardly had any family. My mother, she passed when I was barely a man. I had no brothers or sisters and, don't tell anyone, but there ain't never been cousins. And there sure weren't no woman who could stand a crazy old vet like me."

Devon just laughed. She put a hand on his arm, bringing a slight blush to his cheeks. "You're the furthest thing from crazy I know."

"Is 'at right? Well, don't tell Cooper. He thinks he's doing me a good deed, keeping me in the bar like this, giving me work because I'm an odd one."

"You're not," she said. "And I think Mercy loves you a little bit. I should pay you rent at least," Devon said.

Rawley sipped his coffee then put down his cup. He leveled old blue eyes at her. "Here's the deal, missy. I know how important it is to you to be independent—you wasted no time telling me. What I'd like most of all is for you to find your way. You had a trial or two getting this far, you have a kid... it's high time your luck changes a little bit. It would do me good, being part of someone's luck changing. It'll probably do me more good than you. That old house is paid off. If you want to help with food, you go on ahead."

"That's not very much help," she said.

"You should prolly help with electric while you're at it—you burn lights reading half the night or watching that TV or chargin' up that laptop..."

She laughed at him. She tilted her head toward Mercy. "You're not having any issues with a three-year-old taking over your house?"

He thought for a moment. He sucked a little on his teeth. Then he said, "If I'd a had a normal life, I mighta had grandchildren. Maybe a little one like this here who wants to make green bread. Nah, she don't bother me at all. I get a big kick outta her. You about ready to go home?"

"Yes, please," she said. "I have to get ready for tomorrow. My first day."

He wiped his hands on a towel and reached in his pocket. He pulled out some keys. "You can take the truck. You got a seat for Mercy. You should have a ride so you can get back and forth—my hours just ain't the same as yours. But you're gonna have to take care of your own gas, and it eats a bunch."

She was stunned silent for a moment. "But how will you get around?"

"I told you—I have an old truck I'm workin' on that runs fine. Loud and ugly, but fine."

"Then if I use anything, it should be the old one!" Devon said.

"Nah, that won't work. I need that truck. When my work's done here and things get quiet, I work on that truck out back. I use Ben's old tools—he left 'em along with the truck. It's the most sensible way."

"Rawley," she said, stepping toward him. "This is too much. I could ride into Thunder Point with you in the morning and come home with you at night. I can stay busy till work starts or till you finish. And quiet—I can stay quiet. We won't make any trouble or fuss. Or get in the way."

He pushed the keys at her. "It's a stick. Can you drive a stick?"

"Rawley..."

"Mercy needs her sleep and I get up at five. And she needs a meal, a bath and bed at night. She needs cartoons or some kid show. Let's think about her right now. And when you get a little money saved and get used to this place, maybe you'll find just what you need. For now? It's a ride."

"Oh, Rawley...."

"That truck's a hundred years old. It'll work another few. I'm done talking about this now."

Devon was a little hard on Rawley's transmission going up the hill on her way to Elmore. She didn't dare look in the rearview mirror—she didn't want to see him wince or cringe. But once she got going, once she was on the highway, she not only did fine, she found it exhilarating. She felt so free, driving herself and Mercy, headed to a safe and secure place.

Once she got back to Rawley's, after giving Mercy some lunch and settling her with thirty min-

utes of cartoons before her afternoon rest, Devon
was back on the computer. She was researching
Oregon driver's licenses and laws concerning custody to see if Dr. Grant was right. She also looked
at the Washington State records of birth and her
college transcripts. Although she had a Washington driver's license somewhere, now that she was
in Oregon, that license wouldn't work for long. To
get her driver's license in this state she'd have to
take a test and provide documentation. And she
was thrilled to find that all she had to do was apply
to receive a copy of her birth certificate, which
she could do online, if she could get a credit card.

Then she read about custody and found Dr.
Grant had it right. Certainly as an E.R. doc he
would have run into domestic situations from time
to time, so he'd learned all about this.

Devon came to several sudden conclusions. She
had done nothing wrong by taking her child out
of a commune in which the biological father was
conducting illegal business. He would never seek
legal help to get Mercy back—not only did Jacob
believe he knew everything, he didn't trust courts
or law enforcement or government. Then there was
his elaborate marijuana growing operation. Devon
had no idea who he sold it to or how the business
was handled. There were new faces around the
commune from time to time and the men who
lived there came and went with regularity. And, of

course, one of these days Jacob would be caught and he would go to prison.

What she now knew with blinding clarity was that his "cult" was a front for his drug operation. It was a perfect distraction to have a God-loving, hippy-dippy, granola-natural, free-spirited commune that only appeared to live off the land and to do so modestly. Devon also realized that each woman there, including herself, had been targeted and recruited very carefully by Jacob himself. Devon shuddered at the reality of it all.

The next day Devon went to work and Mercy went to Dr. Grant's house to play with his children, Jenny and Will, watched over by Gabriella, the sweetest and most beautiful nineteen-year-old Latina she'd ever met. Gabriella had known Dr. Grant and his family since she'd been a small child. They had a good arrangement—she managed his household and he paid her college tuition—organizing their schedules to accommodate his work and her class schedule.

Devon quickly learned the routine in the doctor's office, which could be boring at times, since it was so slow. She scheduled a few appointments; improved his filing system; updated his computer files and even swept, mopped and dusted the office.

Devon brought her lunch from home but she

took her coffee breaks across the street at the diner where she could count on seeing some of the women she'd met. Many people passed through the diner and in no time she'd become a familiar fixture. Sometimes, when it was just Gina Mc-Cain and herself in the diner, or maybe Sarah as well, she found herself revealing parts of her story.

She shouldn't have been surprised when those women both chimed in with their own stories of bad relationships with men. It was almost like a rite of passage, surviving relationships that were not meant to be.

Spencer often found a reason to stop by the new clinic. She shouldn't have been surprised as she knew he was very curious about her. But he claimed he was just interested in how the doctor could help out with physicals for the members of the football team and the other high school athletes. Devon prepared a flier for Spencer complete with a price list. Scott was pleased with her initiative and Spencer took some fliers back to his office at the high school. He stopped by a couple more times to pick up more fliers. "You haven't been back to the beach lately," he said. "And the weather's been perfect."

"I've been working," Devon said with a laugh. "You know, you can take more of these fliers and then you won't have to keep coming back here."

He counted out ten fliers. He grinned handsomely. "I'm good with these for now," he said.

And he was back two days later for ten more. Although the doctor's hours were posted on the door, Spencer always seemed to stop by when Scott wasn't there.

In fact, a lot of the townsfolk stopped in from time to time. They wanted to know if the practice was going well and if Dr. Grant had patients yet, and if Devon was getting along all right. Between the diner and the practice Devon grew into the town, and the town grew into her.

After just a couple of weeks, Scott was impressed enough with her job performance that one day, out of the blue, he said, "I'd say your trial period is over and we can increase your pay."

As her new life fell into place, Devon grew more comfortable. She always kept her eyes sharp but never saw so much as a suspicious vehicle drive through town. She made a trip to the DMV, took and passed her driver's license test, and now had ID to go with the rest of her new life. Once she had socked away a thousand dollars in her savings account she indulged in a few things for herself. A blow dryer and a nice circular brush, and a few cosmetic items she hadn't used in years. Now the proud owner of a credit card, she bought some things online where they were often cheaper, but were delivered right to her door.

Along with the other changes, her appearance began to take on a new and improved look. She began to feel like the person she could barely remember.

"Why, Devon," Lou McCain said. "I knew you were a pretty thing the first day I met you. But, child, I love what you're doing with your hair these days. And if I'm not completely mistaken, you look like you've gained a little confidence."

A lot of confidence, Devon thought to herself. A large part of that came from realizing she could get a good, stable job and do it well but, perhaps, a larger part came from having women friends again. It was great just having friends to talk to about everything and nothing—from failed love affairs, new romances, family issues, even politics. The best parts of Devon's week were those days she took a coffee break at the diner with Gina, Sarah, Carrie, Lou and Ray Anne. She missed her sisters at The Fellowship. They hadn't always agreed or gotten along, loyalties shifted and adjusted, but they had relied on each other.

When Devon found out Ray Anne was a real estate agent, she said, "I've been very happy staying with Rawley, but I'd really like to have my own place. And I don't want to overstay my welcome."

"Yeah, I bet old Rawley is just hats and horns all the time," Ray Anne said.

Devon laughed. "He's actually a gem."

"Talks your ear off, does he?"

"One-on-one, he has plenty to say," Devon said. "And he promises we're not in his way and that we can stay as long as we like, but I think Rawley would like having his house back. Even though we're comfortable there, I'd like to be closer to Dr. Grant's practice and Gabriella. In fact, just about every street in town is close enough to be able to walk to and from work—that would be so nice. I just don't have much money. Do you ever come across a room for rent? Or a garage apartment? Maybe furnished? Or anything like that?"

"Not often. But I'll put the word out. What can you afford?"

She shook her head. "So little," she said. "A few hundred?"

Ray Anne said, "Whew. That's going to limit the possibilities."

"I have no furniture," Devon said. And rather than explain how she'd been living, she simply said, "I left everything behind, just so I could get out."

"Hmm, I did that once," Ray Anne said. "My first husband. I was young, he was a real ass with a drinking problem and I needed to get that behind me. I asked for nothing—I just signed everything and ran for my life. I had to start over. It wasn't easy but, once I was on my feet, everything was mine."

Devon was quiet for a minute. Then she said, "First husband?"

"I had three of them. The first one was a drunk, the second was much older and more stable, and he was controlling to the point of being abusive, and the last? Twenty years older than I was and cheating with every young thing he could round up. He had a lot of money so all the girls in their twenties were lining up to give him a go. But, after the first marriage, I never left with nothing again. I figured out a few things. Now I at least have a nest egg."

"Wow," Devon said. "Just when you think you're the only one in the world who had lousy luck with men..."

That made Ray Anne laugh. "Well, don't believe everything you hear, but I've also had some good luck here and there. Maybe it didn't pan out to be happily-ever-after in the white picket fence ideal, but I had good times with good fellas. So—how'd you get hooked up with Mr. Louse?"

"Oh, that," she said. "I might as well have been wearing a sign that said, 'Hi, my name is Devon and I have nothing, no family and my self-esteem is at its lowest ever.'"

"That'll do it," Ray Anne said.

Then, in the second week in July Ray Anne called Devon and said, "There's a duplex at the end of Sarah's street. It's for rent. It's small—only two bedrooms. And I'll warn you right now—it needs a lot of love. But it's only four-fifty a month. And everything in it works—appliances, wiring, plumbing. I might be able to talk the landlord into a few improvements, but he's stubborn. He just wants to forget it's there, which is why I handle the rental for him."

"I want to see it," Devon said instantly.

The duplex was located on one of the higher elevation streets in Thunder Point. The street itself was a bit of a mixed bag with a few large homes along with many that were small and old. Some of the properties were pristine and fussy while others had been left to ruin. The duplex, unfortunately, was one of the latter. There were weeds in the yard, cracked and broken sidewalks and the place had a neglected air about it. There was a broken-down overhang at the front of the house and the view from there was beautiful—Devon could see the entire bay and the mountains beyond. There was a speck off in the distance—that would be Cooper's place.

"That's a little scary," Devon said, pointing to the overhang.

"One of the things I think I could get repaired, if only to avoid a lawsuit."

If the outside looked bad, the inside was a disaster. Trash, peeling paint, holes in the walls—mostly from doorknobs that hit the walls when the doors had been swung wide. A few walls showed signs of suspicious holes—as if someone had thrown something or punched them. "Who lived here?" Devon asked.

"Four nineteen-year-old boys who had to be evicted. Mr. Dunwoody—and the neighbors— would like a quieter tenant next time around."

"And who lives on the other side?"

"Mrs. Marissa Bledsoe, an elderly widow, a little on the weak and wobbly side. She can't handle much in the way of upkeep, but she's pleasant and good-natured."

Devon looked at the filth, the scarred hardwood floors and the chipped and peeling paint. The place even had a bit of a smell to it, of what, she wasn't sure. The bathroom was a horror—there was a shower curtain that was disgusting and the tub and tiles were filthy. The toilet was older than she was, and there was a large chip in the porcelain tub.

The kitchen was almost as bad. Fortunately the newest item was the refrigerator and since the electricity had been left on, it was only dirty. Nothing had been left to rot.

Behind her Ray Anne was saying, "I know you left your things behind but I can help you find inexpensive secondhand items. Once the floors are scrubbed clean, they'll be safe, but you'll need area rugs—this place gets pretty chilly in winter."

"Will he paint and repair the walls?"

"He says if he has to put any work into it, he wants seven hundred."

"What about the damaged overhang?" Devon asked.

"I think I can talk him into that—it looks dangerous. And the agreement reads that if anything doesn't work or leaks, he has to replace or repair it. But it's four-fifty, as is. I'm sorry. I shouldn't have wasted your time. It's horrible."

Devon had been thinking about the layout—a small but functional kitchen, a good-size living room with a pretty little fireplace, two nice-size bedrooms and a rather large, disgusting bathroom. And a view to die for.

"I think it's beautiful. I'll take it!"

Six

Midafternoons on a weekday were a quiet time at Cooper's. Perfect time to have a little sit-down, and Landon and Spencer were asked to join Cooper and Sarah for a talk. Rawley passed the four of them as they were seated around a table on the deck and he headed back to his kitchen.

"You're welcome to join us if you want the latest news," Cooper said to him. "We're having a status update meeting."

"I don't do meetings. It ain't in my contract. I'll tend bar and serve. Anyone want anything?"

"I'm good," Spencer said, wondering what this meeting was all about.

"I'll have a Coke, Rawley," Landon said.

"'S'at right?" he said, and went inside. But he didn't come back.

"How'd that work out for you?" Cooper asked with a laugh.

"You need better help around here." Landon leaned back in his chair lazily. "Just give us the update," he said. "And be sure you clock my time."

Cooper looked at Sarah. "Do we have to be married before I can cuff him?" he asked.

But Landon got a wop on the back of the head from Spencer. "I don't have to marry anyone to do that. I'm his new coach. Now can we get to it? Please?"

"All right, we're getting married," Cooper said.

"We know this already, Cooper," Spencer replied.

"Soon. Two weeks from Saturday. Carrie said she'd cater a party right here—could be very nice. We'll have a quiet ceremony out on the beach," he said, taking Sarah's hand. "Then have a little sunset party on the deck, on the dock, on the beach."

"How lovely," Landon said, bored to tears.

"Landon, how would you like your own home?" Sarah asked him.

"So you're moving out on me instead of moving Cooper in with us?" he asked.

"Something like that," Cooper said. "We've been knocking around plans for the past couple of weeks. Sarah's going to be flying the rest of the summer. At least that's the way it looks right now. But she's short—her schedule is already lightening up and they have a brand-spanking-new Lieutenant Commander on his way in to take over most of her duties. So we started talking to builders. And we're going to build. Right there," he said, pointing to the steep hill next door to the bar. "Nice big picture window, big deck, stairs to the beach, big kitchen. We'll be excavating around the lot, making room."

"You're going to *disturb* the wildlife?" Landon asked. Cooper had been trying to respect the wishes of the departed friend who had left him the beachfront property; Ben had wanted the promontory on the other side of the bar left to the birds and flora—a natural preserve.

"The land between me and Thunder Point doesn't have any wildlife except beetles on it," Cooper said. "I'm going to develop it. At least some of it. I have to—I need a couple of decent roads. That's the price of a house. And I want a house." He reached for Sarah's hand. "Sarah's going along with me on this, at least until she figures out what she wants to do. While she's having a little time off to think, she's going to be a general contractor. She's going to help me build us a house."

There was quiet for a few moments and then it was Spencer who broke the silence. He cleared his throat. "I couldn't be happier for you both, but what does this have to do with me?"

"You've been hunting for a house," Cooper said. "You hoped to get into something with a bigger kitchen and bathroom before football practice started and you ran out of time to look. I think we can help with that. Consider it another temporary situation, but Sarah's place won't move in the wind, it's in town, and it's small but nice."

"Oh, yeah?"

"Wait a minute," Landon said. "I might get enough of Spencer at practice, no offense."

"No offense taken," Spencer said. "You're not my dream roommate, either."

"Landon, let's talk about you having your own place," Sarah suggested.

Landon sat up straighter, but suspiciously. And hopefully. "Like an apartment?"

"Like the toy hauler, where Spencer and Austin have been staying."

He glanced at it, thought for a moment. "Hot! Can I move it? Like somewhere *else?*"

"No," they said in unison.

He slunk back down in his chair. "Well, it's better than sleeping in the same place with you two, I guess." He glanced at Spencer. "They're embarrassing."

"You poor abused thing," Sarah said. "You have a terrible life. Your big sister is going to know how late you stay out and how many people you have in your 'apartment' until you move away. I don't know how you will live."

"Spence, why don't you and Sarah run over to

her house, take a look," Cooper said. "It might not be what you want long-term, but while you're still trying to figure out if this is the right town and school for you, it might just work. It's close to everything. Drop-dead view of the bay."

"I'll take you over in the Razor," Sarah said. "It's on a month-to-month lease and it's cheap. Three bedrooms, but the third is like a closet— only big enough for a small bed or a desk and a shelf. I've been using that room to store boxes of stuff I have no room for."

"Now?" Spencer asked.

"Now," she said.

"Come on, Landon," Cooper said. "Let's get to work."

When everyone stood, Landon muttered, "I came this close to having a bachelor pad..."

Driving across the beach, Spencer found himself feeling guardedly optimistic about this opportunity. He'd been all over this little town. Some of the neighborhoods were quaint, some very nice, some pretty run-down and worn-out, but one thing was a constant—property didn't become available very often. He'd looked at several rentals and even a few houses for sale, but nothing met his needs— they were either pathetic dumps or far too big and pricey for a high school football coach. And as a transplanted Texas boy, he was getting pretty well hooked on this Oregon beach and the lifestyle here.

As Sarah drove them up the hill to her house, he recognized the neighborhood. Yes, he'd driven up and down this street a few times; it was a pleasant, well-kept area—large pines behind and between the houses. Sarah's place was one of the smallest on the block, but as they pulled up in front of it, what really caught his attention was the view from the front of the place. From right outside the front door he could see the entire bay, all the way to Cooper's bar and beyond.

"If I were going to be here one more summer, I'd put a small patio right here," Sarah said.

"One thing I've figured out about this town—it is all about the view and Cooper's in the catbird seat. And to think he fell into it."

"Well, want to just stand here or go inside...?" Sarah asked.

Right then Ray Anne's car pulled up in front of the house. She rolled down the window to wave a greeting, and from the passenger side, Devon opened the door and stood in the street, waving over the top of the car. "Sarah! I found a house! Sort of! Right down the street!"

Sarah walked toward the car and Spencer found himself following. "What house?" Sarah asked.

"A duplex," she said. "At the end of your street."

"What duplex is that? I didn't know anything was vacant in this neighborhood."

"That old Dunwoody place," Ray Anne said. "You know—it's looking a bit...needy?"

But Devon's face was absolutely shining. "It's going to be beautiful!"

"There's lots to do," Ray Anne said. "It's past its prime. But it's a solid little place with a very nice neighbor."

"There isn't anything to do that I can't handle," Devon said, beaming. "I didn't think I'd get this lucky! This fast! It's going to be wonderful. We're going to love it."

Ray Anne just shook her head and laughed. "Oh, if only all my clients were this easy to please. Have a great day. We have to go find Devon a bed."

Spencer watched as they drove away. The first time he saw Devon, he thought she was cute. As the days became weeks, she grew more beautiful to him. Striking, in fact. And that laugh—it cut right through him. He couldn't seem to stay away from her and there was no logic to it.

He shook himself. "Let's have a look inside, Sarah," he said. "In case I haven't said so, this is really nice of you."

She unlocked the front door and entered, looking at him over her shoulder. "We have to look out for each other. We're combining families here."

"It's all good," he said. But it wasn't all good. He had no regrets about coming to Thunder Point. It was a great move for a lot of reasons and he was more than a little anxious to meet and start working with his colleagues and the team. Everyone he knew was growing deeper connections—Austin had gained a second father and soon, a stepmom and stepbrother. Cooper had gained a son and would soon add a wife and brother to the mix. Sarah and Landon were expanding their intimate circle. But in the midst of all these people, Spencer was alone.

He missed his wife. The past few years she'd been so sick, but he often missed the girl he'd married. It had been so long since he'd seen or held that girl.

The house was unremarkable, but had so many of the things he wanted—a large kitchen, a comfortably big bathroom, a living room with a fireplace, a backyard, a view. It was a simple house. Nothing flashy. Not the kind of house one aspires to. Not what he'd build if he could. Certainly not what Cooper was going to build next to Ben & Cooper's.

And yet it was perfect. Just what he and Austin needed.

"This is great, Sarah," he said. "If you're sure."

She laughed and asked, "How many houses do I need?"

He grinned at her. "Two weeks, huh?"

"I was a hard sell," she admitted. "But I'm ready."

"Is Cooper trying to tie you up before you can change your mind?"

"Not exactly," she said with a laugh. "He wants to get married on the beach before he brings heavy equipment in to excavate the hillside for building. He doesn't really know how much of a mess that's going to make. Getting him to wait two weeks was a challenge. Cooper's been married in his head for a while now."

"That's…kinda sweet. Who would figure Cooper for sweet?" Spencer dropped a hand and gave a pat to the head of Ham, who had come to greet them. "I guess the dog won't stay with the house?"

"Cooper would be devastated. He might be marrying me for the dog. But I assure you, some of the dog hair will probably stay with the house."

"One phone call gets my household goods en route. You want to think about this?"

She shook her head. "I'm ready to move."

"Where are you going to put all this stuff?" he asked.

"I'm going to store a few things, put a couple of things in the RV or Cooper's loft apartment and then get rid of a lot. Cooper has me convinced my new house deserves some new furniture. Need anything?"

He shook his head. "I have more coming than I need as it is. Maybe we'll have a big yard sale?"

"Maybe," she said with a laugh.

When they were back in the Razor, he said, "Drive me past that place Devon just rented."

"Sure. I'm curious, too. I've driven by it before, but never thinking it would have anything to do with me or a friend of mine." And she whirled down the street, past a lot of perfectly lovely homes.

At the end of the street, Devon's new place stood out like a wart on a nose. The grass was tall and mostly dead with a few green sprouts here and there. The driveway was covered in brown pine needles and the windows were streaked and filthy. The other half of the duplex was neat, except for the lawn, which was also a wreck. But the driveway on the other half was swept and the windows were clean. But that didn't help the overall effect much. "What a dump," he muttered.

"Holy crap," Sarah said.

"Hold up a second," he said.

Spencer got out and went up to the house. He cupped his hands around his face and peered inside. Then he turned back to Sarah. "Who the hell lived here? Hell's Angels? It's horrible," he said. "Filthy. Holes in the walls. Stains everywhere. Cigarette butts ground into the floor. A lightbulb instead of a fixture. It looks like a crack house."

Sarah came up beside him and pressed her face up against the front windowpane. "Ew," she said.

"She's got her work cut out for her. It looks like a fixer-upper."

"What the hell was she so happy about?" Spencer asked.

"Maybe this looks a lot better than what she had," Sarah said with a shrug.

"But she's staying with Rawley, right? And he's a little different, but Cooper said he's dependable and a good man even if he's not the most talkative. And he has a good, clean, sturdy house with plenty of room for them...."

"It's not always just about houses, Spencer. Maybe this represents more than that to her. You should ask her."

He thought about that for a second. "Maybe," he said. "If I run into her."

Spencer didn't run into her, at least not for a few days. He didn't go by the doctor's office or the diner. In fact, since seeing that god-awful duplex, he'd been trying not to think about her. For something like that to make her smile, to make her happy meant her previous circumstances must have been so much more pathetic than she let on. And that made him just plain *sad*. It was crazy that a beautiful young woman with an adorable little girl had escaped something bad only to land in that disgusting hovel. It amazed him to consider the idea that she might see this as breaking free.

But he couldn't get the girl off his mind.

He nursed a cup of coffee at the bar while Sarah and Cooper looked at their building plans— not just for a house, but for the whole ridge that stretched between his place and the town, including roads. Austin was in the RV watching TV, laying around and eating cereal out of the box. Landon had taken one of Cooper's kayaks out on the bay for an upper-body workout and would come in for his work shift after that. There were two kayaks rented, two paddleboards, and since Spencer had been in the bar, six people had been in for coffee. Four of them took coffee cups down to the beach and dock; two customers sat on the deck and enjoyed the morning view.

Despite all this activity, Spencer couldn't get the girl off his mind.

Rawley came into the bar from the kitchen. "I need a little time, Coop. You okay here alone?"

"No problem, Rawley," Cooper replied without looking up.

"Could be gone for a spell."

"I got it," Cooper said, still studying the layout in front of him.

A minute later, Spencer heard Rawley slam something into the bed of his truck outside. Then he was back in the kitchen. Next he was struggling out the door with a box full of stuff. Then he was back, then out again with a load of cleaning implements—mop, broom, rags.

Cooper finally looked up. "Rawley, what the hell are you doing?"

The old guy stopped short, mops and brooms and stuff in his arms, and said, "Every night I beat Devon and the little one home and you know why? Cause she works all day, then takes the little one to that shit hole she rented. They eat a sandwich she packed up and then Devon tries to make a dent in the filth and damage of that house while her daughter either looks at her books or sits with that old lady neighbor next door. It just ain't right. I'm going over there. See what I can do."

As if he had been hit with a cattle prod, Spencer was off his stool. "I'm in that with you, Rawley. Let me get my shoes and tell Austin I'll be gone awhile."

"Take your own car," Rawley said. "I'm putting in some serious time." And he was gone.

"Can you manage Austin?" Spencer asked Cooper.

Cooper turned to Sarah. "Can you handle Austin? The bar should be quiet. It's a weekday..."

"But I want to go!" Sarah said. "I'm embarrassed I didn't think of it!"

"Okay, we have a problem," Cooper said. "I can close the bar for a few hours, but we got us a kid."

"Landon will help out," Sarah said. "We'll just tell him not to serve alcohol and to keep an eye on Austin."

"Yeah," Spencer said. "What does he get for that? Double pay?"

"He gets me to not hate him," Cooper said. "If we're helping out a friend, he can just suck it up." And with that, Cooper went out on the deck and split the morning calm with a piercing whistle.

By the time Spencer was back on the deck in jeans and shoes, Landon was coming up the stairs to the deck. "What?" he asked.

"We're heading out to help a friend," Sarah told him. "We'd like you to keep an eye on the bar and Austin. Austin's watching TV right now—don't let him get away. And just don't sell alcohol. Cooper will be back before five."

"What friend?" he asked.

"Rawley's cousin," she said. "Devon. She rented a house down the street from us and it needs... help."

"Help because she shouldn't have to live in a completely demolished dump," Spencer said. "Austin goes no farther than the dock. In a life jacket."

"Gotcha," Landon said.

They headed out in two cars and when they arrived the front door was standing open. Rawley's old truck was backed into the driveway with the hatch down and there was the sound of pounding coming from inside.

"No moss growing under that old boy's feet," Spencer said as he stood outside the front door with Cooper and Sarah. Rawley was already involved in patching a hole in the wall with drywall he'd obviously brought along. There were a couple of cans of paint sitting on the floor.

"What've we got, Rawley?" Spencer asked.

Rawley looked up. "Bag the trash. She's got it in neat piles in each room. We got nasty kitchen appliances and while you're at it, pull 'em out from the wall and clean that nasty stuff under 'em. We got a bathroom that a vagrant wouldn't use. We got walls to paint, trim to scrub and paint, windows to wash. Leave the fireplace till last—she don't need it this summer."

Sarah walked across the living room and peeked into each room. "Cooper, that bathroom is yours. It's awful. Spencer, why don't you help me in the kitchen."

Spencer took a look at each room. "Yep, Cooper gets that bathroom." And then he got started pulling out appliances. While Sarah worked on cleaning the inside of the refrigerator, he bagged the trash and threw it in the back of Cooper's truck. A little over three hours later, the kitchen appliances were clean and Spencer was washing the walls so he could paint them while Sarah got started on cleaning out the cupboards.

And then they were interrupted when Landon and Austin pulled up in the Razor with a cooler strapped to the back.

"Lunch!" Landon announced.

Work stopped at once while Landon opened the cooler to reveal sandwiches and cold drinks. Austin carried a grocery bag full of chips and snacks.

"What did you do with the bar?" Cooper asked.

"Put the closed sign on the door, just like you used to do before you had slave labor," Landon replied. "Wow, this place is a wreck."

"And it's already a lot better than it was," Spencer informed him.

After some serious hand washing, they sat on the living room floor in a circle, all of them, and ate the sandwiches. And then they went back after it with a vengeance. By four-thirty Cooper and Rawley were leaving to take care of the evening crowd down on the beach. Sarah was looking over her handiwork—she'd cleaned all the windows while Spencer painted the kitchen. The floors were clean but ill-used. She scuffed a toe on the floor. "I guess that's what rugs are for," she said. "And, if Devon is interested, I might've found a home for some of the furniture I can't keep."

"I'd been thinking the same thing," Spencer said.

"Looks damn good in here." Sarah turned full-circle. "I'm going to walk down the block, let Ham out and take a shower. See you back at the beach?"

He laughed. "Remember, I still live at the beach."

"Maybe not for too much longer."

When Sarah was gone, Spencer stayed behind. He started to envision furniture in the rooms he could see. A table for four in the kitchen. A sofa and chair and bookcase in the living room. A toy chest. A blackboard on the kitchen wall by the back door for schedules or shopping lists. A thick rug in front of the fireplace. He'd never been much for decorating; it had never mattered to him very much. For some reason he wanted this little nest to be safe and cozy for Devon and Mercy. He wasn't entirely sure what she was running from, but he wanted her running *to* something decent.

He could have left. He should have left, but he stayed. It was almost five when she arrived with her daughter. He went to stand in the open doorway and when she saw him, she looked confused.

"Spencer?" she asked. She was wearing her scrubs and tennis shoes. He backed into the house wordlessly and let her enter. She put her hands over her mouth in awe. "Spencer!" she gasped.

He realized what she thought and said, "Oh, no—I didn't do this. I helped, that's all. It was Rawley. He wanted to help out so the rest of us came along. They had to get back to the beach—

people start showing up, looking for drinks and sandwiches and deli pizza at about four."

"Who did this?" she asked in a soft voice. "Who?"

"Well, it was Rawley, Cooper, Sarah. And I helped."

She looked him over. "Helped?"

He was a dirty mess. He laughed. "I did everything Rawley told me to do."

She glanced around. "My God..."

"The bedrooms aren't done. Well, they're swept and mopped, but Rawley's got some paint for the walls. It's boring. It's just 'renter's white.' But I think he's finished patching walls. And if I could just brag a little, I hauled trash and painted the kitchen...."

"Oh, my God," she said. "It's immaculate. It's shining." And then her eyes filled with tears. "I can't believe you guys did this for me."

He gave a shrug. "You're Rawley's cousin, so I guess we're all family. And it's not like I had to work today...."

She looked down for a long moment, frowning. Just what she didn't want—another extended family. She wanted *friends*. Spencer couldn't know how much the idea of everyone being one big family caused her to cringe inside.

Mercy came in the door carrying her books and her blanket. She stood there, oblivious. Apparently a three-year-old couldn't see the improvement. Then Devon lifted her eyes to Spencer's face. There were tears on her cheeks. "Do you know how long it would have taken me to get this far?"

"Yeah." He laughed. "I do."

"You're not going to understand this, but I've had great kindnesses given me but the price has been... Well, never mind that. 'Thank you' will just never be enough." She wiped the emotion off her cheeks.

"Devon, I want you to stop right there. There's not going to be a bill. It was just us being good neighbors, that's all. I don't want you to think you owe anyone anything."

"Thank you," she said.

"But you'll probably want to start with that— just 'thank you.' The rest of the bucket brigade is at the beach. I need a shower. I have to check on Austin, make sure he hasn't driven anyone crazy. I'm going to take off—I'm really ready for a cold beer." He headed for the door and she stopped him.

"Thank you, Spencer."

"I was glad to help out."

Seven

Devon drove to Cooper's to thank the rest of the cleanup crew and, as she thought about it, she had to acknowledge that there was a difference between people helping one another in a small town, and relying on each other in a commune. And she had so much to give in return—even managing the doctor's office, she could be of help every day. She could extend herself the extra mile, making sure those people who called or came in received the best she had to offer.

Then she remembered something she had known long ago—that kindness wasn't only demonstrated by giving material things or labors. There were the simple gestures that people forgot, that were so important—a little extra time, a smile, patience, conversation, gratitude. These were the things Aunt Mary had valued, she had never had much by way of material wealth but she'd been one of the most generous people Devon knew.

She reminded herself of these things as she walked into Cooper's, holding Mercy's hand. She went first to the kitchen to find Rawley. "You wonderful sneak," she said. "I can't believe what you did!"

He turned from the sink. "I just meant to put a dent in it for you," he said. "But all them others just jumped in. Looks darn good, don't it, though?"

"Darn good. Thank you. You are certainly my guardian angel."

He grinned at her and if she wasn't mistaken, flushed a little bit. "Ain't no one ever called me that before."

"Can I buy you a beer?" she asked.

"Girl, I don't drink nothin'. I don't make all that much sense without ever takin' a drink. Those others, though—they'd prolly take your beer money."

She just laughed at him.

He bent at the waist and peered at Mercy. "Wanna help old Rawley wash up dishes?"

Her little face lit up and Devon said, "Oh, Rawley, she's just going to make a big mess."

He scooped her up and planted her on the step stool in front of the sink. "I reckon. There ain't no sharp things in there, I know what I'm doing." He tied an apron around her neck and it fit her like a long dress. "Why don't you take a break for once. Sit out on the deck and count seabirds."

Devon wandered back into the bar. Cooper was alone behind the bar and he was smiling at her. She leaned on the bar. "How can I thank you?"

"You just did."

"I can't even buy you a beer in your own bar," she said. "I'll think of something special. Something that will show you how much it means to me that you'd take on that cleanup job for someone you barely even know."

He leaned toward her. "Listen here, you've already done enough for me. For us."

"But I haven't done—"

His voice was lowered when he talked, as if this was just for her. "I've known that old boy in the kitchen for almost a year now. He's a curmudgeonly old coot. He hasn't had an easy life, he doesn't trust people quickly. He's been mostly alone and hardly anyone knows how big his heart is. I'm maybe the best friend he's got and he makes me work real hard for a few words. But since you and your little girl have been around, Rawley's a whole new man. Almost can't shut him up. And he's got a twinkle in his eye that I haven't ever seen before. He's been needing someone to take care of—he's been needing family. And I wouldn't be saying this but it's pretty plain—you're not just good for him, you're good to him. That matters to me, Devon."

"He's a good man," she said.

"He is that, hard as he might try to keep it a secret."

She leaned toward him and in a hushed tone said, "I'm not his cousin."

And Cooper whispered back, "I know."

"He told you?"

Cooper shook his head. "I guessed, that's all. It was awful sudden, you showing up, but as long as it works out..."

"I would never hurt Rawley."

"That's coming across loud and clear."

"I can't really talk about..."

"About why you cut off your pretty hair and won't talk about where you've been? Look, hardly a one of us doesn't have stuff to get over, so you don't have to explain. I could make you blush with my past. In fact, let's leave that alone. There might come a time you want to talk about whatever it is, but know this—it doesn't really matter that much. What matters is that you find what you need, that Rawley is happy, that your daughter is okay."

"That's what's important to me, too."

"Then we're bent on a single purpose. Now, what's your pleasure? Coffee? Soda? Wine?"

She sniffed back some emotion. "Can I have a beer?"

"You got it," he said, pulling a bottle out of the cooler. He popped the top and put it on the bar as she was struggling to open her wallet. He put a hand over hers. "Devon, I'm not taking your money. Don't be ridiculous. The families of folks who work here eat and drink for free. Now find a place in the sun to relax—Rawley says you've been working day and night for a week."

"I could just kiss you," she whispered.

"I'll take that," he said with a handsome big grin. Then he leaned across the bar, presenting her with his cheek.

Devon sat on the deck with her beer. Down on the beach she saw Spencer throwing the football with Landon. So much for his shower. He was wearing the same jeans, but without his shirt or shoes. He had apparently been distracted by a little ball practice. He had amazing shoulders and arms, which she wished she hadn't even noticed—but there was no denying it, he was a beautiful speci-men. His boy, Austin, was fooling around on the paddleboard, very near the shore. There were a few people out on the water—a couple in a small skiff, rowing around the quiet bay. Two people were on paddleboards, taking them farther out into the bay.

Her eyes went back to Spencer and Landon. They threw long, powerful passes. This was the coach and his star player, and they were impressive. She could hear them shouting at each other and laughing. She just couldn't believe she was here. Feeling for the first time as if she was actually living a normal life. Not just that, but in a setting millions of people would envy—the beauty of the rocky sea, the long peaceful beach. It felt as though right up to this very moment, this very second, she had worried and wondered what was coming tomorrow, that she'd been a little afraid each day that somehow the clock would be turned back and she'd find herself again behind that fence.

Sarah came out to sit beside her. Ham was by her side and Sarah sat down beside Devon. "What did you think of your duplex?"

"I was speechless," she said. "You guys are my magic fairies. I don't know what came over you."

"I had a day off." She shrugged. "I'm going to pay for it by sitting alert for the next two nights, but that's okay. I'm almost done. I'll be on paid vacation by the end of the summer."

"How do you manage that?" Devon asked.

"Well, you give the Coast Guard ten years, accumulate a lot of leave, fall in love with Cooper and marry him." At that precise moment he appeared at her side, handing her a glass of white wine. Sarah laughed. "He promises to serve me and pamper me for the rest of my life."

Cooper disappeared again and Devon said, "I'd marry him for that."

"Watch it, now, I saw him first."

"And when is all this going to happen?" Devon asked.

"It's beginning to happen right now. I'm moving in with Cooper. Spencer is vacating the RV and taking my rental house in town. Landon is taking over the RV as his bachelor pad, under the watchful eye of his diligent and suspicious sister—I even have a new pair of binoculars. And a week from Saturday we're having a wedding, right here, on the beach. Will you come?"

"Oh, my gosh, seriously?"

She nodded. "It's going to be very laid-back, just like my Cooper. By the way, I'm getting rid of a couch. Interested?"

"Sure," she said, sitting straighter. "Are you selling it?"

"No," Sarah said, smiling. "Hopefully I'm moving it down the street to your house where it will find a good home."

Three days later Sarah's couch appeared in her living room along with two side tables and some lamps. A couple of days later she noticed a moving truck pulled up in front of Sarah's house—Spencer was moving in. He had a dinette set he didn't need anymore moved into her kitchen. Then Sarah offered her two beds. "Not like you got them off craigslist," she said. "They're almost new and I'll give you the mattress protector to go with them.

And some linens I can't use anymore." Spencer
gave her a dresser and chest that had been in his
last guest room and, just like that, her little house
was ready to move in to. Then Sarah and Spencer
had a huge yard sale and Devon went, picking up a
few extra items—kitchen things, a set of old dishes
that looked fine to her, even a couple of things to
hang on the wall.

She ordered a few towels, a couple of blankets,
pillows and some flatware online.

When she embraced Rawley at the front door
of her little house, she said, "We will see you almost every day."

"Yes, you will. If you don't come by Cooper's,
I'll check on you here so don't go thinkin' you're
done with me. Me and Mercy, we bonded."

Rawley went to the Farmers' Market in Myrtle Creek one afternoon. He just roamed around,
looking at the crafts and produce stands, taking his
good old time, observing. He felt like a man in a
foreign country, checking out the status of things.
And then he saw what he was looking for—a produce stand run by a couple of farm girls with long
single braids. They were selling strawberries, early
pears, root vegetables such as carrots, onions, red
potatoes and scallions. There was leaf lettuce,
butter lettuce, beets, peppers, small, early hook
squash, little zucchini and green beans. They had

small cucumbers for pickling and some fine looking tomatoes. He gave a tomato a gentle squeeze—soft and meaty yet firm. "What fertilizer you use on these?" he asked one of the girls.

"We have livestock, so we make our own blend—all organic, all clean," the smiling girl said.

"Wish I could get my hands on some of your fertilizer. I got me a couple tomato plants—they're healthy and strong and still don't produce like this. Where does all this come from?" he asked. "You grow it yourselves, right?"

"We have some property down the river. In two weeks we'll have larger squash and in late summer the melons will start coming in. Plus apples and the tomatoes will keep coming as long as the weather holds."

He had never paid much attention to these ladies before, but now he was looking at them in a whole new way. The three young women did the selling and behind them, in the back of their booth, looking as if they were there to do heavy lifting, were two large men in jeans and boots. They looked friendly, but they didn't chat with any of the customers. They stood back, arms crossed over their chests, wearing half smiles, talking only to each other.

On their display stand they had big jars—old-fashioned pickle jars with hand-lettered labels: Veterans, UNICEF, Save The Children, Police and

Firefighters Fund, St. Jude's Hospital. Well, covered their bases, didn't they? Rawley thought to himself. He tried to remember if these were the same charities they had been supporting the last time he stumbled on them. He took out a couple of dollars for the Veterans jar and asked, "Does any of the money you earn go to charity?"

"If there's anything left after we pay the bills we donate," the young woman said. "The Fellowship supports a number of worthy causes."

"The Fellowship, yeah, that's right. You have a produce stand on the road back by the river, don't you?" he asked.

"Not open every day, sir. We don't get a lot of traffic back there so we're only open about four afternoons a week and always on the weekend in the summer."

"Gimme a couple of big bags of these tomatoes," Rawley said. "And a bag of them green beans. You ladies do a right fine job."

"Thank you, sir."

"And you weave them things?" he asked, pointing to a display of shawls and throws.

She laughed happily. "Yes, sir. Charlotte does that—and she taught some of us how to knit and crochet. That occupies us on all those cold winter nights. Would you like to look at them?"

He wandered down to the end of the stand and picked through them. The prices on them were pretty high. "Wow, you're awful proud of these. Seventy-five dollars?"

"They're handmade, sir. And original designs."

"I'll have this one here. I have an elderly neighbor lady who would really take to it."

"Perfect. I hope your neighbor loves it."

They wrapped up his vegetables and throw. Rawley paid in cash and left. Instead of going back to Cooper's to work, he went to the doctor's office. Devon was sitting behind the counter at the desk and looked up, surprised to see him.

"What a surprise! I hope you're not sick."

"Never felt better," he said. "I brought you a couple of things." He put his parcels on the table. "I split up the beans and tomatoes, kept half for myself. Then there's this," he said, giving her the tissue-wrapped parcel with the throw.

She smiled at the beautiful vegetables, but when she saw the throw she frowned. "Rawley, what have you done?"

He gave a shrug and a fairly handsome smile. "Just checkin' on things in Myrtle Creek. I thought you might like knowin' it seems to be business as usual. Not that I expected to see anything amiss. But they're still there, sellin' their tomatoes and woven things, wearin' their overalls and braids." He shook his head. "Devon, we'll be careful, but it's gonna be all right, I think." He gave her a gentle smile. "I think you got yourself a new home."

She came around the counter, stood on tiptoes and kissed his cheek. "Thank you, Rawley. I not only have a new home, I have a table and chairs. When can you come to dinner?"

"I reckon there's time tomorrow night. Wednesday nights ain't so busy at the beach."

"That would be great. Consider yourself invited."

Devon had become a familiar face at the thrift shop in town. She was very careful with her earnings, but she was able to pick up some wonderful things for Mercy. Children grew out of clothes so fast that secondhand items tended to be in very good condition.

She didn't worry much about things for herself—she had her work uniform of scrubs and she was very happy with them. For the weekends she had her shorts and jeans and a few other casual things. But there was a wedding coming up and she found herself picking through the women's secondhand clothing, just in case she saw something suitable.

And there, hanging all wonky and kind of tied on to a hanger, was a sundress. She untied the straps and held it up…and fell dead in love. It was navy blue with pink flowers, along with a bit of white and yellow. It tied over the shoulders. She hadn't worn anything like that in years and without even looking at the price tag, she hugged it.

"I guess that means you like it," said the woman who ran the thrift shop.

"If I can afford it, it's meant to be," she said.

The lady lifted the tag and smiled. "Can you manage fifteen dollars?"

Devon let out a breath. "I can."

She was so excited about her "find" that she went straight to the diner to show Gina. "But of course I don't have shoes. I guess I can wear my tennis shoes—that won't look completely dorky down on the beach."

"You can," Gina said. "It's a beach party—anything will work. But you can also wear flip-flops—that's what the bride's wearing."

"Seriously?"

She nodded. "You're going to love it. We're wearing strapless, breezy summer dresses and Cooper and Mac are wearing Tommy Bahamas island shirts and sandals. I predict we'll all be barefoot in no time. One thing you could use—a wrap. The beach gets chilly at night, even in summer. Do you have one? Because I have a few—nothing too fancy. I can loan you one. I have a yellow wrap that I think might go with this dress."

"That would be so wonderful, thank you. How's Sarah doing? Is she getting nervous and excited?"

"Nervous, yes, but not about the nuptials. Cooper told his family about the wedding and they're all coming. All of them! Not only are they getting a new daughter-in-law and sister-in-law they've never met, they haven't met Austin yet. In just a few days, this place is going to be raining Coopers!"

Sarah had to take a week of leave to be available for Cooper's visiting family and preparing for the wedding. Everyone started arriving on the Thursday before the Saturday wedding and she met them all except a couple of nieces and nephews who had been unable to attend. But there were promises of another summer visit before school started again.

Cooper's family met Austin and Spencer with caution, clearly trying not to overwhelm them with their sheer numbers. But once the kids got out to the beach and on the water, the adults began to relax.

Sophie and Hank, Cooper's parents, not only brought gifts but a cooler packed with Sophie's lasagna, homemade bread, extra sauce and meatballs. Apparently she was afraid Cooper wouldn't be able to make sure they were all fed. As the Cooper clan arrived in Thunder Point, things loosened up considerably. Cooper got a lot of teasing about falling into this fabulous property when everyone had always considered him just a wanderer who couldn't put down roots.

On Friday the preparations began in earnest; the Cooper family helped by stringing lights around the beach, attached to poles that were stuck in the ground. Sophie brought out the lasagna and Rawley added a huge green salad and compared recipe details with Sophie. Rawley tried to excuse himself from the family dinner, but he was denied and told to go find Devon and Mercy and make sure they were part of what appeared to be the groom's dinner. Anyone else who happened to be at the bar or on the beach was invited to partake. The McCain clan was there in force, and the place was jumping with kids and teens and adults everywhere.

"How many people will be coming to this wedding?" Cooper's sister, Rochelle, asked.

"No one knows," Sarah said. "We had a very loud disagreement about that. I wanted to write out some invitations and Cooper said no. He wanted to tell our friends—both from town and from the Coast Guard station—and anyone else who wandered by would be welcome. Poor Carrie, our caterer—she's going to have to wing it. We obviously didn't have any RSVPs."

"It's a beach wedding," Cooper said. "If they come, they get a party."

"I hope we don't run out of food," Sarah said.

"We won't," he said. "Carrie knows more about catering in this town than any other person. The only thing we have to worry about is rain."

"It wouldn't dare rain," Sarah said.

It was quite early on Saturday morning when Sarah heard a vehicle on the beach and took her coffee outside to the deck. It was Carrie, delivering some items for the wedding and the party. As she surveyed the scene below she saw the bandstand that had been positioned at the base of the hill with reels of extension cords that would be run up to the bar to power the speakers and electric instruments. There were a couple of long tables for food and drink set up near the staircase to the beach. And finally, an arch covered with fresh flowers. Sarah put a hand to her chest and sighed deeply, feeling a rush of tears come to her eyes. It was beautiful.

She heard a sound and, thinking it must be Cooper, she turned. But it was Sophie, carrying a cup of coffee.

"Come and see," she whispered.

Sophie joined her at the rail and saw the beautiful arch. "Oh, Sarah," she said.

"Carrie said she'd think of something. She's an amazing woman. I was all for just getting married privately, maybe up the coast. But Cooper said he wanted to be married on this beach and that he'd take care of things." She shook her head. "He surprises me at every turn."

Sophie slipped her arm around Sarah's shoulders. "We haven't seen enough of our son the past twenty years. He's spent quite a few years traveling, no interest in claiming a permanent home. Now I see a changed man, Sarah. And he's happier than I've ever seen him. I expect that's because of you."

"He's made me happier than I've ever been," she said. "I have no idea how all this happened. I came here to be alone, to lick my wounds after a failed marriage. Cooper's not only gained a son in Austin, but he's become a role model to my brother, Landon."

"And I think that, finally, after all these years, I won't worry about my son finding what he wants and needs to complete his life." She kissed Sarah's cheek. "Thank you. As the mother of a painfully independent son, thank you for coming into his life. I can see you're a very good match."

"I'm going to do everything I can to make him happy. He already makes me happier than I thought I could ever be."

They were hugging and drying their tears when Cooper came outside with his cup of coffee. He looked at his mother and his bride and said, "Oh, brother."

Eight

Devon couldn't remember the last time she'd attended a wedding. It was probably back in her college days. And she'd certainly never gone to a wedding like this! Although children were welcome at the wedding, Scott convinced her they should leave them at home so they could be put to bed at a reasonable hour. "We're going to drink and dance and have fun!" he insisted.

She drove Mercy to Scott's house where she was spending the night with Jenny and Will, leaving Devon and her boss free to go to the wedding. When they arrived at the Grant home, complete with all Mercy's overnight gear, she was actually happy to see that Gabriella's boyfriend was also there. Devon was introduced to Charles, also a college student.

"You're okay with Charles spending the evening with Gabriella and the kids, aren't you?" Scott asked.

"I'm relieved, in fact," she said. "She's not just a nanny or au pair or babysitter, but a completely normal nineteen-year-old."

"You don't have to worry about that. Gabriella has a very active social life when she gets time to have one. Follow me in your truck. We'll just park at Cliffhanger's and walk across the beach, if you're up to it."

She stuck out a foot, showing off her new flip-flops. "I'm ready," she said, smiling. "I even live close enough to the beach to walk home if it comes to that. You never know—I could have the time of my life tonight."

He peered at her. "How long since you've been to a party or a wedding reception?"

"I can't even remember. A very long time."

A lot of people had the same idea—the marina parking lot was full. After they parked, he looped his arm with hers to walk her across the beach. "We're going to have some fun tonight. I don't want to see you picking up Mercy before morning—just enjoy yourself. You look very pretty tonight, Devon."

She flushed slightly. "And so do you, Dr. Grant."

Even though it wasn't dark yet, the sparkling lights twinkled in the dusk, casting a glow over a wide area of the beach. There were no chairs set up, but there was a runner that led from the bottom of the steps to the arch and a box on the side of the bay where the preacher would stand. The band was set up and they were playing some soft, classic tunes—"I'll Be Seeing You," "Deep Purple," "Will You Love Me Tomorrow." People were milling around with plastic cups, visiting, laughing and generally getting into the party mood. The sky had never been more beautiful, the bay was calm and dark, the air warm and there was only a slight breeze.

Scott Grant pressed a cup into her hand. "Lots of people here I've never met before," he said.

She grinned at him. "It turns out I know a lot of them. I've already met Cooper's family." She grabbed his hand and dragged him around the gathering at the beach, introducing him to those people he didn't know. They eventually found Rawley behind one of the long serving tables, wearing a shirt identical to Mac's and Cooper's, as if he were a part of the wedding party. Even Austin had a matching shirt. Austin was running around the beach with a kid about the same age, kicking up sand at the water's edge.

Gina wore a powder-blue strapless summer dress and held a lovely bouquet; Mac stayed close to her near the bridal arch, chatting with a man who must be either the minister or justice of the peace. He wore a Hawaiian shirt and sported a long ponytail.

The sun lowered. The lights twinkled. The band played and the sky was clear and deep, speckled with stars.

Devon's happiness at being included was almost too much to bear. People thought of her as a regular girl, worthy of their company. She pulled her yellow wrap, her borrowed wrap, around her shoulders. It was all so beautiful and happy....

In the small apartment above the bar, Sarah turned in front of a full-length mirror mounted on the closet door. Her dress was identical to Gina's except that it was pink. The contrast with her tanned skin and dark hair was perfect. She had a delicious bouquet of roses, calla lilies, baby's breath and periwinkles—all white, yellow and blue.

Cooper leaned against the wall, appreciating the vision she created and she grinned at him. "Will this do?" she asked him.

He took a couple of lazy steps toward her. "I've never seen you more beautiful. You ready to do it? It's a long contract. Ninety-nine years."

She put her hands on his shoulders. "Just ninety-nine?"

"My little commitment-phobe has gone, I think. I have something for you."

She laughed and shook her head. "You can't possibly give me one more thing, Cooper. You're giving me your life, your beachfront property… you're taking on my brother and supporting us both…."

"It's just something for you to wear to bed on our wedding night…."

"Aw, that's very sweet…"

He pulled a small box out of his pocket. He popped it open to display a pair of diamond stud earrings. She sighed and touched one. "Not a nightgown?" she asked.

"We have absolutely no need for a nightgown. Just these."

She pulled her earrings out of her ears and began inserting the diamond studs. "There are a bunch of Coast Guard down there as well as more townies than I can count. It might be very late before you get to fully appreciate these earrings."

"No, it won't," he said. "I don't care how much they eat, drink and dance—we're going to escape and lock the door. Spencer and Landon have charge of Austin. Carrie, Gina, Mac and Rawley have charge of the party. They're under orders—shut it down before dawn."

"Dawn?" she asked with a laugh.

He lifted her chin and put a soft kiss on her lips. "I want everyone to remember this night as much as I will." He put out a crooked arm. "Come on, Mrs. Cooper. Let's tie the knot. And start our new lives."

She slipped her arm through his and went downstairs. Before exiting the bar, Cooper stopped and flipped the lights on the deck on and off a few times. Then when they stepped outside, the music changed abruptly and the band began to play "The Way You Look Tonight." As they descended the stairs to the beach, their guests applauded. There were a few whistles and catcalls as well, making them all laugh.

And then they stood in front of the floral arch, facing the preacher in the Hawaiian shirt and ponytail. The young man said a few words about commitment and partnership, the standard vows were exchanged, promises made, and then, per Sarah's request, a Native American blessing.

And then Cooper was invited to kiss his wife and the beach came alive with cheers. Mac, the best man, was handed a glass as were Cooper and Sarah. There was no elaborate toast, just a brief salute to Mr. and Mrs. Henry Cooper and followed by many a "Hear! Hear!" And then the funky little band made up of middle-aged men broke into "I'm in the Mood for Love," punctuated by the popping of champagne corks.

While Sarah and Cooper stood in front of the

arch, there were the flashes of cameras and most of the guests made their way over to congratulate them. When the receiving line was exhausted, Sarah and Cooper were first in the buffet line. A neat stack of beach blankets were stacked at each end of the long serving table and Cooper handed a plate to Sarah, grabbing a blanket at the same time. He spread it on the sand near the bottom of the stairs to the deck and soon others joined them, while still others continued to stand or spread their blankets on the other side of the band. A group of eight or ten teenagers including Landon and Eve took their blankets and set up some distance away from their parents and elders. Gina and Mac ended up beside them and when Cooper caught sight of Spencer trying to corral Austin as well as a couple of plates of food, Cooper motioned them over to join their party.

Not everyone needed blankets—there were several rocks and driftwood trunks scattered around that made for handy chairs. And before the first wave of guests had enjoyed the food, the dancing began—mostly by those people over the age of thirty. The music was not the teenagers' style at all. Cooper's mom and dad twirled around the sand a little bit and once the eating was mostly done, Cooper took his wife onto the outdoor dance floor.

Cooper didn't have possession of her for long—

her USCG friends and coworkers were present and wouldn't let her rest.

After dancing with his mother and sisters, Cooper gratefully returned to the blanket, sitting down beside Spencer. He noticed that Austin had already abandoned them for Landon's party, a safe distance away.

"I guess you couldn't convince Rawley to come as a guest tonight," Spencer said.

"Not a chance. I'm lucky I got him in that shirt, the only thing that identifies him as part of the wedding party. But have fun? Never." Cooper laughed. "He's a cautionary tale," Cooper said, nodding at the man behind the serving table. "He's exactly what I was destined to become if I stayed as solitary as I'd been."

"You throw a good party," Spencer said. "You should do beach parties regularly, even when you're not getting married."

"Makes sense," he said. "I have to hand it to Carrie—she sure can pull a party together under difficult circumstances, can't she?"

"Where'd she get that band?"

"They're a bunch of local guys. One's a mailman, one's a crabber and I don't know who the third one is. Not exactly *American Bandstand,* but you can't complain about their tone, right?"

"If you like ballroom music."

"Get out there, Spencer," Cooper said. "Wrap your arms around something soft. Give Sarah a whirl, because after tonight you can't touch her."

Again Spencer laughed, shaking his head. "Yeah, I think I'll just enjoy the view."

"Looks like the new doc is circling a target," Cooper said. He nodded toward the other side of the bandstand to where Scott Grant reclined on a beach blanket and Devon was kneeling in front of him, talking animatedly with her hands, making him laugh.

Spencer had seen them arrive together. They came to the beach arm in arm. Then she held his hand, pulling him all over the beach, introducing him to people he hadn't yet met. Then they spread their blanket together.

Were they already a couple? he wondered. It would only make sense. They spent every day together. And Dr. Grant—he seemed like a pretty nice guy.

But Devon, she was something else. Her transformation since the first day he'd seen her was remarkable. She had arrived here as a skittish and shy runaway from some kind of cult or something. She didn't know he had overheard her when she was telling—or rather, trying not to tell—Rawley that first morning. By now Rawley might know the details, but Spencer didn't. Still, the changes in the girl were impossible to ignore. Or forget. She'd become a cute, efficient, fun-loving sprite with a quick wit and spontaneous smile that just lit up her whole face. She must be feeling safer, more confident. She had a glow about her and he was inexplicably drawn to her.

She's a blonde, he thought. His wife had been blonde. Maybe he was just hot for blondes....

And of course, that was the last thing he was in the market for. He'd laid his young wife to rest just a few months ago, after a long and ravaging illness. Now he was concentrating on raising his son, starting a new career, making a new home. There was no room for romance, especially with a woman hiding a weird and mysterious past.

Someone approached her—one of the Coast Guard guests, he believed. He gave her a half bow that made her laugh, held out a hand and took her out in front of the bandstand to dance. There was a little more laughter, some barefoot twirling. He found himself smiling, glad she was having a good time. He couldn't believe there was anything creepy or sinister about her—she seemed so transparent, except maybe for that part of her life she was fleeing. For no logical reason whatsoever, he was glad her flight had brought her here, because he believed this to be a safe place and populated with the kind of men who had the strength to protect her and her little girl, if that became necessary.

He shifted his gaze to Cooper, who was making the rounds, dancing with the women in his family and with friends from town. Sarah was being passed around pretty liberally as well—lots of cutting in going on out there. Then there was Gina and Mac, the newlyweds, locked together in a sweet, close sway...until they were disrupted by Mac's aunt Lou and her steady, Joe, and partners were exchanged. But that didn't last long—they were back together for the next song.

He looked for Austin, who hadn't moved in quite a while. He was still sitting with the teenagers, Landon, Eve, Ashley James and a young man by the name of Frank. When Spencer had decided to come to this town, he had no idea it would include kids like Landon. He was an expert on high school kids, especially athletes, and Landon and his friends were A-list, no question—smart, healthy, responsible and very patient with ten-year-old Austin. Landon was bunking with Spencer and Austin while Cooper's parents borrowed the RV as their guestroom and he was a perfect houseguest.

Spencer wandered over to the outdoor bar for another beer and, while standing there, he talked with a number of folks from town. Yeah, this was a town excited about football season and it made sense. Their high school teams did well and were worth bragging about. People wanted to warn him about competing teams and ask him if he had some secret weapon. They wanted to go over details of performance in previous years and talk about their stars. Finally he was dragged out to dance by Ray Anne and, with beer in hand, he spun her around a little bit.

"Wow," she said, "you can even dance!"

"I've chaperoned a ton of high school dances," he explained.

She tapped his beer bottle with a long, pink, manicured finger. "No beer at those dances, I bet."

"Not where I could see it," he answered with a laugh.

"Hard to believe times have changed so little since I was in school. It's been a couple of years."

"Has it now?" he asked, playing dumb.

Dance over, he found himself standing around with Coach Rayburough, Cliff and Mac. The talk was football, of course. And his eyes kept drifting to Devon—she either danced or visited with women friends or sat on the blanket. It wasn't late, but inevitably the party dwindled—people started leaving.

Spencer was tackled around the legs by his son. Austin looked up at him and said, "Can I go home on the Razor?"

"Who's driving?" Spencer asked, joking.

"Ha, ha. You know."

He looked around and saw Landon was saying his goodbyes, shaking Cooper's hand, giving his sister a kiss on the cheek. Then Landon was striding toward Spencer. "Eve and I are going to head out. We'll take Austin home in the Razor, if it's okay with you. If it's not, I'll walk him and Eve will drive the Razor. Or we could leave it for you."

"As long as he has his seat belt on and you go slow," Spencer said. "Don't hit any wedding guests. That's bad luck."

"For sure." Landon laughed.

"We'll swing by and grab Eve and Ashley on the way home," Mac said. He glanced at his watch. "Half hour or so?"

"Come on, Mac, it's Saturday night!"

"You gonna bring 'em home?" Mac asked.

"Yeah, later! After Spencer gets home." Then he looked at Spencer and said, "There's no hurry on that...."

They were walking off in the direction of the far side of the beach, Austin with four teens. And then the saxophone player spoke into the microphone and said, "We'll give you a couple more, then this old band is packing it up...."

Spencer handed Mac his beer bottle and said, "Excuse me." He walked across the dance area. He was thinking, *Get a few beers in me and I'll do any stupid thing.* In front of him Devon was talking with Scott Grant as he folded up that beach blanket. "Almost missed my chance," he said, holding out a hand to Devon. "The band's shutting down."

"Aw, that's nice," she said, putting her hand in his. Then she looked at Scott. "If you want to go, I'll see you in the morning when I come for Mercy. I can get across the beach on my own."

"Got your whistle?" he asked.

She laughed at him, but Spencer, half expecting an argument, said, "I'm her neighbor—I'll make sure she gets home."

And then to his surprise, Scott Grant said, "Okay. Later, then."

Probably shouldn't have done that, Spencer thought. He already knew he found the girl intriguing and attractive and complicated—spending more time with her just didn't make sense for a man in his position, single father, recently widowed, vulnerable. But then he put his hand on the small of her back, brought her gently up against him, and that's where all thinking ended. He was vaguely aware of someone in the band singing *You're just too good to be true, can't take my eyes off of you....* He swayed with her, their feet barely moving, her head resting lightly against his shoulder, her hair under his chin.

She lifted her chin and smiled up at him. "Did you have a good time tonight?" she asked.

He just nodded and pulled her a little bit closer.

He tried to make sense of this. It had been so long since he'd had his arms around the warm, soft flesh of a woman—that's probably all it was. He'd held his wife in her last months, weeks, days, hours...but that wasn't the same as this. This woman was all too alive. And her hair...the fragrance was just knocking him out.

"What is that fragrance?" he asked her in a whisper. "What do you wash your hair with?"

She looked up at him and laughed. "Baby shampoo."

Okay, he was clearly losing his mind. Baby shampoo? Whatever was filling his senses was much more serious and sensuous than that. The song ended and the next began. He felt her pull back slightly, but he just gathered her up closer. And she came to him. He heard the music, but he was also vaguely aware of the sounds of packing up. Coolers opened and closed, trash was gathered, there was talking and laughing, bottles clinked. He lifted his head, opened his eyes and they were the only couple dancing.

And then, too soon, the music stopped.

"Thanks," he said. "That was nice."

"It was. I'm going to see if I can help before

heading home," she said. And with that she walked right over to Carrie, who gave her a brief hug and shook her head. It looked as if they were just about done with everything they had to do tonight. Once the food and trash was gathered and stowed, everything else would wait until morning.

Spencer went to where Devon had been sitting with Scott and picked up her flip-flops. He stood there at the edge of the party area holding her shoes, waiting. It seemed just about everyone was gone; Cooper and Sarah stood on the deck with his parents, saying good-night. Mac and Gina were halfway across the beach. The band was packing up their equipment. And he had an overwhelming desire to wait them all out, to wait until it was only himself and Devon on the beach, under the twinkling lights.

She was beside him again. "Thanks," she said, reaching for her flip-flops. She slipped them on her feet and they began walking toward the marina. "What a nice wedding. I admit, I cried a little bit."

He said nothing.

"I think the little kids would've liked it, but I'm glad they weren't there. I would've spent the whole night chasing them. And I haven't been to a grown-up party in so long, I can't remember when."

He stopped walking and looked down at her. "Devon. You and the doctor?"

"Huh?"

"Are you with the doctor? Are you seeing him?"

"Scott?" she asked on a laugh. "Oh, my gosh, no!" She laughed again. "I'm sharing his baby-sitter so I can work for him, that's all. He's been wonderful about that—but of course I do pay Gabriella. But seeing him? Spencer, I can't be dating my boss! I can't be dating anyone!"

"You can't?"

"I'm a single mother! I have a lot of responsibility! I can't—"

He stopped walking. He slipped his arm around her waist, pulled her up off her feet and planted a kiss on her, cutting her off midsentence. He moved over her mouth and decided immediately that the taste and texture were perfect. But her arms hung limp at her sides. He lifted his lips from hers. "Me, either. I can't get involved with anyone, either."

"You have a very strange way of demonstrating that, Mr. Lawson...."

"Kiss me back," he said. "Come on, can't you see I can't help it?"

"Seriously?"

"You're beautiful. You smell so good. You taste like heaven."

"And I'm not dating!"

"We'll be friends," he said. "Very good friends. While we figure out if we should date. I haven't been on a date in years."

She laughed at him, shaking her head. "Are you drunk?"

He let go of her, let her drop to her feet. "No, I'm horribly sober. So you don't want to kiss?"

"I think it would be a bad idea. I only kiss boyfriends and I haven't had one of those in…forever."

He shook his head. "You have no idea how much we have in common…."

"Come on," she said, taking his hand. "I'll give you a ride home. And behave yourself."

They were almost to the marina when he said, "Devon, we should…I don't know…spend some time or…" He stopped walking again. "Do you need someone to cut your grass? Help you paint something?"

She shook her head. "What's up with you?"

"I'm very helpful by nature."

She began walking again. "I'll keep that in mind. Thank you."

When they got to the truck, she asked, "Do you want a ride?"

"I think I'll walk. It's just a few blocks. And I should clear my head. I'm not usually so…" He shrugged. "I don't grab and kiss women like that. And I could tell you didn't like it. I think I should probably do some chores for you or something. Prove I'm not rude…"

She put a hand on his arm. "That's all right, Spencer. It was just the twinkling lights and the wedding. Made you feel a little reckless." She tilted her head and he really wanted to dig his fingers into that messy, willful short hair of hers. So he put his hands in his pockets. "Will you be all right?" she asked him.

"I'm fine. Be careful driving home."

Nine

Oh. My. God.

Devon sat in the truck, in the driveway of her duplex. She felt a slight trembling in her extremities and it was not from cold or fear or embarrassment. It was from that very alien feeling of desire that rippled through her arms, breasts, toes...and lips. He'd kissed her. Really kissed her right off her feet. He'd stunned and paralyzed her and it made her want to kiss him back.

Instead she'd scared him away. Which was probably for the best. The last time she'd felt anything like that, it had been for Jacob, much older, much more practiced in seduction, much more dangerous. At least she thought that's how Jacob seemed compared to Spencer.

It had been so long. Of the seven women she'd lived with at The Fellowship, only three of them were regularly sharing Jacob's bed—Charlotte,

Pilly and Lorna. Devon had foolishly believed he had fallen for her—the new girl. And the others didn't tell her, warn her, didn't explain that all the children were his. When she'd realized the truth, she'd wanted to run for her life, and then it was the women who convinced her to stay. "You don't have to accept his advances and we'll take care of you. He might try with you, but he would never hurt you or force you—you're safe," Reese had said. "You're pregnant and have nowhere to go—just stay close to me and you'll have everything you need." By which Reese meant food and shelter and friendship. So at first she stayed because there was nothing else for her, then she stayed because she felt it was safe for her and Mercy. It didn't take long to realize what Jacob was—a manipulative liar who liked having his harem, his kingdom. He was omnipotent and as long as he believed himself to be the Divine Ruler, he was manageable. But she was never his lover again and she could tell it made him angry. Reese made him angry as well, but he needed her medical skills in his camp.

She came from such an ordinary, white-bread background she still couldn't believe she'd allowed herself to be duped into that lifestyle. But they all had. Jacob liked 'em young—early twenties at the most.

She thought Spencer was all the things Jacob was not. She imagined him as generous, guileless, honest and innocent; she knew he was a single father, a widower, a dedicated teacher. She'd been successfully ignoring the fact that he was also hot—built, sexy, sweet. Those deep brown eyes with the golden flecks under sometimes brooding brows—those eyes were deadly. There were plenty of hot men around, but they were all locked into very serious relationships, so they were easy to ignore. A little eye candy, that's all, because all Devon wanted was a way to sort out her life and be free of the kind of entanglements that could mean trouble.

Except Spencer, who was single, as new to Thunder Point as she was, was so kind. She'd always been a sucker for this quality in a man.

She was going to have to ignore Spencer. She had a feeling he could complicate her life.

She should go inside, she told herself. The duplex was dark and although the summer night was mild, it looked cold to her. On instinct, she drove away from her home and across the small town to Scott's house. She parked, knocked softly on the door and waited until he answered. He was changed into plaid flannel pajama bottoms and a T-shirt. He was holding an open book and the house was dim and quiet.

"Devon! Everything all right?"

"Fine. Fine."

"I was wondering how… How's Mercy doing with spending the night?"

"Gabriella said the kids were very good. They stayed up a little later than usual to watch a movie and were in bed around nine-thirty. They're curled up like a bunch of puppies, sound asleep. Gabriella and Charlie went out for a while. Want to check on the kids?"

"Maybe if I could just kiss her good-night…"

He chuckled. "Just down the hall."

She walked toward the bedroom—it was Jenny's room, where the girls napped together. But there were only the two of them there and she circled back to Scott, a little panicked. "Scott, Will isn't there!"

"He's not?" Scott joined her in the hall, then looked in his own bedroom. He laughed. "He's already migrated to my room. Happens all the time."

"Um, this is the first night since Mercy was born that I haven't slept beside her."

She could see he was shocked silent for a moment. Then his voice came gently. "Would you like to take her home, Devon?"

"She'd be so disappointed," she said. "She's been so excited. I'll just kiss her good-night. We both have to grow up sometime…."

"Lay down beside her for a while, if that helps."

"But you're going to bed…"

"Not for an hour or so. It's okay. I'll be out here, reading for a while."

"Thanks." And she went into the bedroom. The little girls were curled around each other, like sisters. She moved them over just enough to lay on the edge of the bed, an arm draping over them, pulling Mercy close, smelling her sweet little-girl smell.

Why couldn't she be tempted by Scott? Maybe because it was obvious he wasn't tempted by her? But Devon didn't want a man at all! Since birth, they'd let her down, every one. After all, her mother had been alone, reaching out to a neighbor to step in when Devon was orphaned. The last man to be kind to her had betrayed her. Men had never proved to be a good idea for her....

Yet she was interested in this one, this Spencer, who was clumsy in his impetuousness, yet he made her feel all soft and gooey inside.

She closed her eyes for a moment. All she really needed in life was to be with Mercy, to be able to take care of her, make sure she was safe, strong and smart. She could do that, given the right circumstances.

And then those deep brown eyes under expressive brows came to mind again and she allowed herself the luxury of remembering their time together that night. Dancing with him and being held close in his arms felt so good. For just a little while, she indulged in that fantasy again—that there was someone for her, someone real and normal and true.

Scott finished the chapter he'd been reading, closed the book and finally decided enough time had passed to go into the girls' bedroom to check not on them, but on Devon. He found what he expected—she was sound asleep, curled around them. He laughed softly to himself. Her sundress was riding up a little, laying bare her strong, shapely legs. Her arm was holding both girls protectively against her.

He grabbed a throw from the living room sofa and covered her, tucking it in around her and she didn't even stir.

This is what he wanted, what he'd been looking for—a pretty young woman with a sharp mind who was completely devoted to the children. Someone dependable and smart; someone fun and energetic. He was ready; he'd been ready for a while. He'd been grieving his wife for almost four years, wondering if he'd ever have another. But he was starting to believe he was ready for someone *like* her. And he'd been looking, trying to find a woman who could slide into the place Serena left.

He found himself wondering—*Does Devon make chocolate chip pancakes? Does she knit or make soup or bread? Did she like being preg-*

nant? The joke on him was that his wife had *loved* being pregnant, yet died of an aneurism postpartum. He'd been in love with his darling Serena since high school; they'd waited a long time to start their family, given the complications of med school and residency. Was Devon the kind of woman who could endure the demands of a doctor's life?

He decided he'd find out. Dinner—they could have dinner together. Let things evolve as they naturally should.

Reese Brolin was prepared to leave The Fellowship with her seven-year-old son, Mark, but in the end she couldn't leave without Mariah, the pregnant twenty-year-old who felt as much like a daughter to her as a sister. Reese was the one who got them all through labor and delivery and she wasn't sure what would happen to Mariah if she was left to the other well-meaning but untrained women. None of them were nurses or doulas.

Sister Laine had offered her this chance. She told her about the secret opening in the fence, the backpack with a change of clothes, the bottled water and apples.

"Did you also help Devon to leave?" Reese asked.

"No," Laine said. "I had planned to follow her, but things didn't work out for me. You should take this chance while you have it. I know you want to go."

"What makes you say that? I have a pregnant girl to deliver. I can't go!"

"You should go, Reese. Take Mark out of here before something happens. I think Jacob is breaking down. It's time to get the children out. Trust me."

"How do you know this?"

"We all know. He's not the same as he was when I first got here. The level of anxiety around here is growing by the hour. Something's going on. I think there might be trouble coming and you know Jacob will fight back. He'll never give up this acreage, his herb farm. You have a chance. You're strong enough and can keep Mark safe. Go south."

And it was then that Reese knew. "You're not who you pretend to be," she said to Laine.

"Don't worry about who you think I am, just take this one chance. And, please, don't talk to anyone about this or it will be very bad for me. Deadly bad. Do you understand, Reese?"

Reese said she did. She had suspected that Laine wasn't one of them. She could sense she was trying to fit in but there was something just a little off. Reese knew because The Fellowship wasn't her first experience in a commune or religious sect. She had been born in Africa to white missionary parents—this was hardly her first tribe.

Laine was a spy and Reese knew it.

In the end, she whispered to Mariah late at night when everyone had gone to bed, "Shh, come with me. I'll explain..."

Mark didn't utter a word, because Reese had told him to be completely silent. She had told him this was important and he mustn't make a sound. She carried what supplies she could and guided her son and her friend to the secret opening in the fence.

"What are we doing?" Mariah whispered as they climbed through the fence.

"Shh," she said. "I'll tell you in a second. Put these things on. Come with me."

They walked out to the road, difficult for Mariah—the baby was a month away and she was big and ungainly, and the brush was thick.

As a child, Reese had been in the thick of African tribal uprisings. Her family had escaped death, and she had seen too much unrest and was no stranger to it. Her instincts were very good; a tribal leader in the Sudan once told her she had the intuition of a hawk and would always know what to do. So, when she saw the road curve where Laine had promised a truck would be waiting, she grabbed young Mariah's upper arms and said, "Jacob is in trouble. There's no doubt the police are coming and he'll fight to keep his possessions. People will be hurt, they will be taken away. If you come with me now, we might escape. If you don't, your baby will be born in jail. I can almost guarantee that."

"No!" Mariah said in a sudden panic.

"Mama?" Mark was suddenly frightened.

Reese crouched down to Mark's level, peering into his eyes. "We have to leave, Mark. We have to leave now or face danger. You have to do as I say."

Then she rose to Mariah. "You can refuse to come with me, but if you do, we are all in danger. You most of all, I think. See that truck? I was told it would be waiting for us. Let him take us to a safe place before it's too late."

"And you'll stay with me?"

Reese brushed her hair back a little. "I'll never leave you, I promise. Never." Reese took Mark's hand, then Mariah's. "Say nothing and trust me," she said, leading them down the road where a dark truck waited.

Reese opened the door and looked inside. The man wore a ball cap, but the hair on his head was short. There was a rifle in his gun rack. He turned his head to look at her and then immediately he started the engine. "Hurry up," he said.

She lifted Mariah into the truck first then Mark, then she squeezed in.

The man pulled away, using only fog lights until he'd gone quite a distance. When he turned on the headlights, she said, "Take us to the police."

"Police it is," he said.

* * *

It was barely dawn when Laine was putting plates and flatware around the long table—enough for fourteen people, and a high chair for a two-year-old. They were six women and four men, including Jacob who sat at the head, and five children including little Liam. The women were busy preparing the meal and rounding up the children. Lorna was making toast and bacon, Pilly was scrambling eggs and Charlotte was spooning oatmeal into bowls for the children. And then Jacob arrived.

"There's a hole in the fence!" he boomed. "Who knows about this?"

The women all looked fearfully at each other. Laine knew, without a doubt, she would be the most suspect, given the fact that she was the newest to this clan.

"Who's missing?" he thundered. He looked around the kitchen. "Where are Reese and Mariah?"

The women exchanged even more troubled glances. Finally it was Lorna who said, "Gathering eggs, I think. That's where they should be."

"There's no one in the henhouse!"

Charlotte stepped toward Jacob. "But they would never leave," she said. "Not Reese—this is her home. This has been her home for eight years! And Mariah is close to having her baby—where would they go?"

Laine braved his wrath. "Jacob, are there any

vehicles missing? Mariah's too pregnant to get far on foot. Shall we go looking for them?"

"I'll take care of this," he blustered, stomping around the room. "Get the children downstairs right now!"

And four women scrambled to do as he ordered.

Laine knew exactly who would be missing, but their lives depended on her ability to be convincing and helpful.

Tears ran down Laine's cheeks and she twisted her hands. "Jacob, Reese and Mark and Mariah aren't here."

He let out a roar, picked up a plate from the table and threw it against the wall. Little Liam in the high chair began to cry and Laine rushed to pick him up. This broke Laine's heart; he was the baby of the house and she desperately wanted to get him on the other side of that fence. She just cried harder as she thought about this.

"Did you betray us, Laine?"

"Me?" she asked on a choked sob. "Why would I do that? If I wanted to leave and knew the way, wouldn't I go? Jacob, they can't have gone far— let's look for them. I'll help. We'll all help."

"There's a conspiracy here," he thundered. "And when I find it, you'll be sorry!"

Laine just held the toddler against her, weeping. But when he turned to leave, she sent daggers at him through the narrow slits of her eyes. If she'd had a weapon at that moment, he might be dead.

A half hour later the men—all four of them, armed—left the compound in three big dark SUVs. Suddenly they were all gone, leaving the women and children behind.

It had taken Laine nine months to be picked up by Jacob. Her assignment was to infiltrate the commune and learn the extent of his fraudulent activities. As well, she was to look for evidence of kidnapping, human trafficking, antigovernment activities and custodial interference. What they *hadn't* known, going in, was that Jacob had developed a large and sophisticated marijuana grow-op. Once Laine had learned the extent of this operation the commune was placed under constant surveillance. At that point her job shifted from investigation to rescue. She had to find a way to get the women and children out before a warrant was served. Crazy Jacob, who said he'd die before facing off with the government, might just kill all of them rather than surrender to authority. This could become another Waco or Ruby Ridge if it wasn't handled with finesse and intelligence.

Laine was FBI. Deep cover. And in grave danger.

Devon felt tickling on her face and opened one eye. Mercy grinned at her. "Mama, you spended the night."

She opened the other eye. Jenny was sitting next to Mercy, both little girls on their knees, giggling at her.

Oh, my, she thought. *This is embarrassing.* "I just wanted to kiss you good-night and I must have fallen asleep right here," she said, trying to get her bearings. She sat up. Someone had covered her with a blanket and she still wore last night's dress. Beautiful. "Where's your daddy, Jenny?"

"He told us to wake you up. He's making clown pancakes."

"Wonderful," she said. She pulled herself up, visited the bathroom, rinsed her mouth and headed to the kitchen. Will was standing on a stool, stirring the pancake batter. The girls were already sitting at the table eating their breakfasts. Scott, still wearing those plaid pajama bottoms and a T-shirt, was flipping pancakes.

"Well, good morning," he said with a smile.

"I'm very embarrassed," she said.

"No need. You were out like a light so I just went to bed." He lifted a handsome brow. "I trust you slept well?"

She chuckled to herself. "Oh, yeah. Just like old times. Wrapped around a couple of little girls."

"Can I interest you in a couple of pancakes?" he asked.

"Sure. That's awfully nice of you, after I disrupted your sleep in the middle of the night."

"Nah, not that serious. I was just reading."

"Where's Gabriella?"

"Sleeping in. I have no idea when Charlie brought her home, but it must have been very late. Sunday is her day off unless I have something going on. I'm on call for Bandon E.R. today and if they call, I'll need her. She usually spends Sundays studying or with Charlie."

"You could just call me," she said.

He leaned toward her. "How'm I gonna do that, Devon?" he asked.

"Right. No phone. I'm going to have to take care of that. Maybe I should take the kids down to the beach, let them see the flower arch, play in the water a little bit. I'd be happy to do that. In fact, it's the least I can do."

He flipped a clown pancake onto her plate and she thought, *This is so normal. I've longed for normal for five years. A few kids, a nice guy in the kitchen, a regular house, work, family...the usual kind of family.* She laughed and said, "So, you call this a clown, huh?"

"My best effort," he said.

"It kind of looks like a...squirrel." She cut off what appeared to be the tail, popping it in her mouth. "Now it looks more like a clown...or a hamster."

When breakfast was over, Devon took care of the cleanup and loaded the dishes in the dishwasher. Then she drove home with Mercy and they changed into clothes for the beach before heading to the marina to meet Scott and his kids. Will and Jenny were toting a mesh bag full of beach toys. "You sure you're up to this?" he asked. "I was called to Bandon. I could be a couple of hours."

"I can handle the three of them, no problem. But I can't get them all home. I just have the one booster seat."

"We can trade cars," he suggested. "Just put Mercy's seat in my car. I'll take your truck."

"Perfect. Now be gentle with her—she belongs to Rawley and he restored her."

The transfer was made and Scott said, "Gabriella is at home, standing by, in case I get stuck at the E.R."

But Devon was leaning into his beautiful new vehicle. She was smelling the car. "Wow. I might just take this baby out for a little spin. Is this new?"

"Pretty new, yeah. You're going to have to drum up some business for me at the clinic so I can pay for it."

"What a great car. I've never in my life had a new car...." She removed the key to the truck off her key ring and handed it to Scott.

"Someday, Devon," he said. "Probably not while you're working for the tightwad doctor, but someday." He took the truck key from her. "This seems to be working out well. Kids and all."

"Kids and all," she said.

With three little kids in tow, she grabbed up the towels, the sunscreen and toys. They went about halfway down the beach before they stopped. Devon spread out their towels and slathered their wiggly, excited little bodies with sunscreen. She laughed at their excitement and told them, "Water's edge, only. No farther than your knees!"

This was Devon's comfort zone—she loved children, especially at this age. She found them precious, hilarious, brilliant, trusting. They could also be very bad, but she'd never wondered what to do—Aunt Mary had had the patience of Job and had taught her well.

They had all played in the water and the sand for about an hour when someone plunked down beside her and she turned to see Spencer sitting next to her.

"Good morning," he said.

"What are you doing here?"

He pointed to the dock. "Austin wants to take out one of the boards and if someone isn't close by to watch him, he gets out too far. He wants to be like Landon—taking that board all the way out to the mouth of the bay. And he's fighting us on the life jacket issue." He nodded toward the littler kids. "The doctor's kids?"

"Yes, he's on call and I volunteered to baby-sit," she said.

"Listen, about last night…"

She laughed in spite of herself. "Regrets, Spencer?"

"If I offended you, I'm sorry. If I didn't offend you, when can we get together?"

A huff of laughter escaped her. "While I'm flattered beyond reason, maybe we should talk…."

"About?"

"About how it might be way too soon for you to think about relationships. Your wife has been gone how long?"

"Not long and yet, a long, long time. And I think you should be aware—I seem to have a drinking problem."

She tilted her head. He hadn't seemed the least bit drunk last night. "Oh?"

"Yes." He circled his knees with his arms. "Apparently if I drink three beers I'll do any damn thing I please. Whether or not it's a good idea."

"I see," she said, laughing. "So this *is* about regrets…."

He sighed. "I can be more suave. You should try me."

She turned toward him. "Spencer, you seem to be a very nice guy, but I warn you—I'm painfully out of practice at this. And it's possible you're just lonely."

He turned toward her. "Devon, my wife was a wonderful woman. I didn't deserve her. That's a fact. And she battled cancer for almost four years. She had brief periods of respite, but every time the cancer would come back harder. Stronger. We fought it together till the end. Was I lonely? Yes, absolutely. If I could've taken it on for her I would have. In the end I was glad she could give up the fight—it was terrible for her."

Devon was quiet for a long moment. Finally she said, "You must miss her so much."

"Of course. But that's not why I danced with you. That's not why I kissed you."

"Then why?"

His eyes darkened; his brows hooded them. "I wanted to. That simple. I really, really wanted to."

Oh. My.

"Listen," Devon said. "We should probably put our energy into a friendship. I think maybe we both have a great deal to overcome."

"I know I do," he said. Then he stood suddenly, whistled and shouted to Austin. "Too far! Get back here!" Then he sat down again. "I really don't know much about you. We'll work on that friendship thing and maybe..." He shrugged. "Maybe you'll tell me about it one of these days."

"Tell you what?"

"Where you really came from. Who Mercy's father is. What you're worried about. Your friends can't help you unless they understand."

Uncomfortable, she looked away. Just briefly.

But it was long enough for her to catch sight of a black SUV with darkly tinted windows driving down the road from 101 to the bar. She gasped. She covered her mouth and then checked the little kids—they were playing at the edge of the bay not fifteen feet away, digging deep holes and filling their buckets with wet sand. She looked back at the car. And she started to tremble.

"What?" Spencer asked. "What is it?"

She gripped his wrist. "Oh, no," she said. "Oh, God…"

"You're afraid of that car."

"I have to go…. I have to—"

"Are they here for you? Looking for you?"

"I have to…" She stood. "I have to…"

"Stop," he said. "Just stay right here. Sit down and don't move. I'll go see who they are, what they want. Don't run—just keep an eye on the kids and Austin."

"I know who they are," she said, her face white as chalk. "I know what they want."

"Then know this. You're safe when you're with me."

Ten

Spencer whistled at Austin, giving him instructions to stay close to the dock, and telling him he'd be right back. Then he took the stairs two at a time to the bar, entering from the deck just as a man entered from the opposite door that led from the parking lot. Cooper was not in sight, probably busy with his family the day after his wedding, and Rawley was behind the bar. He sat down on a stool at the bar.

The man wore jeans and boots and a light blue denim long-sleeved shirt, although it was summer. His sleeves were rolled up to his elbows and his hands and forearms bore a few thin scars, what you would expect from a farmer or rancher.

"Help you?" Rawley asked.

"Yes, sir. I'm looking for a woman, sir. She's kind of tall. Blonde. Around thirty-five or so. She'd have a seven-year-old boy and a pregnant girl with her."

Rawley frowned and shook his head. "She got a name?"

"Reese," he said. "Boy's name is Mark, her son. She has her sister with her and the girl is due to have a baby real soon. They're missing and I'm out trying to track her down...."

"Missing from where?" Spencer asked.

The man didn't answer immediately. "Near Myrtle Creek. Farm near Myrtle Creek."

"You family?" Rawley asked.

He shrugged. "More or less. I've known her a long time. I work the farm and we're all...worried."

"What's she driving?" Rawley asked.

He shook his head. "She didn't take a car. I think she got picked up."

"Got a number we can call if we see her around?"

"You haven't seen them, then?" he asked.

"Hasn't been anyone new around here in a long time. My cousin was here last year, going through a divorce, ye see, but she's gone back to Texas. Anyway, she's way over thirty-five. You worried they been snatched?"

"We're worried in general."

"You talked to police?" Rawley asked.

"It's family business," he said. "If you haven't seen her, I'll just..."

"Wanna leave that number? How long they been gone?" Rawley pressed.

"It's just been a day or two, but there's no reason they should go anywhere. Especially without saying where they were going. It's a mystery."

"I'll be glad to keep an eye out—I'm in this town ever day. And this here guy—he's in town ever day. You'll watch for her, eh?" he said, looking at Spencer.

"Of course. Yes."

"Now. That number?" He pushed an order pad and pencil toward the man and watched while he wrote down numbers. "Anything turns up, I'll give you a call, Mr...."

"Johnson," he said. "Name's Johnson."

"Thing about this place, Mr. Johnson—it's real small. One main street, no apartments for rent, no jobs—most folks are either fishermen, local workers or they hold jobs out of town. There ain't nothing going on.... I been here for years. A couple of women and a kid come here, it's real obvious. We got tourists, mostly for the beach. And I watch over the beach. If your people pass through, I'm bound to notice."

"Thank you, sir," he said politely. "Appreciate it."

Seconds after the door closed, Rawley looked out the back door and Spencer went out to the deck. He was hoping Devon wasn't watching the black SUV—that might tip them off. But she sat on the sand, ball cap pulled down, watching the children and Austin, who paddled by them, remained very close to the shore. *Good girl,* he thought.

Rawley came back behind the bar and wrote down some letters and numbers—license plate. Then he looked at Spencer with piercing eyes. "Devon tell you about herself?" he asked.

Spencer shook his head. "That first morning, when you brought her here, I heard you and her talking. I've never said a word to anyone."

Rawley shook his head. "That's them. From that camp. She's gotta tell Mac now. And Cooper. We can't keep 'em safe if we don't know what or who to keep 'em safe from."

Spencer stood up. "Rawley, let me talk to her. We were just getting around to that when the SUV turned up. She got so scared. I didn't think she'd stay upright."

Devon held her breath and concentrated on the kids, refusing to turn around and look back at the bar. Because of the surf, she wouldn't be able to hear if the SUV departed. Her heart was in her throat; she was afraid as she sat there that Jacob and his men might be sneaking up on her.

She heard a familiar whistle, then Spencer's yell. "Hey, Austin! I'm back." And then he was sitting beside her again. "It's okay," he said. "He's gone, whoever he was. He said his name was Johnson, but I have my doubts."

"How old was he?" she asked.

"Mid-thirties, maybe. He's looking for someone named Reese."

She gasped. "She has a son!"

Spencer nodded. "He said she'd be with a boy and a pregnant girl."

She gasped again. They were getting out—one or two or three at a time. But what of Laine? Was she just helping people to leave and then staying behind? And what about the other women? Laine wondered if any of the others would leave of their own volition.

But were they safe? Would she ever see them again?

"Is he the one you ran from? Johnson?" Spencer asked.

In spite of herself, she gave a laugh. "No, he works for Jacob, the leader of The Fellowship, a farming commune where I spent the past few years. He didn't mention me? They're not wondering where I've gone?"

"He didn't mention you," Spencer confirmed. "It's possible you've been gone so long, they assume you're far away. But what are the chances they'll see you somewhere?"

"Pretty slim, I'd guess," she said. "When I first

arrived, there were more than twenty of us. Lately they've been…leaving," she said.

"The men had some freedom—they left in those big black SUVs all the time. The women went only to the Farmers' Market or the produce stand where we sold what we grew. Everything we needed from tampons to clothing was brought to us. I think it was Reese who made the shopping lists—she tended to run things, whether she was asked to or not. She was the eldest woman there." She blinked. "Are you sure he's gone? That man?"

"I think Rawley got rid of him pretty good. He was convincing—said he'd been in this town and on this beach every day and hadn't seen any women and children that didn't belong here. He said there weren't any jobs or apartments or anything here—a newcomer sticks out—especially a kid or a pregnant woman. He asked for a phone number to call in case one turned up and then he got the license plate."

"That Rawley," she said. "We should never underestimate him."

"There's something about him all right…he sure doesn't look or act like the clever dude he really is." He draped an arm over her shoulders. "I think you're safe. I don't think you have to hide from those people. Just keep your eyes open, all right?" He touched the bill of her cap. "The hat is probably a good idea."

Mercy was suddenly in her lap, whining. Sandy, hungry, cranky. Devon laughed. "A little beach goes a long way—I better get these kids home. I feel lunch and naps coming on. Talk about an interesting morning."

On the way home Devon thought about what had happened and was reminded of the promise she had made to Scott—that if anything suspicious or noteworthy turned up regarding her past life, she would speak to the deputy.

Devon took the kids to Scott's house and moments after she arrived, he was home. She briefly explained what had happened and asked if he would mind looking after Mercy for a while. She then called and made arrangements to meet Mac McCain at his office in town. Scott offered to go with her and have Gabriella mind the children instead, but she wanted to do this on her own. Because she was terrified.

Mac was already at the sheriff's office when she arrived, but he was not dressed in uniform. He wore a short-sleeved knit shirt with his jeans and seemed to have been busy working on some paperwork. He looked up when she walked in and put down his pen. He stood. He gave her a nod. "Devon," he said.

Devon was shaking as she said, "Thank you for letting me interrupt your day off. I have a few things I think you should know about."

He gestured toward a chair that faced his desk. "Are you afraid of me?"

She gave a weak nod. "I don't think I've done anything wrong. At least, not knowingly. But if I'm arrested or sent to jail, away from my baby, my life is over."

"Let's hear what you have to say before we start worrying about worst case scenarios. How about that?"

She took a breath. "Well, it started about five years ago, after I had a run of real bad luck in the job market…" She tried watching his features and expression as she recounted the events up to this morning, when the car appeared. The telling took an hour. Mac asked a few questions. *Were you held against your will? Were you told you would be punished for leaving or attempting to leave? Did you tend, grow or distribute illegal controlled substance? Are there weapons in the compound? Were there statements to the effect there would be danger to anyone who shared the secrets of the commune?*

"Well, I did help gather and mix chicken manure for his men to use in the gardens and by then I knew what was in the warehouses."

He gave her a wan smile. "Do you know what they did with it?"

"I know what he claimed to do with it—he said it was medicinal and used in healing, but he didn't have a permit because he staunchly refuses to have any dealings with the government. By the time he said that it was all medicinal, I knew it was a lie. We lived a rich life in that commune—we had everything we needed. We women didn't have cars or televisions or computers or jewelry, but Jacob had a house of his own, a private residence across the river. I've been there. He has everything a man could want."

"Were you sexually abused?" he asked.

And she looked down into her lap. "No. He never forced anyone, to my knowledge. He seduced. He promised to share his personal utopia and care for us forever. I hadn't been there long before I was pregnant and it was then that I realized all the children there—all tended by all the women—were Jacob's children. He must've thought he was Warren Jeffs with a pot garden."

"Did he engage in sexual activity with underage girls?"

Again she shook her head. "Everyone was over eighteen, at least during the four years I was there. I tried to leave, but he wouldn't allow it."

"How did he prevent you from leaving?"

"Besides a lock on the gate and a couple of men who carried guns? He said Mercy was his daughter and I couldn't take her. The guns were downplayed—everyone claimed they were for protection from government thugs and wildlife. And

I was afraid if I took my daughter and ran, we might be shot."

"Are you afraid for your safety now, Devon?"

"Well, yes, I am. I don't know that I have reason to be—no one has threatened me. I've been here for more than a month and no one has come looking for me. They seem to be looking for Reese, her son and Mariah, but maybe they decided to just let me go. The woman who suggested I run said that if things got scary, I should tell the authorities about the gardens. I know she wasn't talking about the tomatoes...."

He sat a bit taller in his chair. "What woman was that?"

"She was with us about six months, I think. Her name was Laine." Tears came to her eyes. "I loved her. I loved Laine. I loved Reese, too. Reese delivered Mercy. She was so good to me."

He was quiet for a moment. He leaned forward, folding his hands on the top of his desk. "I'm going to tell my boss about this, of course. And that property isn't in my jurisdiction, so my boss will very likely talk to someone in that county. But I haven't heard anything here today that creates a legal problem for you. I have no reason to arrest you. But if it turns out you have valuable testimony, I think I can get protective housing."

Her eyes grew wide. "Like secret witness stuff?"

He gave her a lopsided grin. "Like that, yes. If you need it. And I wouldn't be surprised if someone from the sheriff's department or another agency wanted to hear what you have to say. If that becomes necessary, we'll be very quiet and careful about it. Have you discussed this with anyone else?"

"Rawley. A little bit. He took one look at me and knew where I was from. I'm not his cousin. He picked me up along the road and gave me a place to stay when I first left the commune. I also gave Dr. Grant a few details when I first started working for him." She shook her head. "I have a job now. I really thought my life was getting back on the rails."

"I think things are moving in the right direction for you," he said. "Let's stay calm. I have ways of learning whether Jacob and your old community are being looked at by law enforcement...."

"I have no idea what you can do," she admitted.

He grinned. "It's spooky sometimes. Devon, the very second you think you're unsafe or suspicious or feeling jittery, I need you to call me and let me know. Don't run, please—that will only make things worse. Our offices are next door to each other. We see each other almost every day as it is. We'll check in all the time. Just go about your business, keep a sharp eye, I'll let you know

if I learn something. Now it's time to let the police do their job."

"You're sure I won't get arrested? For just *being*
there? Because I thought there was this whole ac-
cessory thing in the law."

"You have an advantage when you come forward," he said. "If you're not lying, you look safe
to me. I think you can leave this with me now."

She visibly relaxed, as if Mac's words allowed
her to think, for the first time, that the worst of
her worries were now in the past.

Devon was exhausted that evening. Once she
got home she locked up her little duplex, gave
Mercy a bath, then had one herself while Mercy
stayed close and kept throwing beach toys into her
tub. She didn't turn on many lights and they stayed
mainly in the bedroom where they even had their
dinner of mac and cheese sitting cross-legged on
the bed. With all the windows closed up it was getting a little stuffy. By eight-thirty it was getting
dusky and the sun was beginning to disappear behind clouds over the Pacific.

A light knock sounded at the front door. "Stay
right here, please," she told her daughter. With her
heart pounding, she headed to her living room. As
she passed the living room window, she caught
sight of Spencer's car sitting in front of the house.
She leaned against the door and asked, "Spencer?"

"It's me."

She opened the door. He stood there in sweat-pants and a sweatshirt that had the sleeves and neck cut out; his hair was all spiky and he had a shadowy beard. He smiled at her, showing those excellent white teeth and she nearly melted into a puddle of goo. She was about to ask him what he was doing there when she saw he had a toolbox in one hand and a couple of big sacks from Home Depot in the other.

"Sorry—it's kind of late. And I have a couple of things I think you'll need."

"What?" she asked.

"Well, let's see. Some of these paper shades. They're supposed to be temporary while you're waiting for your fancy custom blinds or shutters to be installed—but here's a secret. They last a long time. My last neighbors—young couple living on a shoestring—had them in their windows for two years. They don't look bad, either. And you can't see through them. If you stand between the window and a bright light, there's a slight silhouette." He handed her a second, smaller bag. "Better locks. Really good locks. But this is the most important thing." He handed her a box. "An iPhone. With a GPS and all kinds of bells and whistles."

"Oh, Spencer..."

"That black car really scared you. I thought these were the few things that could make life simpler and more secure for you." He leaned aside to smile at something. Mercy was peeking out of the bedroom door to see what was going on. He grinned at her.

"Aren't you supposed to be in bed?" Devon asked her. And Mercy scampered back to the bedroom. "Where's Austin?" she asked.

"Home. I have my phone and I'm just down the street. He's locked into some computer game that's slowly destroying his brain cells. He'll call if he needs me and I'll be back in an hour. I'm taking him to Dallas tomorrow and his grandfather is meeting us there to take him the rest of the way to San Antonio. He's going to visit with his grandparents, cousins and friends from our old neighborhood before school starts. Oh, I also have this," he said, pulling a bottle of wine out of a big bag. "You might need a little sleeping aid. Trust me, when I'm done here, no one's getting inside without making a lot of noise."

"I don't think anyone will try to break in, but this is all so...perfect. But that phone—it must've cost a fortune."

"Listen, you have to have this, even if no scary black car is looking for you. You have a child, a job, friends...you live alone."

"I've been taking care of business from the clinic on the office phones. I check in with Rawley. I make calls for Scott. It's been working, but now..."

He put the box in her hand. "Now you should have this. It's a safety precaution. I already programmed my number into the phone. I'm just down the street. I can be here in less than a minute."

Her eyes drifted over him and she hoped he didn't see the attraction there.

He smiled. "I saw that. You like me."

"Don't think just because you buy me presents..."

"Isn't this better than grass cutting? It's very practical. I've always been a practical guy." He put down all his stuff and got out his drill and tools. "I'm the kind of guy that always changes the oil when it's supposed to be changed. I put the toilet paper on the roll. I pay the bills on the due date. I think it's the teacher in me."

Why was that so sexy, she asked herself.

He knelt before her front door, getting started, measuring. "Do you have a pair of scissors? You can cut those paper shades to fit—there's a tape measure in my toolbox. Put 'em up where you need 'em most. And when we're done here, you should call Rawley, let him know you have a phone now and the doors and windows are reinforced. Is it a little stuffy in here?"

"I was nervous about having windows open,

even though I haven't been threatened or approached or anything...."

"Ah. I got some window locks you can adjust—you can have your windows open a few inches. Safely."

With her arms full of paper shades, she sat down on the couch. "I talked to Mac. He was very nice. He'll be looking into that...situation. But I'm not supposed to talk a lot about the details...some of the details, anyway."

"I'm not going to ask you any more questions, Devon," he said, working on the door. "I just wanted to do something that would help you feel safer."

She didn't say anything to that. He had voiced the thing most on her mind every day—how to feel safe.

She got the tape measure and scissors and went to work cutting the blinds to fit the biggest window in the duplex. She measured and cut, then Spencer said, "Before you put that up, let me get the locks on that window." After about forty minutes Spencer was almost done. The doors and the windows all had strong locks on them and the windows were covered.

After checking on the sleeping Mercy she found Spencer sitting on the couch, packing up his toolbox that sat on the floor in front of him.

"You look like you just came from a workout," she said.

"In a way. Football practice starts in the morning. I've already been over at the high school most of the day getting ready for the year ahead—inventory equipment, settling in my office, that sort of thing. You're probably going to be seeing a boatload of high school boys come in for physicals this week."

She sat down at the end of the couch. "We already have a lot of appointments booked. Aren't you going to Dallas tomorrow?"

"I don't have to be at practice the first day—they're just going to get equipment issued and paperwork passed out. My assistant, the former coach, and the equipment manager will handle it. But first thing Tuesday morning, the torture begins." He grinned evilly. He looked around the small room. "How's that? Locks and shades."

"And phone. I'll figure it out tonight."

"I hope it makes you feel more comfortable here."

"You know what? I've struggled with safety my whole life, sometimes not even realizing it. Sometimes this need to feel safe is the bane of my life. I can't make peace with it."

"You can't," he said. "We can do everything right and shit still happens."

"I guess you know, huh?"

"Healthy young wife, stricken with cancer… Yeah. Shit happens."

"How do you handle that?"

He shook his head. He smiled slightly. "I live. That's what I do, Devon. I live. I asked myself— if I could build a bunker for me and Austin, and live there for the rest of our lives protected from the sun's rays and all car accidents and maniacs and slippery floors, would we emerge as very old men and feel like we'd won? Like we'd beat the system? Or would we crawl out of that bunker and look around and say, we had long lives, but empty lives?"

"But do you ever worry that you haven't been cautious enough with your son?"

"Not anymore. I made a decision—worry doesn't work. The only thing that will work is my best—and we might still have huge challenges. I don't cut any corners, don't take any chances, especially with Austin, but being afraid to do anything fun, anything that brings happiness isn't going to be the answer—I know that. Jesus, Bridget didn't do anything wrong or foolish or irresponsible. And living in a bubble wouldn't have helped her. There was a valuable lesson in that."

"And how am I supposed to make peace with all of it?"

"Lock the doors. Pay attention. Call me if you hear a noise." He smiled at her and reached out to touch her nose. "Everything is going to be all right."

"You're sure?"

He gave her a nod. "I'm just not sure how fast, that's the only detail."

Eleven

After the first night with locks and blinds and a phone, Devon began to grow more confident. The next night she slept and the night after that, she slept even better. The high school boys began to keep their appointments with Dr. Grant and, to her extreme pleasure, he asked her to run the patient histories, create their charts, weigh them, take their temperatures and blood pressures and, for those who had insurance, she filed the paperwork.

She remained vigilant, watching her surroundings both at home and at work, but she didn't see anything or anyone suspicious and, over the course of the week, she began to relax. Gabriella reassured her that she was very careful about things like keeping the doors locked when she was minding the children, so Devon did not worry about Mercy during the day.

When Friday came, Devon took an early lunch

break, leaving Scott at the office, and drove to the high school with her lunch. From the parking lot she could hear the football team shouting, grunting and groaning. She walked toward the bleachers and smiled as she heard Spencer's voice rise above the rest. "Hump! What're ya, tired! Move it! Drop and give me twenty! Sorenson—you lazy bum, let's see some *action!*" And he would just use his whistle. A lot.

She went to the bleachers and sat there, taking out her drink and her sandwich. After pushups, he had a couple of them passing the ball, a few running a couple of plays, a few players—suited up in pads—smashing into each other with him yelling, "Harder!" He was jogging all over the field in his sweats and sleeveless T-shirt, sweat staining the shirt, and she hadn't really noticed until today— what a fine male butt he had. He was full of gestures—rolling his arm and shouting, telling them to rev it up. Leaning his hands on his knees, bending over and shaking his head as if someone had a long way to go, demonstrating some footwork by rapidly running in place, knees high.

Spencer was all over the field, sometimes yelling, sometimes slapping a player on the back or giving an approving knock to a helmet. She had headed this way because she was curious, but her curiosity was quickly giving way to an onslaught of other feelings. She was enjoying watching him.

At first glance she wouldn't have thought he had such power. Such strength. And his energy was impressive. Some of the boys on the field were as big as he or even bigger, but he ran them ragged.

Devon had been an athlete herself at one time. She might still be an athlete, given half a chance. She should have been prepared—his sweaty, muscled, graceful movements appealed to that part of her. She loved sports, always had. And she'd been very competitive in high school. She hadn't had time for more than working out and running in college—with classes and a job, she'd been too busy. She thought about how fun it would be to play some fierce volleyball or soccer. A pickup basketball game would be fun, as well.

Then she realized, if she was still here in Thunder Point when Mercy started team sports—which was not too far away—maybe she'd be one of the parents who coached!

From the corner of her eye, she saw a woman run onto the track from the far end of the football field. A jogger, she was long and lean with a glorious copper-colored mane, a full bosom, a tight fanny and…and she wasn't wearing much. Devon coughed suddenly, nearly choking. The runner was wearing a sports bra and tight briefs, almost bikini style, more what you would see on a beach volleyball court than here at a high school football field.

Maybe she was in training, Devon thought. It

wasn't track-and-field season but that didn't mean a person couldn't train year-round. She could be training for a marathon.

She ran past the bleachers and all the way to the far end of the football field, where she ended her run and began to walk around in a circle, hands on hips, cooling down. After a couple of minutes of that, she began stretching out, touching toes, sitting on the ground, one leg outstretched, reaching for her foot. Then with legs spread wide, she stretched, touching first her left foot, then right.

Devon stole a glance at Spencer, but he wasn't watching the runner. He was watching his team. One young man was gaping openmouthed at the woman. Behind him Spencer pulled the towel from around his neck, wound it up real tight and snapped his player in the butt, getting a yelp out of him. The player whirled around, rubbing his backside.

Devon laughed in spite of herself.

Spencer blew his whistle twice and shouted. "Mile and a half, then hit the gym for weights!"

The team converged on the assistant coach and equipment manager, returning balls and other training aids, grabbing water then running around the track as a unit. Spencer noticed Devon sitting in the bleachers and he lifted a hand in a brief salute, which she returned. Then he went about the business of gathering up gear with the assistant

coach and equipment manager. There was a util-
ity vehicle nearby, a modified golf cart, and all
the gear was loaded onto it. Meanwhile the team
rounded the curve once, twice, three times...

This would be a good time to take off, Devon
thought. She'd only taken a little over a half hour
for her lunch break, but she didn't want to be a
distraction. Like some people did, for example.

Back in the gym Spencer worked the team
hard, supervising their weight training, then he
loaded them up on protein drinks and water and
sent them to the showers. He needed an athletic
trainer pronto—someone who could wrap strains
and weak spots while he concentrated on the team.
Coach Rayburough said he had always trained a
student to do this work. At Spencer's last high
school, they'd had a certified professional with student assistants. Most college teams had physical
therapists, trainers and orthopedists. But Thunder
Point was operating on a shoestring. This town had
a lot to recommend it, but it was not a rich town.

Spencer decided to ask Scott Grant about doing
a little volunteer time with the team. Spencer could
cope with practice injuries, but game night was another story. He couldn't stop the game and couldn't
turn a wounded young athlete over to distressed
parents. He would need medical assistance to help
with those issues.

Then there was that woman—Miss Benjamin—whom he had recently learned was a high school history teacher. "What the hell is she doing on my practice field every day?" he asked Rayburough.

"She better be trying to get your attention," the older man said. "If she's not, I think she's close to committing a felony."

"Can't we get her to stop that? To say that football is not on the team's collective mind when she shows up would be an understatement."

"Why don't you ask her? In fact, why don't you take her out for a drink and ask her—that might be all she needs."

"Ah, no." He shook his head. "No, she's not my type at all. She's a little too out there for me. She couldn't be more obvious if she was sending me private pictures on the internet."

Rayburough looked him up and down then shook his head. "You're a strange man, Coach. I'm older than dirt and I don't mind looking at her."

"I know pole dancers who are more discreet. She could wear some fucking shorts around those seventeen-year-old boys. What's she like in the classroom?"

"How would I know?"

"I'm going to find a way to get her to stop, without ruffling her feathers or getting her in trouble." She pissed Spencer off but—even he almost had a woody, so those boys must be a hot mess right now.

"Now, I gotta have a trainer—where can I get one right away?"

"Put the boys on the job," he said. "They'll bring you one or recommend someone they know. There are plenty of boys who couldn't make the team but love to be part of the action. And if you need me, I'll train him."

Spencer handed Rayburough a notebook. "I put together a weight training supplement that I think these kids should be on. How's the overall nutrition on this team? They typically get enough protein? They have to force carbs, but they need protein to build muscle. You have any way of watching that? Because we need a little more muscle on that field and I want them well fed and hydrated."

"I print out a workout diet guide every year—I think you'll find most of these boys get great support from their families. They'll provide what you ask for—they need the scholarships."

Spencer decided right then he was going to do a little investigating. He could probably ask Landon for input. There was no way a player would come to him and confess he wasn't getting enough food. But if there was anyone from a family who couldn't afford the five eggs or broiled beef or steamed legumes or cheese and cracked wheat, Spencer knew ways to supplement that would get a player strong and healthy. He wasn't going to have anyone collapse out there.

The locker room was filled with wet, half-naked boys, the showers still running. Spencer blew his whistle. It became instantly quiet as a church, even the water stopped running.

"I'm going to be here at eight tomorrow morning and at two tomorrow afternoon. It's not a training day but anyone interested in talking about the best nutritional program for energy and body building should show up. And, after a short discussion about that, I'm willing to talk about some plays. I brought my playbook. I'm pretty sure my last team had a few you've never seen. This is *not* required—I know many of you have work and family obligations—don't worry, I'll catch you up next week if you have to sit this one out. This is entirely optional. Hey, good workout today, men. If you keep showing me your stuff like that, we'll go far."

Eight o'clock the next morning, the entire team was crowded into the locker room, waiting for him. Once he got over the shock of seeing them all there he realized that any of their parents or bosses would have excused them for anything to do with football.

Now the pressure was on....

Because school would start in less than a month, Dr. Grant's clinic was pretty booked on Saturdays. The only serious situation was a laceration on the palm of a fisherman who carried a good many scars in roughly the same place. Devon helped with the treatment and the cleanup and then she sat down and put her head between her knees for a few moments. Scott laughed at her.

Blood bothered Devon, it always had. Once she cut her finger, pretty deeply, and had to lie down on the floor with a towel wrapped around it until she was no longer faint. "I'll get better," she told Scott. "At least I hope so."

Around three that afternoon, Spencer came into the clinic. "Hey," he said, smiling. "I have an appointment with the doctor."

She looked at her computer screen. "I don't have you down on the schedule."

"Yeah, I know. I just called him. He said he can give me some time. And then, I was wondering, do you have plans for tonight?"

"Me? Plans?" At least she didn't laugh out loud.

"You. Plans. I was thinking something simple. Relaxing. How about I bring a pizza over to your place. Or, I could take you and Mercy out for pizza, or something else if you'd like. I'm guessing you don't have plans to go to the mall or a movie or something…."

Devon gave him a smile. She was a little surprised—she hadn't seen or heard from him since she'd seen him on her lunch hour a day ago. With school starting soon she knew he'd been busy. "Pizza would be nice. I'll give Mercy her mac and cheese and bath and we can have the pizza. It will be very quiet. There's no TV or anything."

"Just what I'm looking for. Seven too late?" he asked.

"Just late enough. I need a refresh. It's been a long day in here. There was even blood!"

"Ewwww," he said on a laugh. "Never expect that in a clinic, right?"

"Scott's not with a patient right now so you can go back. I think he's either in the office or the break room."

The minute he was gone, she leaned her chin in her hand and smiled. She'd been thinking about him a lot but hadn't expected that he would be thinking about her. He had a full and busy life.

The phone rang only twice while Spencer was talking to Scott, then they came out to the front together and Spencer was thanking him. Then he said to Devon, "See you tonight."

"Sure," she said.

And he was out the door.

Scott stood there beside her desk. She finally looked up at him. He lifted one eyebrow and asked, "Date?"

"Well, I don't think it's exactly that. We're going to have a pizza together tonight."

"I know you've been out of circulation for a while, but that's a date in my book."

"Spencer is a friend. And neighbor."

Scott shook his head. "Devon, friends and neighbors date..."

The realization came to her slowly. She had gone to the wedding with Scott, danced with him and yet had not considered it a date. But this time she knew it was, because she wanted it to be. When you want a man to be your date—whether it's champagne and flowers or pizza—it's because you're hoping it might go somewhere. *And where,* Devon McAllister asked herself, *where do you think it's going to go?*

Her brows were drawn together fiercely, she could feel it. Then she heard Scott say, "Devon, I know you have problems to sort out, but the world won't stop turning if you laugh. Have a good time. Enjoy yourself."

"I guess that's right," she said.

"Are we done for the day?" he asked.

"You are," she said. "I have some charts to enter. So as long as I'm here, I'll answer the phone and add appointments to your roster for next week."

"And I'm going to grab a cup of coffee, then head home. I'll probably see you there when you pick up Mercy. Unless you'd like her to stay over so you can be alone with—"

"No! I mean, no, thank you. It's not that kind of date."

Scott could've had his cup of coffee at the clinic—they had a pot on. Or he could've gone out to the beach bar and had a beer to go along with his self-pity. Instead he went to the diner where he found Gina behind the counter and only a few teenagers in a back booth.

"Hey, I don't usually see you this time of day," he said, sitting in front of her.

"I'm usually long gone by now, but I'm covering for Ashley until four or so. She's been out on the bay with a couple of her friends and Eric, her father."

"That must be kind of interesting, being reunited with her father."

Gina laughed. "There's no 're' about it—Eric took off when I was three months pregnant. We were kids…he ran far and fast. I found him last spring when I was looking for medical history for Ash—I realized I knew nothing about his side of the family and thought I'd better get some basic information. That got the ball rolling and they wanted to meet."

"I didn't realize," Scott said.

"I raised her alone, with the help of my mother," she said.

"What's it like, seeing him again after so long?"

She shrugged. "He just says a quick hello if he's going to be spending a little time with Ashley. And he's not too intense about it—he sees her every couple of weeks. They're developing a nice friendship, I think. But for me? Amazing how much water has gone over the dam. Life goes on."

Not always, Scott thought. "You know, you and I had a couple of dates, right before you married Mac..."

She smiled. "We did."

"Got any girlfriends? I'm not doing that great in the dating department. And I'd like my life to go on..."

She tilted her head and smiled sympathetically. "Scott, are you sure you're ready?"

"My wife died almost four years ago...."

"I know. But everyone is different. Maybe it's taking you a while—no shame in that. Be patient—when the perfect woman comes along, everything will fall into place."

"How am I going to know the perfect woman if I don't even date a potential perfect woman? I was just building up to asking Devon if we could go out to dinner and someone jumped in line ahead of me!"

Gina laughed.

He put his elbow on the counter and leaned his head into his hand. He groaned. "Shit. I'm pathetic, right?"

Gina poured him a cup of coffee. When he finally looked up, she was smiling. "Scott, you've known Devon for a while now. She's worked for you for over a month. You keep her three-year-old in your home. If you had the hots for her, it wouldn't have taken you this long."

"It takes hots?"

She nodded gravely. "It takes hots. Right now you've got a real cozy deal—a nice new clinic, a good babysitter, from what you say an excellent clinic manager, plenty of time with your profession and your family, everything covered, everything handled. You're free and clear—when the right woman shows her face, you're ready. You'll know it in minutes. Until you're really ready, you might not recognize her."

"What makes you think I'm not ready?"

Gina smiled. "You really want to hear this? Be sure, because I'm not real crazy about saying it."

"Lay it on me. Please."

She put her hand over one of his. "Our two dates? Were very enjoyable. You're a very good date. And I was interested in your life, your relationship with your wife, and your kids. But you talked about your wife through two entire dates."

He was stricken silent for a long moment. Really, he was shocked. Had he done that? He rubbed the bridge of his nose with a thumb and forefinger. "Jesus, did I do that? Aw, I'm sorry, Gina."

"You don't have to apologize. I was in love with Mac. I had been for years. I just didn't think he felt the same way, which is why I was very happy you asked me out to dinner. And I mean it, I enjoyed myself. I like you. But I knew right away, you're not ready to move on. Scott, I think you need to give yourself permission to accept some things—your children are young. You were with your wife for a long time before they came along, before she died. I know you'd like to be in a nice stable relationship again and I know you're frustrated, but you're not ready. You still want to be with your wife. Until you run into someone who makes you see a whole new possibility, a whole new kind of life, it just isn't going to happen. And lucky for you, too, because if you force this you and the new wife are going to have a third person in your marriage."

He just looked down. "You might be right. But this is getting old."

She surprised him with a laugh. "Tell me about it," she said. "I spent sixteen years between lovers."

"I don't have that kind of time," he said glumly.

"Oh, Scott, you have as much time as it takes. Let yourself off the hook. It's okay if it takes a while to be ready to move on."

"Got any suggestions on speeding up the process?"

"I'm sorry. No. But can I reassure you about one thing? As long as it took you to ask me out, as long as you've been working up to asking Devon out, neither of us was The One."

"Really? And how does that explain Mac?"

"Well, the short version of that story is that not long after we met, he kissed the daylights out of me and we were both a little overcome. I was ready for that, more than ready. But Mac, whose wife had left him with three small children, was terrified. And he had this secret plan—he was going to use sheer willpower to keep away from any kind of romance with me until he felt safe, like until our girls had graduated from high school and were college bound." Then she smiled very widely. "I think my couple of dates with you might've made him decide to take a risk or two. When it came down to a choice between being together or being alone and safe, he took the chance." She sighed. "We were in love from the start. We just had lives that were too complicated."

He lifted his coffee cup and sipped. "You should be a bartender," he said. "Does everyone tell you their troubles?"

"Pretty much," she said, pouring herself a glass of ice water. "And I don't tell anyone anything. But in a few more years, when I finish my master's, I'm going to start charging for my advice."

Spencer arrived right at seven, balancing a pizza box on one hand and a six-pack of cold beer in the other. And the minute she saw him, she could feel her eyes light up, which made her cheeks blush just a little. He came inside and saw Mercy sitting on the sofa in her nightgown with a couple of her books. She looked at him and said, "What's that, Pencer?"

"Pizza. Are you going to have a taste before you go to bed?"

She nodded and gave him a shy smile.

"Then come on, we'll have it in the kitchen."

She jumped off the couch and hurried behind Spencer. He was right at home, putting the pizza on the table, opening a beer and asking Devon if she'd like one. The pizza smelled so good she thought she might drool. She closed her eyes and just inhaled, making him laugh. "You don't splurge on pizza, do you?" he asked.

She shook her head. "But I make decent meals, just inexpensive ones. Oh, God, that looks so good. Brings back memories of school days and lots of pizza." She grabbed plates, napkins and a knife to cut a small slice for Mercy. "Do you need a fork?" she asked him.

"Seriously? No way. That's just wrong. It's a hands-on dinner—just hands." He sat down next to Mercy and gave instructions to her. "This is how you do it," he said, lifting a slice and aiming at his mouth.

And she copied him, but the bite she took was very small and suspicious.

"She's had pizza before, just never from a box."

She took her own bite and almost swooned. "Love pizza. Love, love, love pizza."

"You okay with the toppings?"

"Oh, yes," she said, chewing happily. She swallowed and said, "I want to hear all about your week. Your team, your training."

"I saw you sitting in the bleachers during one of our practices. What did you think?"

"You work them hard. But they don't look too bad. I wasn't there long but I saw some decent passes, a few good kicks. And you looked pretty... relentless."

"Most of those boys have been weight training in the off-season. They're eager, that's for sure. I had a good team in Texas, and a good booster club, but let me tell you something about this town— football is important to them. It's necessary. It took me two days to see what Coach Rayburough meant about this high school and this town. They don't have all the advantages of a bigger school in a bigger, richer town. We'll go into this season with less training equipment, fewer personnel and with a team that has more personal responsibilities than the typical player. The academic requirements to play here are set higher, most of them have part-time jobs and family responsibilities, but they're committed. And determined. I called a meeting this morning—purely optional on a Saturday morning. Just a meeting to talk about nutrition, weight training and some plays they probably haven't seen, and every single one of them was there." He took another big bite of pizza. Then he told her about the trip he made to Bandon to a big health food store to buy a special grain-and-nut mixture, heavy carbs to mix with fruit and yogurt as a start-up fuel. They talked about the importance of minimizing fat in their diets and doing all the other things to ensure their diets provided the correct sustenance for them to work hard on the field.

He would be talking to interested students about taking on training positions on the team, and told Devon he had asked Scott to be the team doctor on a volunteer basis.

And she was completely intrigued.

"I'm boring you," he said with a laugh.

She shook her head. "Not at all. I love football. It's as complicated off the field as on."

"This team is going to go up against some big, talented kids. Kids with better equipment in some cases. It's going to take more than a good playbook to keep these boys safe, strong and healthy."

Mercy wandered away, back to the sofa with her books and the blanket she liked to sleep with while Devon and Spencer finished the pizza and continued their conversation. When he took a pause she dared say, "I wasn't the only one watching your practice. Do you have an admirer?"

He frowned. "Ms. Benjamin? The half-naked history teacher?"

Her eyes flew wide and she gulped. "Teacher?"

He took a drink of his beer and nodded. "Showing her body to the student body. I'm surprised she's getting away with that in a small town like this."

"Oh, boy, you're not happy."

"I have a plan. I'm going to remove her audience. When she shows up in her little tiny panties, we're leaving the field. If I have to, I'll change the practice schedule."

"Kind of sounds like you don't like little tiny panties...."

His eyes darkened. "Depends who's wearing them. And no matter who's wearing them, sharing them with twenty-five young men during a training session isn't exactly classy." He tilted up his bottle again. "Did it bother you?"

She shrugged. "I played volleyball in high school. Our uniforms were kind of skimpy. But not that skimpy. And I ran track—again, we didn't want much wind resistance so our gear was fairly brief."

That made him smile. "You do like sports."

"What's not to like? Someday, when I get things together a little better, maybe I'll get back into it."

"No athletics the past few years, I take it?"

She laughed. "I lived on a small farm. Trust

me, my muscles were worked plenty. But I'd rather play soccer or softball or run to get my exercise." She turned to look into her little living room. "My pizza girl is out like a light," she said with a laugh. "I'll take her to bed and tuck her in."

When she returned to the living room, Spencer was lying flat on his back on the floor. "Spencer!" she said, leaning over him.

"Did I mention my back is killing me? To say nothing of my knees, calves, shoulders?"

"Did you hurt yourself?"

He rose up on his elbows. "Yes. It's the same at the start of every season, trying to keep up with boys half my age, trying to make them feel inadequate and competitive so they'll push it a little harder. Quite frankly? I'm getting too old for this shit. But, God, it gives me a rush. Every new team gives me a rush but they're killing me."

She laughed at him. "Sounds like you're the one who needs off-season training."

"That's just it, I keep up. I work out. They still hammer me when football training starts."

She got down on her knees. "Roll over. And remember I don't do this for everyone."

He lifted one brow in question, but he rolled over.

She started to massage his shoulders, first softly, then with more depth and strength. "I don't think there's anything better than muscles that are stiff and sore from a good workout." He groaned appreciatively and she laughed. "One of these years you're going to have to stop showing off in front of the high school boys."

"I have this fantasy—that each one of them thinks I can take him down if I want to. Don't give me trouble, boy, because I can sack you."

"Ego," she said, drilling her fists into his back.

"Hmm. Don't stop. Don't ever stop. Lower." He stretched his arms out above his head. And she worked his back harder, deeper, half tempted to try walking on it.

She went after the small of his back, which was tight as a drum. "You take anything for this?"

"Two Advil, one beer. I'm thinking about another beer." Then he yawned.

"Don't fall asleep on me," she said.

And then in a swoop that she didn't see coming, he rolled, grabbed her and she was on the bottom looking into those deep brown eyes as he leaned over her.

Those dark eyes seemed to glow a little bit. Her hands rested on his biceps and she was frozen, gazing.

"I didn't know we'd end up like this," he said.

"Kind of seemed like your intention...."

"The first time I saw you, six weeks ago or so, with your overalls and long braid, I didn't know

I'd kiss you. I didn't expect to be holding you. I wasn't looking for anything…"

"I know," she said softly. "You're a pretty new widower. I understand."

"I don't want to pry for personal details, but is he out of your life now? The man? Mercy's father? Are you free from him?"

"I hope so."

He tapped her chest above her left breast. "In here?"

That startled her; she didn't realize just how much of a mystery her life was to him. "Oh, Spencer, that was over almost as soon as it started. I was afraid and confused and…I was vulnerable and he was very protective and loving. I didn't realize he was a liar, that he didn't care about me, only about possessing me, making me a part of his vision, his family, his 'Fellowship.' I haven't been with anyone since Mercy was conceived."

"And now, Devon? What now? Because I think you know—my feelings for you are getting stronger…."

She didn't have to even think about it. "I just want a normal life. Like other people have."

He smiled into her eyes. "Really?" he asked. "Normal like who? Like Rawley, an old Vietnam vet who spent a lot of the past forty years homeless, battling PTSD? Or like Gina, who had a daughter at the age of sixteen and raised her alone? Like

Scott Grant whose wife died just after the birth of his second child? Leaving him the single father of two? Or maybe a normal person like me—widower who shares his son with another father? We're all just a bunch of flawed people, trying to slap together decent lives with the few tools we have."

She just stared at him, her mouth open slightly. She could feel her eyes threaten to tear and she swallowed. "God. I don't know if I'm just completely naive or really insensitive. I'm not the only one who has challenges."

He gave her a little kiss. "Your challenges haven't been small," he said in a comforting tone. "Look how far you have come."

Twelve

The landscape of the hill behind the beach took on a ravaged appearance as the earth movers came in and began a complicated excavation for the new Cooper residence. The old switchback road from 101 to the bar was closed and would eventually disappear while two new roads would take its place, making things safer and more accessible. While he was at it, Cooper was enlarging his parking area, which would allow people easier access to the bar and the dock.

These two roads were going to cost a small fortune. And that was not even considering the additional cost of a custom home. So why was he standing on the beach every day, watching those huge, noisy, exhaust-spewing earth movers and dump trucks with a big stupid grin on his face?

And he wasn't alone on the beach by any measure. *Everyone* arrived at one time or another to watch the action. Sometimes there were ten people standing on the beach near him, looking up at that vast hill. This was a momentous event for Thunder Point—the development of new land. The town and the whole north promontory was pretty well developed and there were some who had hoped Cooper would sell this land to a resort or hotel chain but, mostly, people were just happy to see it improved. All of this development was bound to be good for the town.

Cooper had talked to a developer, of course. He had it in his head that he'd sell lots along the beach for single family residential. It was even within his power to lease those lots with restrictions on the size and architectural style of each structure. "I'll be the homeowners' association," he told Sarah. "No one's putting a purple shed with a neon sign that flashes Girls Girls Girls on my beachfront."

He planned to put some classy picnic tables and grills on the beach. Not a ton of them, but a few. He had an idea that once this part of the beach was further developed, and the new roads were built, they'd have more visitors in the bar. And if they had more visitors, he would be able to add more kayaks and boards as rentals.

During the dog days of August, there weren't a lot of people on the beach, at least during the weekdays, so work progressed nicely. And the beach, while the road crew wasn't working, was completely unaffected.

He had a vision for this hillside development. Given it was a hill, tall multilevel houses were practical. Lower-level garages and even wood shops or rec rooms would fit perfectly on the lowest level with most of the living space on the second level. Then lofts or second levels could be built on top of that. Anywhere from twenty-five hundred to four thousand square feet, these family homes would have large oceanfront decks and staircases to the beach. That style of architecture was not only most practical but would maximize the use of the land.

Even though he had an idea of how many single family lots this stretch of beach could handle, he was still focused on one—his. Theirs.

Mac drove the sheriff's department SUV across the beach, stopped, got out and just stood with Cooper for a while, looking at the roadwork, as he did almost every day. After several minutes he said the thing he said every day. "That's gonna make a difference. But the beach might get busier."

"As long as it doesn't look like Fort Lauderdale at Spring Break, I'll adjust. Maybe they'll buy sandwiches and drinks from me."

Rawley came down from the bar to stand with them and stare up at the site. "Damn fancy, you ask me."

The men looked at him. "I didn't hear anyone ask. You hear anyone ask, Mac?"

"I like fancy," Mac said. "I'd kill to have one of those parcels. I don't need much—those kids will get their own lives eventually. But I'd take one of those windows. Or the deck—I could use a deck like that as long as it had an ocean out in front of it."

Cooper looked at him. "Maybe you ought to go see the bank."

Mac laughed. "I walk into a bank in this uniform and they smile, thank me for the service to the town and offer to set up a little checking account for me. They know what I make, what I'm worth."

"We'll look at the map together. You pick out one of the lots. I'll make you a deal."

"I don't want a deal."

"Why not? I can do whatever I want," Cooper said.

Mac sighed. "Because I don't want to be sitting out on that deck having a beer with you," he said, lifting his chin toward the bar, "and have you remember you cut me a deal and be all butt sore about it."

"I'm not like that," Cooper said.

"You might get like that."

"Tell you what," Rawley interrupted. "I'll buy

one and I'll cut you a deal. I'll be dead by the time I get around to complainin' about it."

Cooper and Mac turned together to look at him. "*You're* going to buy a lot?" Cooper asked.

"I could," Rawley said with a shrug. "If it made a difference in my life."

"But I thought you didn't have any money!"

"Did I ever tell you that?" Rawley wanted to know.

"You were going to sell your truck to bury your father!"

Rawley shrugged. "I'm a practical man. My dad, he socked away a little here and there. Over time, it piled up. I got no bills and a steady job. And I have another truck. I never thought it was a good idea to sell that old house. My dad died in that house—it's good enough for me to die in."

"And I paid to bury your father," Cooper grumbled. If Rawley had enough money socked away to buy one of these beachfront lots, he sure wasn't broke, yet he'd let on that he'd have to sell his truck or house to pay for a burial. He sure played broke.

Rawley slapped a hand on Cooper's back. "That was real neighborly, Coop. I didn't forget to thank you, did I?"

"No," he said. "You were very polite."

"That's a relief. My dad would be spinnin' in his grave to think I was ungrateful."

"Why didn't Ben leave this whole thing to you?" Cooper asked him.

"I had little use for it. All I wanna do is run errands and mop up now and then. I ain't innerested in dividing it into parcels and talkin' to a lot of people about what they can put on 'em. For that matter, I ain't the friendliest proprietor and have no intention of getting any friendlier. I reckon Ben made the right choice, all things considered. You're the talker, not me."

And then he just walked back up that long staircase to the bar. Once he was inside, Mac started to laugh.

"It's not that funny," Cooper grumbled.

"I think it's hilarious," he replied.

The landscape of the town was changing in many ways. School would start the week before Labor Day. Lou McCain, who had shared a house and parenting responsibilities with her nephew, Mac, for ten years, was ready to move on. Since she taught middle school in Thunder Point, she could continue to help with the kids even if she lived elsewhere. She was the perfect person to make sure they got to and from school, and when Mac or one of the seventeen-year-olds, Ashley or Eve, or Mac's new wife, Gina, couldn't carpool the kids to games or lessons, Lou would find a way to help out. But at the age of sixty-one she was ready for something new.

"I'm getting married," she announced at dinner one night. "I'm moving in with Joe this week before school starts and on Labor Day weekend, while you're cooking burgers on the grill, we're leaving town."

There was silence around the table for a moment. Then Mac said, "Alone?"

"I'm over twenty-one," she replied starchily. "And so is Joe, though he's not quite as far over twenty-one as I am." Joe was African-American, ten years younger and a State Trooper who occasionally worked with the sheriff's department. So far there hadn't been so much as a blink at the biracial connection or age difference.

"I mean no wedding, no reception, no friends or family along for the ride?"

She shook her head. "We're looking forward to going somewhere alone. I'm not changing my name, either. I've been Lou McCain a long time. I don't want to learn how to change my signature. And I'll still help with the kids regularly. I mean— they're as much mine as anyone's."

"They are that," Mac agreed. "Well. Congratulations."

"We have to get this done before football starts," she said. "If you think I'm missing a Thunder Point football game, you're crazy."

* * *

In Cooper's apartment, the plans for the new house were always handy, usually rolled up and standing at attention in the corner. Sarah thought Cooper was a little addicted to them. He spread them out a few times a day, made too many calls to the architect and contractor. He had pronounced this as Sarah's special project, her responsibility since she was leaving the Coast Guard but, so far, he hadn't been able to let go of it for thirty seconds.

While they were lying in bed late one night, he pointed out to her that she was almost done with flying. "You have one more week," he said. "Then you're all mine."

"There's a farewell party and you have to go. This time, no shots."

"That hasn't been a problem of mine," he pointed out to her, since the last time they attended a Coast Guard party she was the one who got drawn into doing shots and he'd had to practically carry her home.

"Then it's you and me. Mr. and Mrs. Cooper, beach bar entrepreneurs. We'll be looking at colleges with Landon, going to Friday-night games, paddleboarding on the bay. What else are we gonna do?" she asked.

"Build a house," he said.

"Right. You seem to be all over that project.

So—what's the anticipated date of completion on that?"

"The date they promise or the date it will probably actually be?" he asked. "Because the rule of thumb is that it always takes longer and costs more than they tell you."

"Let's go with your best guess on when we'll be in there," she suggested.

"I'd say June at the latest now that the roads are almost complete. They're in but not paved. Damn, those suckers are pricey!"

"So, do we have money problems?"

He ran a knuckle over her cheek and smiled. "Not yet."

"Are we going to have money problems?"

He lifted his brows. "Need something?"

"Do you promise not to laugh?"

"I never laugh at you, babe. You laugh at me, remember. But I take you oh-so-seriously."

"I want to get pregnant. I want us to have a baby. I want me to have a baby and you to be the daddy. I want to throw away my pills. I want to just go for it. I've wanted it for a few years and never dared. But with you, I feel safe. I'm ready. I'm almost thirty-four and I want to have a baby."

Cooper's eyes got a little glassy. She thought he might be going into some kind of fugue state. He gave her hand a little squeeze and got off the bed and went to the corner. He gathered his rolled-up plans and came back to the bed. He unrolled one after the other until he found the floor plan he wanted to look at.

"What are you doing? Can't you leave that alone for ten minutes and talk to me?"

He shook his head. His index finger ran over the lines. "Here," he said. "We can add a bedroom or two here."

"Shouldn't we talk about it?"

"I just don't know how many bedrooms to add," he said. "We know I'm fertile, even when I'm trying not to be. You're the x-factor here. So how do you feel? Feel like one? Two? Three? Because I can still take the lot next door."

"What are you doing? Are you crazy? The second I suggest throwing away my pills you're building on three more bedrooms?"

He rolled over the plans and grabbed her arms, pulling her against him. He kissed her deep, hard and convincingly. And long. He didn't release her mouth for a long, long time. When he finally did, his voice was a little hoarse. "This is it for me, sweetheart. And I hope it's it for you. This beach, this town, this house. If you want to fill it up with kids or raccoons, there's no way I can say no to you—so why don't we add a bunch of bedrooms?"

"Do you want a baby?"

"I want one with you," he said. "And I'm ready to get started."

She laughed at him. "We'll mess up your plans. Besides, I haven't thrown away the pills yet."

"No worries. I can always use the practice…."

Spencer, Devon and Mercy had dinner together most nights. Austin was still with his grandparents, but would be back in a few days to get ready for the start of school. Devon would pick up Mercy at the doctor's house and they went home to freshen up. Then either Devon would make something simple at her house and Spencer would join them or, with Mercy in her pajamas and toting a couple of picture books, some color crayons and a coloring book, off they went down the street. "Does Pencer know I don't like that pizza in the box?" Mercy always asked.

She laughed. "I think by now he gets it. But don't worry—Spencer has peanut butter."

"I like peanut butter," she said.

But Spencer had a nice surprise for Mercy—he usually served her favorite meals. Tonight it was spaghetti and meatballs. So while they ate, Devon and Spencer always talked about football practice, or her busy office, with all the kids showing up for physicals and immunizations. They covered town news, updates on the transformation on the beach and anything else that came up. After dishes were done, Mercy was found on the sofa, reclining on her special blanket, leafing idly through her favorite book or watching an old kids' movie on the hand-me-down DVD player that was once Austin's. That was the best babysitter Devon had ever come across.

"I should take her home and put her to bed," Devon said.

"No, you don't," he whispered, leaning into her and kissing her neck. "Not until you have to. Settle Mercy in Austin's bed with her movie and come back here. I have a surprise for you."

"I have a feeling I'm not going to be all that surprised," she said with a smile. More kissing and snuggling, is what she assumed. They'd been sneaking kisses and caresses here and there for a week or more. But it was so wonderful to hold hands with someone, to not have to hide the affection. She had finally owned up to Scott Grant, who had asked, "Is it that kind of date yet?" And she'd said, "It is," with a flush and a smile.

Devon went back to the living room where she found Spencer waiting on the couch. "Spencer, there's a bell on the bedroom door!"

"I know," he said, grinning. "It wouldn't be safe to hang it around her neck."

She sat down beside him. "How's your back feeling?"

"As bad as my legs and arms, but I'm up to this, trust me."

With his arms around her waist, he pulled her

closer and covered her mouth with his. Her entire insides began to smile and she was so overwhelmed with gratitude for having found this man. She put her arms around his neck, leaned back and opened her mouth under his. He moaned; she sighed. She was melting inside; she was melting into him. His hands, large and callused, were roaming up and down her back, then they were in her hair, pulling her mouth hard against his, then they were on her butt.

She broke away just a little bit and said, "As surprises go, you're pretty predictable. We make out like teenagers every night. And there's a three-year-old in the next room," she whispered. "Thank God you have good brakes."

"Here you go. If you say yes, I lined up a baby-sitter for your house tomorrow night. A couple of them, actually. Landon and his girlfriend, Eve—Mac's daughter. I asked them to babysit so I can take you out," he said.

"Out?"

"Dinner?" he asked. "We can stay close. Maybe a bite to eat at Cliffhanger's? Walk on the beach? Whatever you feel like."

"Alone?" she asked.

He smiled at her. "I'm sure there will be people around. But we can spend a little time here without a three-year-old in the next room, if you feel like it."

She bit her lip. "I'm a little nervous."

He pinched her chin with a thumb and forefinger. "Listen to me, Devon. You don't ever have to be nervous with me. I'm not going to push you into anything. Here's what I want—I want you to always feel safe and comfortable with me. If you're not ready for more than this, then I'm not ready."

"Spencer? Are you planning to break my heart? Because I'm starting to care about you enough to take risks that a month ago I swore I would never take."

He shook his head. "Here's the thing—I don't want you to take risks. I'm a sure thing. You can put a stop to this anytime you want to. I'm not pretending anything, honey. I didn't think this would happen. But I'm glad it did."

"Well, there's no stopping it now," she whispered. She put her arms around his neck and held him fiercely while she kissed him for a while longer. Reluctantly they finally broke apart, knowing it was time to get Mercy into her own bed. He followed her home to make sure there were no problems. Once the doors were locked behind them, Spencer made his way home.

He was an angel. Not just a very nice man, but he was almost perfect. He was the best of sweet and gentle. He was a fierce warrior who drove his team hard, while nurturing them at the same time.

He pushed those teenage boys to the limit, but he also drove himself just as hard

But they were both skirting the issue—they both really wanted to make love.

But she was very nervous. It didn't exactly just dawn on her that she hadn't had a normal relationship with a man yet, even though she was twenty-eight and a single mother. There had been some high school and college romances, some of them quite satisfying even if they weren't real long-lasting.

And then Jacob came along.

Her genuine worry was—what if she didn't know how to have a normal relationship now? What if she had this lovely, sexy man and screwed it up? The temptation to back off, to run, was always so strong in her. She knew it came from a lack of confidence and she had been trying to overcome it for the past few years.

Although Spencer had been through so much himself, he was so much braver and surer of himself. He knew what he wanted. He wasn't afraid of taking a leap of faith. And he didn't seem to be worried that she wasn't quite there yet.

She was nervous all day, anticipating her evening with Spencer. Scott Grant asked her if anything was wrong and she said no, only that they were so busy and she didn't want to get behind.

Finally the big night arrived and, as promised,

Landon showed up with Eve and a couple of old board games. Devon wore her best jeans for their date and was so relieved that Spencer showed up in jeans, as well. She hoped he didn't notice her jitters. Something about a babysitter and a date out in public made this seem official and she so hoped he wouldn't regret it.

She was completely unprepared for the mood at Cliffhanger's—they greeted Spencer like an old friend. They got a table in the bar, ordered a beer and a wine and that was the end of their date as she had expected it. Just about every person in the bar and the dining room stopped at their table, gave her a friendly hello and then either began questioning Spencer about the football team or giving him advice.

"Oh, hi, Devon. So, Spence, who's starting?"

"You know who—you saw every one of them last year. Although I do have a sophomore who's going to really surprise you. With the right encouragement, he could follow in Dupre's footsteps."

"Team captain?"

"Landon Dupre—it was unanimous. He's got strong leadership skills and is completely up to the job."

"Got a game schedule yet?"

"It's being posted and published in two days— clear the calendars."

When their crab legs arrived, they were left briefly alone. Devon said, "Everyone knows."

"That we're out to dinner? Yes. That we might make out like rock stars after dinner? Yes. That I hope I have a girlfriend? It's obvious."

"They think we're doing it," she said.

He leaned toward her and just smiled. "They hope, just like me and you."

"Spencer!" she said on a laugh.

He took a drink of his beer. "I haven't been here too long, Devon, but there's something I know about this town. Unless you're a really bad person or someone who stirs up a lot of trouble, they just hope things work out. That's all. They want their kids to be safe and make something out of themselves, they want their neighbors to get by all right, they want their friends to be happy and they want to be blessed with work. Everyone around here seems to work real hard. They seem to always be pulling for the good guys. It's so uncomplicated."

"If we get together, you think it won't get complicated?" she asked.

"From time to time it will," he said. Then he shook his head. "I'm not going to waste a lot of energy worrying about it."

She sipped her wine. "Why can't I be more like that?"

He shrugged. "I know you have good reason to worry about things like this, but I think that's

going to pass. Pretty soon you'll realize there's
no fence around you here. You have nothing but
choices—it's all up to you. Plus, you're well-liked
here. You help the doctor, have a sweet little girl,
have friends who care about you—nice friends.
You even have old Rawley coming out of his shell.
As time passes, you're going to relax into a new
life and things will work out. With any luck, I'll
get to be a part of it."

It seemed as if the second they were done eating, people were swarming by the table again. Cliff
came from behind the bar and actually pulled out
a chair, sitting down to talk to Spencer about some
of the records that had been set in previous years.
And when the waiter brought their coffee, he took
a seat, as well. He had some opinions on the team
he was sure Spencer would want to hear.

Devon relaxed. This gave her strange comfort,
this familiarity. No one seemed suspicious of her;
they all seemed very accepting. A couple of times
she put in her two cents' worth on football matters
and that seemed to be met with surprise—a girl
who knew a lot about football? Then they offered
their approval that she should be so knowledge-
able. Spencer was right again—these people were
just plain good folks. They were a tight bunch,
however, and if she did anything mean or dam-
aging to their football coach, they'd behave very

differently. Spencer hadn't been here much longer than she had, but he'd clearly won them over.

And it appeared they'd be having coffee with these folks for a long time.

Her cell phone rang and she grabbed it in a panic. It was Landon. "Is everything all right?" she asked.

"Everything is fine," he answered with a laugh. "Can Mercy have some ice cream before bed?"

She was speechless. "Oh, sure," she said. "Not too much, though—we don't want a bellyache. How is she behaving?"

"She's good. We're playing a little Candy Land. And eating ice cream."

"Okay. Thanks for calling."

She just gave a smile and nod to Spencer's questioning eyes. And then the men continued to talk football. It made her smile to herself—any other woman would probably say, "Nice date, buster." But Devon was so reassured by the easy acceptance and sincere camaraderie.

Finally, reaching for Devon's hand across the table, Spencer said, "Much as I'd like to hang around, Devon's got a sitter and we should probably get going."

"Right. Sure." Cliff pushed back his chair, the waiter stood up, one of the bar patrons gave a nod.

"Tell you what—I'll stop by for a beer one of

these days. We'll carry on this discussion later," Spencer said.

"You do that," Cliff said, sticking out his hand. And then he nodded. "Take care, Devon. See you around."

"You bet."

She let him hold her hand on the way into the parking lot. He stopped beside his truck and put his hands on her waist. "You were a very good sport about that."

"I had fun. I think you're the most important person in town. At least during football season."

"It was obvious right away the town gets behind all the school events. And they love their football." He pulled her closer. "Walk on the beach? Feel the need to get home? My place?"

She touched his cheek with her palm. "How about your house."

Thirteen

Spencer had left on only a dim kitchen light. He pulled Devon in the door and it was barely closed when he pulled her close and just held her for a moment. He looked at her in the faint light, touching her face softly, gently. The light bounced off her golden hair and her blue eyes twinkled. He touched her lips with a finger. "This is as alone as we've ever been, I think."

She nodded, slipping her arms around his waist.

He kissed her lightly on the lips. Then her forehead, her chin, her cheek, her neck, her ear. Then he was on her lips again, but his touch was so tender, almost hesitant. And he was kissing her slowly, very slowly. His fingers were in her short hair, running it back from her face, sweet and tempting, kiss after kiss. And then he licked her lips open and took her mouth firmly, but his touch was still achingly slow, gentle.

He pulled away a half inch. "What do you think?" "I think…yes."

He smiled into her pretty eyes. His hands circled her waist while hers went around his neck and he lifted her off her feet, straight up, so that she was looking down into his eyes. "What do *you* think?" she asked him in a whisper.

"I was at yes a long time ago."

She put her hands against his rough cheeks and kissed him, deep and hard. Tongues played and he reminded himself for the hundredth time, *Easy, young man.* It had been so long since he'd held a woman with the intention of making love. Years, possibly. He was already aroused. No surprise there, he'd been aroused since the first week he'd known her. In fact, the minute he'd seen her transformation from overalls and a long braid to more fitted clothes and that sexy, floppy short hair, he'd wanted to get his hands all over her.

He walked toward his bedroom while she clung to his neck. He put her feet on the floor, sat her down on the bed, then went down on one knee to take off her shoes. He kicked off his own and rolled with her onto the bed, claiming her mouth now with more power. "I'll go slow," he said softly. "We'll take our time with this." Then he wondered if he was saying this for her benefit or his own. Since he was desperately close to wanting to ravage her completely, he wondered if he would be able to make good on the promise he'd just made.

But he wouldn't allow himself to even fantasize about taking her hard and fast. If he ever wanted to see her again, be with her again, he was determined to make her feel safe, good, right. Satisfied. Respected. Cared for. And with that in mind, he started touching her perfect breasts on the outside of her clothing while the zipper in his jeans threatened to break wide open.

And God bless her, she began touching him, his chest, his hip, his denim-clad erection. And he groaned with equal parts misery and jubilation. She unbuttoned his shirt so she could caress his chest and he slid his hands under her shirt. He hadn't lost his touch—he had that bra clasp opened in one flick.

And he heard her softly laugh right before she claimed his mouth again.

He felt like a randy teenage boy, wondering how far she would go, how far he should go. He unsnapped her jeans and with his hands on her hips, began to push them down. She lifted her hips a bit to help and in spite of himself, he growled deep in his throat. When she kicked off the jeans, his hand instantly went to her panty-covered crotch while he dove at her neck, licking, sucking, moaning. She was a little damp and he thought, *Yes!*

With no more thoughts of an inexperienced

teenager, he pulled her shirt up and away, made the bra disappear and slid those panties off. Holding her breasts in his hands, he licked one, then the other, his hand parked on her mound, one finger sliding a little deeper, massaging, circling, testing.

So ready...

He felt her tugging at his jeans and he said, "Got it," and stripped off his clothes as quickly as he could. He gave his throbbing member a rub and she brushed his hands away and put her own on him. That growl came out of him again and he pulled her close. "Oh," she said. Then she said, "Mmm," and massaged him, gently at first, then with more strength.

He rose over her, took her mouth in a long, deep kiss and said, "I meant to go slowly for you."

"We can go slowly later."

He smiled. "You think so, huh?"

"I want to feel you inside."

He rolled away briefly, just long enough to reach into the bedside table and get a condom. He had it applied in record time and he was over her again, pushing her down onto the bed, edging her legs apart with a knee, probing gently. And then he pushed inside in one long, slow, fluid motion. He held still inside her, listening to her breathing—deep and rapid. She dug her heels into the bed and pushed against him.

He brushed her hair back from her forehead. "Okay?"

"Very okay." She wiggled a little bit beneath him.

Okay, he thought. And he began to move, slowly at first, holding her mouth, then her nipple, then the other nipple, sliding in and out. He grabbed her butt and shifted their angle so that he'd be connecting with her clitoris; he picked up speed and she began to moan and gasp loudly, fiercely, gripping his shoulders, digging her nails into him, riding him as he rode her. "Come for me, baby. Come for me."

She threw her head back, her eyes rolled back, she pushed against him so powerfully she nearly lifted him, and it came. She closed around him, pulsing, drowning him in liquid heat. "Like that," he whispered. "Just like that." He kept at her until the pulsing slowly ebbed, until she began to relax beneath him, and then he went after her with all the passion he'd been storing, three, four, five hard strokes.... And he was overcome. His eyes watered; he ground his teeth; he throbbed himself empty. It was beyond what he had remembered.

He held himself over her, mindful not to crush her with his weight. It took a few moments for him to catch his breath, to open his eyes, to see her smiling up at him.

"Like that," she whispered. She smoothed her hand from his cheek to his neck. "Just like that."

He smiled at her. "We did that pretty well for a first time."

"My toes curled," she said. "I think maybe I had a blackout."

He laughed. "You all right?"

"I'm very all right. You?"

"I'm going to probably be a pest now," he warned her. "It's going to be even harder to be away from you."

"That's okay, Spencer. I'm happiest when we're together."

Spencer pulled the cover over them and Devon lay in his arms, her head against his shoulder. She'd been so worried, so nervous, and she needn't have been. Spencer loved her in a way that made her feel crazed with desire and yet cherished. She turned her head and looked up at him. "Spencer, what does it mean to you when you make love with someone?"

He seemed to consider this for a moment. "Do you want the real honest answer?"

"Of course! Please!"

"Well," he said, gently stroking her back, running his fingers down her spine, "in younger days, before I found a woman I wanted to commit to, it meant pleasure. It meant getting deeper, excuse the pun."

She couldn't help it, she giggled a little.

"I hear there are a lot of dogs out there who will sleep with any woman. I was never cursed...or blessed...with that quality. Sex was always important to me. Meaningful. I always hoped I'd found someone I could love with a purpose. It didn't always work out for me, and it wasn't always my choice, either. I had some short flings where I wasn't the right man for her. I had a few longer affairs that sputtered out and it was no one's fault."

"And with me?" she boldly asked.

"I think you know." He leaned over and kissed her brow. "I'm falling in love with you."

"Isn't it a bit soon for that?"

"Soon? We've known each other two months. I painted your kitchen. I don't go around painting kitchens for women I don't care about. I've been alternately trying to stay away from you and trying to get closer to you since June."

She lifted her eyebrows. "You were trying to stay away from me?"

"I wasn't exactly successful at that...."

"But why, Spencer?"

"Besides worrying that I wasn't ready? That I could be rebounding after Bridget's death? You were secretive. Mysterious. Obviously a little frightened and of what, I wasn't entirely sure. But it isn't too soon and I'm not rebounding and I can wait until you're ready to talk about what happened to you because over the past few weeks I've come to the conclusion that whatever you're keeping to yourself is a very small piece of who you are."

"It already seems so long ago and far away, and yet something will happen like the appearance of that black SUV and I worry that it will be lurking forever. I'm ready to tell you anything you want to know."

He smiled at her. "Is that so?"

She nodded. She whispered the story of how an offer of help had turned into four years and a child in a commune with a morally superior cult leader. She explained how her desperation for safety and comfort and well-being had seduced her into believing in him and turning over her independence, her soul.

"Did you love him? A little bit?" he asked when she'd told him the full story.

"It passed very quickly. If you love a person who's using you, you're sicker than he is."

"And you ran," Spencer said.

"I had a brief window of opportunity and had to take it. There might not have been another chance and I was a little afraid that what he said was true—that some government agency would take Mercy from me and send me to jail for being a part of his illegal operation."

"And now?"

"Mac doesn't think there's any danger of that, but I'm going to have to cooperate with anyone who wants information that might lead to his arrest. He's guilty of a lot."

He rubbed her back. "There's probably a special place in hell for a man who risks rather than protects children, any children. I'm glad you're out."

"I might be haunted by it for a long time. I worry about the ones I left behind. Only a couple of the women there are completely under his spell—most of us just wanted peace and safety for our families. I worry about what might happen to them. Eventually he's going to be brought to justice."

"We all have ghosts, honey. Over time we make peace with them—they're part of a past that was difficult."

"That's all I want, for it all to be past."

"And, Devon? What does it mean when you make love?"

She smiled at him. "It means I risked my most valuable possession next to my daughter—my heart. It means I love. And hope I was right."

He pulled her close, kissed her deeply and whispered against her lips, "I'm always on your team. I'm always your loyal friend, no matter what. If you decide you're really in love with me, even better. But, Devon, you can count on me either way. I give you my word and my word is good."

"I never doubted that," she said. "I could feel it."

He grinned. "Then I guess you wouldn't mind feeling it again," he said, moving on her.

Cooper was on dad duty because Spencer was embroiled in football training and a couple of pre-season scrimmages. He flew to Dallas to meet Austin at the airport and fly the rest of the way home with him. Austin's maternal grandfather, Dale Cunningham, flew up with him to Dallas and he walked with him to meet Cooper's arrival.

Shaking his hand he said, "I hope you've been taking your vitamins."

Cooper laughed. "Good visit?"

"You bet. And I think I've aged ten years. His grandmother is in a coma."

Cooper laughed again. "One of these days I'd like you and Mrs. Cunningham to fly out to Oregon to visit. It's not fancy, but we have a good time and some of the best sunsets on the coast. I'm building—the place should be ready by late spring next year. Sarah and I will be in a bigger place on the beach. More room for company, but don't wait that long. We can always manage something with a door that closes."

"Thanks, Cooper. You and Spencer working everything out all right? Getting along?"

"Who wouldn't get along with Spencer? He's a pussycat—as long as you're not playing ball for him."

Dale chuckled. "I hope you have a good trip back." He ruffled Austin's hair.

"We're going to stop on the way home from Eugene and get some school things."

"Grandma might've put some new school clothes in the suitcase."

"Aw, she didn't have to do that!"

He laughed. "Well, she did have to. His legs and feet grew while he was visiting. The kid's a weed."

"Thanks, Dale. It's appreciated."

Dale Cunningham bent down. "Gimme a hug, kid. Your old grandpa has to get on a plane home."

Austin obliged.

"Say thank you, Austin," Cooper advised.

"Thanks," he said.

"Call when you're home safe."

Once Austin's grandfather was on his way to his plane, Cooper dropped an arm around Austin's shoulders. "We've got about twenty minutes before boarding, bud. Let's hit the bathroom and grab some fast food for the plane. It's a long flight and there won't be any food on board."

"Will it still be light when we get home?"

"Barely. Why?"

"I wanna get out on the bay. Just for a little while."

"You'll have plenty of time tomorrow. We

should call your dad, let him know we connected and are on the way."

"I called him once already," Austin said. "Can I have pizza?"

"Sure," Cooper said. And while they waited in the food line, Cooper texted, The package has been delivered. They had about three minutes to spare when they got back to the gate and were immediately boarding. Cooper's phone chimed and he looked at the response, Tell the package I'm ready for him to be home.

"I think your dad missed you," Cooper said with a laugh. "He said he's ready for you to be home."

"I think maybe three weeks is too long," Austin said. "They need *naps.*"

"Everyone who hangs out with you seems to need a nap. What do you suppose the common denominator is there?"

"I'm gonna have a new school," he said. "It could suck."

"It's a good school—it probably won't suck. You'll make friends easy."

"Why?"

Cooper shrugged. "One of your dads is the football coach and the other one owns the beach bar. We're cool."

"Yeah, I have two dads," he said. "I don't care, you know, but it's kind of weird…"

"Not nearly as weird as you think. People get

divorced and remarry all the time. There's the original dad and the next dad. Happens all the time. At least both your dads are very cool." Then he grinned stupidly, very uncomfortable with this ten-year-old's dilemma. "Same thing with moms. I think Sarah is now your stepmom. And a lot of people have seen your dad around town with Devon, who I think he likes."

That got Austin's attention. "Does she like football?"

"Yeah. She does. I think she knows more about football than I do."

"I know more about football than you do," he said, grinning his crooked-toothed grin. And Cooper thought, *We're going to have to set him up with braces soon. Do we split the cost on that?*

"Watch it, now. I know a lot about football. The town's gonna look so different, you'll think I took a wrong turn. The hillside on the beach is a wreck, there are two new roads getting finished, in another week or two, they're going to start the foundation for the new house. They'd like to get as much done as possible before they get weathered out. And, of course, football officially starts. Your dad says he's got a good team…and everyone in town has an opinion or some advice for him." He cleared his throat. "I'm looking forward to watching Landon play."

"Who'm I gonna sit with?" Austin asked.

Cooper had a flashback. He'd been the new kid a lot growing up and there was a pang of memory about being at the end of a lunch table...alone. Walking to classes...alone. Wondering who would be his friend and half the time making a bad choice.

"Well, you're not obligated, but I always sit with the McCains—Gina, Mac, Aunt Lou. Sometimes other friends and their kids join us. Once school gets started you'll probably find your own gang of kids you want to sit with, but Gina and Mac always go early to get a good spot and it's not torture, sitting with us. We bring a cooler and snacks. And you seem to be a bottomless pit. So until you get acquainted, you can count on sitting with us."

"I like to meet up with my dad after...sometimes the team goes out."

"I can make sure you meet up with your dad..." And with a pathetic swirl in his chest he thought, *Maybe I'll even get invited along.* Then he realized, he was merely mirroring Austin's feelings. Empathizing. Poor kid—he must feel very vulnerable. "Most of the kids you've seen around the beach will be in your school."

"I didn't get to know 'em or anything."

At least for Austin, it was doubtful he'd face this issue again. He'd probably graduate from Thunder Point high school. Cooper sought a happier subject. "Landon's been at practice every morning, but afternoons he spends at the beach. I bet he can be talked into taking you out on the bay. You're about ready to try out your own board, aren't you?"

That got a grin. "I already have. When no one's looking. No one except Landon."

"You *think* no one's looking," Cooper said. "Was your visit with your grandma and grandpa great?"

He shrugged. "Pretty good. Being at their house… It made me miss my mom…."

"I guess it would," Cooper said. "We'll get your grandparents out to Oregon for a visit, get Grandpa out on the dock, fishing. Get Grandma on the back of that Jet Ski."

Austin laughed at what must have been an amusing mental picture.

"Think you can show 'em how to get up on a board?"

"Bet I could," he said. "I'm gonna need something, Cooper. Pretty soon I'm gonna need a wet suit, like Landon has."

"Put it on your wish list. We got birthdays and Christmas and grades…"

"Grades?" Austin asked.

Cooper shrugged. "Sometimes when you get impressive grades, little rewards show up here and there."

"Really? That doesn't usually happen."

"What happens? When you get something like straight A's?" Cooper asked.

"You get to live," Austin said.

Funny, that's what had happened at his house, too. But it was different when your mother was dead and you had to go to a new school. "There you go," Cooper said. "One more reason it's cool to have a spare dad."

Devon bought some princess decals and paint and Mercy helped her decorate the second bedroom in the duplex.

Mercy needed her princess chamber—her own bedroom. Helping to decorate the walls interested her in having her own space, which gave Devon *her* own space. Devon's routine had changed, especially now that Austin had returned from Texas. The perimeters of her life had grown and now included important time with Spencer. They saw each other for at least a little while every day, but at night when their kids were settled, they talked on the phone. Devon was pleased to know Mercy had made a positive transition to sleeping in her own bedroom. They now had separate beds and separate bedrooms and Devon could not be happier about it.

Devon and Spencer came out as a couple in Thunder Point. At first she was reluctant to go public, but she soon realized no one was surprised.

They now held hands in public. Spencer would drop an arm over her shoulders and give her a brief squeeze. There was the occasional chaste and socially acceptable kiss.

As they shared more and more of their lives together one evening Spencer reported that Austin had seemed a little unsettled after his trip to Texas and that he had asked Spencer if he "missed mom." Spencer had answered that he would always miss her and always wish she hadn't gotten sick, but that it was all right to make new friends, that it took nothing from Bridget's memory to have more people in their lives.

He later confided that Austin had told him they looked at a lot of pictures while he was in San Antonio, old pictures from when Austin was a lot younger. There were many pictures of his mom, back when Bridget was vital and healthy and rosy-cheeked. Austin told his grandparents that he didn't even remember his mom like that. And that had made Grandma cry and Grandpa got all moody and coughed a lot.

"I had to have a talk with them," Spencer told Devon. "It was not what I wanted to do, but I had to. I understand their grief. I can't imagine losing a child, no matter how old that child is. But we have to let Austin move on. A ten-year-old has a hard enough life without being filled with sadness all the time."

"Oh, Spencer, how did they take it?" Devon asked.

"Very emotionally. They're sorry I was unhappy with them. They only wanted to be sure Austin remembered his mother. But I explained that we have all those pictures and they're available to Austin if he asks for them. He knows where they are. They'll belong to him someday and hopefully he will show them to his own children. But I can't send him to Texas for a fun visit only to have it fill him with dread because it won't be fun, it will be sad. Of course they promised not to do that again. But Cooper has a solution—we need to send the Cunninghams plane tickets and get them out here."

"Will it upset them to meet me?"

"Because we're together? A couple? In love?" he asked her, smiling. "I hope not, but their feelings won't change anything. We all need to move forward."

That was all Devon wanted, to move forward and with each day she put Jacob and the commune farther and farther behind her. She wanted a new life, this life. She loved the doctor's office, loved Gabriella, the town, the beach, and most of all, Spencer. She had visions of one day being a real part of this Thunder Point family, being a family with Spencer and Austin.

School started and Austin was the new kid and friendless for about two hours after which Spencer's house and the beach hosted new friends on bikes. The Tuesday after Labor Day school resumed in earnest. There would be no more holidays until Thanksgiving, but there would be football games. Two a week during most weeks. Devon had not been this excited about how she'd spend her time since she'd been in high school herself.

But before she could attend her first football game the first week in September, a dark-colored sedan pulled up in front of the clinic one morning. Two men wearing sports coats over knit shirts emerged and came inside.

"Devon McAllister?" one of them asked.

She felt her face lose color. She nodded fearfully. She was alone in the clinic.

The man who had asked her name pulled a thin wallet from his breast pocket. "Douglas Freeman, FBI. You're going to have to come with us."

Fourteen

"**W**hy?" Devon asked weakly.

"We'd like to ask you some questions. There must be someone here who can cover for you."

"Not today, I'm here alone, with the doctor's cell number for emergencies."

"Why don't you go ahead and give him a call, Miss McAllister. Let him know that there's been an emergency in your schedule and you're going to be away from the office."

"What is this about?"

"I think you know. We'd like to ask you about your last residence."

"Will I be long?" she wanted to know, and helpless, she began to tremble. "Will I be back?"

"Possibly. Possibly not," Douglas Freeman said.

Having seen the car parked in the street, Mac walked into the clinic, hoisting his gun belt as he entered. "Gentlemen," he said. "Can I help?"

There was a lot of badge flashing, but Devon went to him instantly. "They're taking me somewhere. They won't say if I'll be back. Mac, what about Mercy? What does this mean?"

"You can bring your daughter, Miss McAllister. She'll be taken care of."

"I don't want her to be taken care of by strangers in a strange place!" She turned to Mac and whispered, "Are they putting me in jail?"

Mac took a deep, irritated breath. "Come on, you guys. Lighten up. If you just want to ask her questions, tell her where you're taking her and when you'll bring her back." Then he looked at Devon and said, "They're probably just taking you to an FBI Field Office or maybe a police department. You don't have to go with them unless they arrest you, but if you want to cooperate with them, you should at least listen to their questions." He gave the agents a brief glare. "They're just trying to intimidate you."

One of the agents glared back. "We don't need your assistance, Deputy."

"This woman is my friend and neighbor!" he snapped. "She came to me with information that I passed on to the sheriff, who I presume involved you, so stop acting like the goddamn Men in Black. Devon is kind and cooperative and responsible. Tell her how long you'll need her today.

And you're welcome to use my office if that will help."

"We have a location. And Miss McAllister will be brought back if she wants to come back."

"Why wouldn't I want to come back? My daughter is here!"

"All right, look—there's no reason for all this anxiety. Tell me where to take her," Mac said to the agents.

"This is our investigation, Deputy."

"Understood. And I'm the law enforcement officer who brought you Devon's information. If you want more information, she should be comfortable and feel safe in helping you. Where are we going?"

They exchanged looks. "Coquille sheriff's department," Douglas Freeman said.

"Well, that's easy. I could have saved you some time. Excuse me." He plucked his phone out of his pocket and called one of the deputies who worked for him. "Steve? I have business out of town. Can you cover the town? Thanks, I owe you one." Then he called the dispatcher and signed out for Coquille, leaving Deputy Pritkus in charge.

Devon used her cell phone to call Scott. "Dr. Grant, I'm going to have to leave the office. Mac is taking me somewhere to be questioned about you-know-what. Can you make sure Mercy is with you or Gabriella? I don't know how long I'll be, but I'll keep in touch. I'm planning to be back

here as soon as possible. What should I do with
the clinic?" And then she said "okay" a few times,
a thank-you and disconnected.

"That wasn't quite as cryptic as I would have
liked," one of the agents said.

"I'm getting that," Devon replied. "I'm also getting that you get jollies out of frightening people,
for which you should be docked pay." She texted
something quickly.

"And what's that about?" he asked.

She finished, hit Send and turned her phone
around. She had sent a text to Spencer. Going with
the police to answer questions about the commune. Back later.

"Are you done notifying the public now?"

"I'm going to turn off the coffeepot and some
of the lights and lock the door. I'm going to ride
with Mac. I'm happy to help, but you guys just
give me the creeps. I guess you never heard that
story about honey versus vinegar." And with that
she walked to the back of the clinic to close it up.

"FBI is taking priority on this case," Mac explained as he and Devon made the drive to Coquille. "And, just so you know, they can be very
proprietary. It's their case."

"That's been made perfectly clear," Devon replied. "They better be a lot nicer to me or this
isn't going to go as well as they think. I don't trust

mean people, even if they have badges. After four years with Jacob, I could say *especially* if they have badges. He spent four years trying to convince us that anyone associated with the police or any government agency only existed to hurt honest, hardworking people. I knew that wasn't true, but these guys kind of make me wonder..."

Devon continued, "I knew Jacob was a fraud... but he seemed a harmless fraud with plenty of good food on the table and a nice place for me to live in."

"How did you know?"

"Aunt Mary, the woman who raised me, was devout. We went to church and bible study a lot. I'm not as religious as Mary was, but I know my scriptures. And Jacob didn't."

"Maybe his interpretation was intended just to meet his own needs," Mac said. "Using religion and the bible to his advantage?"

"That is definitely true, but he was so far off the map, anyone who knows their bible would know he was just making stuff up. As time passed, I began to see he wasn't so harmless. The women in that house—some of them became dependent on him and believed every word he uttered."

"But you didn't?"

"No, but I still didn't have anywhere to go or any money or any driver's license or anything. A couple of people just walked off while we were at the Farmers' Market, but they didn't leave children behind. I could've done that, but I would never leave my baby." She shrugged. "I was stupid. I got myself into it."

"You were hungry," Mac said. "And scared."

"The nights were cold back in Seattle," she said softly.

She glanced at Mac out of the corner of her eye and saw his jaw pulse. It was quiet in the car for a while. Then Mac said, "Devon, that's not going to happen again. You're a part of the town. You have friends. You've been a friend. Tell the FBI what they want to know. That bastard has preyed on frightened young girls long enough."

Devon was taken to a small interview room with a table and a few chairs...and a recording device. Her two agents, McGrump and McGlower, were there, of course. But she was relieved to be joined by a pleasant young woman, also a special agent, who asked most of the questions. Emma Haynes was her name.

The process was grueling. She had to go through every detail of how she was first introduced to Jacob and The Fellowship. Then she was asked about everything she knew of the background and personalities of every woman in the family. She had to describe the men, who had changed over four years—only one had been with Jacob the entire time Devon had been there and his name was Brody, big strong Brody, and he was mostly sullen and private and quiet.

Then she had to try to describe Jacob's evolution from the man she'd originally met into an angrier, more paranoid man; a man who believed he had to protect his domain from outsiders and the invasion of government and their foolish laws and punitive taxation. There were many questions about the treatment of the women and children, even more questions about the growing of marijuana.

The interview went on for hours and Devon did her best to recall as much information as she could about every detail of life at the commune, including the little she knew about the actual grow-op.

"Can you remember how many times you were in Jacob's house?"

"Four times. Within two months of my arrival." Then followed a painful recounting of how she had been foolish enough to believe that Jacob loved her. She had listened to his grand plans and had believed every word.

The agents then turned the questioning to matters concerning the role of the women at the compound. Again, Devon was open and honest with the agents.

"Some of the women were more agreeable than others," she told the agents. "Jacob never forced anyone to sleep with him, but he did belittle women who weren't inclined, painted them as not very giving by nature. The only woman brave enough to argue with him or disagree with him was Reese—the oldest in our house. The only women to clean his house were Charlotte and Priscilla, and only when he was in his residence. When Mariah joined us and Jacob began to seduce her, Reese fought with him. But he overpowered her and it wasn't long before Mariah was pregnant. Getting a woman pregnant thrilled him."

"You must have hated him," Emma said.

Devon laughed. "For a little while. Until he started to complain about how impossible his life sometimes seemed, managing a home full of women and children who were expected to be gentle and get along. We didn't always get along. But we all had one thing in common—no other resources. Nowhere to go. More than hating him, I felt like such a failure, such a fool. I felt like I had nothing and no one except the women I lived with. I'd still be there if I hadn't wanted a different kind of life for Mercy."

"Tell us more about the barns where the marijuana was grown. Was it an acre? Quarter acre? Concealed? Did you have any contact with the plants or the transport or sale of the plants?"

She'd seen inside the buildings through open doors; she knew what it was but none of her duties had anything to do with it. That was mostly up to the men. The women tended the vegetable gardens, livestock, chickens, household chores and children.

She had to list the names of people she could remember leaving the family—there were quite a few over four years. But no women who had children while they were there were allowed to leave with their child. So they stayed.

Question after question, and the only one who cajoled pleasantly was the woman, Emma Haynes. She seemed to be just slightly older than Devon, maybe early thirties.

"We're going to take a break," Ms. Haynes said. "I'm going to get us some lunch. Anything in particular you'd like, Devon?"

"Anything would be fine."

"Is there anything you don't like? Something I should avoid? I'm thinking about a half a tuna sandwich, small salad and cola."

"Sounds perfect. I'm a little worried about Dr. Grant and Mercy."

"Why don't you take a few minutes to check in. You can use your phone—you're certainly not suspected of any crime. If you could say as little as possible about our line of questioning, that would be appreciated. I don't need Jacob to be warned that we're looking at him."

"Don't you think he knows?" Devon asked.

"I think he suspects," she said. "I'll get your

lunch. Make a couple of phone calls and ease your mind."

"How much longer will I be here?"

"We'll have you home for dinner, Devon," she said. "If we need any more information from you, we can get in touch later. One long day of answering questions seems like more than enough to expect from you. And we're grateful for your cooperation."

"Can I have some privacy?" she asked, glancing at McGrump and McGlower.

"Absolutely! Gentlemen?" Emma gestured toward the door.

They seemed to leave the small room reluctantly. Although it made Devon smile to herself, knowing that anything she said within these walls was being listened to. Still, having a couple of "suits" bearing down on her like that was most disconcerting. Plus, she found them beyond rude. If they wanted her continued cooperation, they might try being a little more civilized.

She called Scott, told him where she was and that the police had many questions about the commune, which she was doing her best to answer helpfully. He assured her that Mercy was fine and probably didn't even know her mother was out of town. "And don't worry, Devon—as job security, I'm saving all the paperwork for you."

"You are a givin' man, Doctor. I always said so."

"Just call me if you need me."

Then she texted Spencer, told him all was just fine, that she was answering questions for the P.D. and would be home by dinnertime. He texted back that he would leave school and come for her if she needed him.

She was so lucky. She had Mac, who she thought might still be in the building waiting for her, Scott, who would guard her child and close up his business if she needed him, Rawley, who literally gave her a second chance...and Spencer, who loved her.

During lunch she was alone with Emma Haynes and Devon asked her questions about her work. Emma went from a degree in criminal justice to a master's degree to the FBI and loved going to work every day. "Look at the people I meet, the wrongs I can help right. What's not to love?"

"Well, can you settle down and have a family?" Devon asked.

"Sure, though my job might change. Right now I not only travel a lot, I also am regularly reassigned to new field offices. The hard part for someone like me is finding the right man. My whole world seems to be filled with men in law enforcement."

"Well, if they're all sourpusses like the two who picked me up in Thunder Point today, I can see your problem."

She laughed. "There you go." She took a drink

from her soda and said, "The afternoon is going to
be taxing, Devon. We need your help in creating
a diagram of the compound, the buildings, the location of weapons, of marijuana, fences, et cetera.
We'll help you with the drawing—I have an artist
coming to join us. This is important."

"I understand. I'm afraid, Emma."

"For your safety?"

"No. For theirs. There are friends in there. Children. Small children. I would never forgive myself if I told you things that would lead to them
being hurt."

Emma gave her hand a squeeze. "This is why
we're so exact with the questions we've asked. We
don't want any injuries. We will not take any action that will hurt innocent people."

She took a deep breath. "Okay. Let's do it."

Devon was exhausted by the time the afternoon
came to a close. She had done her best to help develop a rendering of the compound she'd lived on
and the interior of each of the buildings. She told
them as much as she knew and remembered. In
the process, she had her first experience with Red
Bull to keep her going.

"Too bad for you I'm not some sort of suspect,"
she said. "I'd admit to anything right about now…"

"There's one more thing before we take you
home," Emma said. "Sit tight, I'll be right back."

Devon wondered how much more they could possibly want to know. Just then the door to the little interview room opened and Devon looked up to see Reese standing there. She jumped to her feet so suddenly her chair tipped over; she gasped and tears sprang to her eyes. She rushed into Reese's comforting arms, holding her fiercely.

"There now, little darling. I guess this means you're glad to see me?"

Devon backed away slightly and looked into Reese's smiling eyes. She touched her hair, now shortened like her own. But while Devon had cut hers short, leaving her with that slightly wild mop, Reese's blond hair curled at her chin. Reese was beautiful beyond words; Devon had always loved her, since the first day they'd met.

"I didn't know they had you, too."

"They don't have me, darling. I came to the police and asked for help. I'm living in a safe place in another city. I'm looking for work. I'll stay there until this whole thing is resolved."

"How can it be resolved?" Devon asked.

"It's important to get the women and children safely out of there before there's any kind of conflict between Jacob and the law. I have no idea how that can be done," Reese said. "The police don't confide in me."

"Pilly will never leave him," Devon said.

"I worry about that, too," Reese said.

"Where is Mariah?"

Reese smiled and her face lit up. "She's with a family. She delivered a healthy son just last week. She's safe and has a good place with people who can help her rebuild her life. I left Mark with her for the day."

"I'm working for a doctor in a little town not far from here and I saw one of them come in the black SUV," Devon said. "They were asking if anyone had seen you and Mariah." She shook her head. "They never asked about me. I think maybe they don't care that I'm gone."

"Oh, Jacob cares. He was in a rage. They left and went looking for you. I have no idea what went on there when I left with Mariah and Mark. I hate to think about it. I managed his family for him and Mariah was not only the youngest woman there, but she was pregnant. I can imagine Jacob just about lost his mind." She shook her head sadly. "Devon, there's so much more history to that place than you know—we'll talk about it someday."

"Will we see each other again?"

"Of course," she said, giving her hair a pat. "I don't know when, but we will see each other again. Tell me about your life now. Are you safe? Happy?"

Devon nodded. "It's been amazing. An old guy

picked us up and took us in. He kept us in his home for a little while."

Reese frowned. "Does he dominate you?"

Devon smiled. "He's nothing like Jacob, nothing at all. He said he'd had hard luck most of his life and he was just giving back. He pointed me in the direction of a possible job and I got it. I found a small place to rent, I share a babysitter with my boss, filled the little house with secondhand furnishings. I put in a lot of hours for the doctor, but I do a good job for him and he lets me know he sees it. It's a small place—people get to know each other easily."

"You should probably get some counseling...."

Devon laughed. "I'll see if I can work that into the budget someday."

"I want you to think about it. Jacob worked so hard at making all the women think they had nothing, no options, no ability to do anything but exist inside his fence. That's a lot to overcome."

"Are you in counseling?"

She nodded. "It's helping. I'll tell you more about that when we see each other next. We really can't be in touch right now, but I hope it won't be too long before..."

"Why?" Devon asked. "Can't we talk on the phone sometimes? Maybe meet here? Jacob would never come near a police building!"

"If we want the FBI to finish what they started, we need to just live quiet lives until it's over. Then we can see each other again. I hope it's not too long."

Just as she suspected, Mac was waiting for her to take her home. He had gone back to Thunder Point, but returned for her. When they were in the department car he asked, "Was it okay?"

"It was the most exhausting day of my life," Devon said. "They wanted details about each person that I'm not even sure I remember accurately. Basically we were slaves and we had a mostly benevolent master."

"Mostly?" Mac asked.

"Mostly. Let's face it—he's a drug dealer."

Mac tapped his wedding ring on the steering wheel. "I think, a major drug dealer."

She pulled out her phone. How had she lived so long without this ability to communicate so easily, so rapidly? "And I miss some of the women and kids so much," she said to Mac.

She texted her boss and Spencer to say she was headed home. By the time Mac pulled up in front of his office, the clinic was dark. "Listen, Devon," he said, "what you did today was brave. And it was right. You could've given us all a different name, hidden right in plain sight, started a new life here and disappeared from your past. Coming to me, cooperating with the feds, that was brave."

She gave him a weak smile. "I hope it was also smart," she said.

Fifteen

Cooper's little apartment over the bar had one bedroom. When it was his turn to keep Austin overnight so Spencer could have a life, Austin slept in the same room with Cooper and Sarah—on the pull-out sofa. It was not optimal. Not only was there no nooky on such nights, but Austin snored like a freight train. He also flopped around on that bed like a fish on the dock.

Cooper wanted to impose on Landon to keep the little guy in the toy hauler, but when he even led up to such a request Landon cleared his throat, lifted a brow and smirked. Then Austin asked Cooper, "How old do I have to be before I get a man cave?"

"Very old," Cooper said.

The upside was, Austin did make friends right away because Austin was connected with one of the most important people in the town—his own dad. Kids from school only had to see him at the first high school football game to get the message—Austin's dad was the coach and Austin sat with Mac, Cooper and the others. But instead of Austin being lured away to hang with kids his own age, all the kids who liked the new kid wanted to sit with the in crowd.

"But I thought you enjoyed having Austin around," Sarah said.

"I do. I'm nuts about Austin. But I would like to have him sleeping down the hall. So I can be myself."

"You're a sex maniac," she said.

"I thought that was your favorite part," he said, grinning lasciviously.

"You're hardly deprived," she pointed out to him.

"True," he could admit. In fact, since Sarah had bid farewell to the Coast Guard, her days and nights were her own. The September air was still mild and autumn on the beach brought a whole new energy—the after-game campfires had begun and the night was alive with the sounds of teenagers. Cooper dimmed the lights in the bar by ten o'clock to keep the action down on the beach rather than running up and down the stairs for drinks. But he liked to sit with his wife on the deck and watch the partying. Thunder Point had scored a big win over one of their rival schools tonight.

"I think I was deprived by not growing up on a beach like this one," he said. "They have so much fun down there." He grabbed her hand. "We're a little crowded here, but I like the nights. Especially football nights."

"I have almost as much trouble coming down after watching Landon play as he does," she said.

"Let me get you a glass of wine," he said, moving as if to get up.

"No, thanks."

"Anything? I'm going to get a beer."

She shrugged. "Water would be good."

"You got it," he said, going inside. He grabbed a beer and bottled water and was back on the deck before he began to wonder. He handed her the water. "No wine?"

She shook her head. Then she smiled.

"Are you already pregnant?"

"I think so," she said. "I haven't taken a test yet, but I think so. Boy, I give you a job to do and you don't waste any time." And she laughed.

He sat down beside her and just looked at her beautiful face. He was stunned. He reached a gentle hand to tenderly cup her cheek and jaw and she covered his hand with hers. "When will we know for sure?"

"I could try a pregnancy test now, but in several more days or even a week, the results will be more accurate. I'm barely late."

"Are you okay with this?"

"It was my idea, remember."

"God," he said reverently. "I've never been a father this way."

"Maybe I should ask if you're okay with it," she said.

"I must be," he said. "I want to carry you upstairs and make love to you. Now. I want to, I really do."

She laughed at him. "Cooper, does everything translate into sex for you?"

"Everything to do with you," he admitted. "I can't wait to tell my dad. And Mac—Mac is good for cigars. Landon's going to get a kick out of this. And Rawley, who thinks I don't know what I'm doing—"

"Let's wait a little while," she said. "Early pregnancy can be kind of iffy and I don't want to get everyone all excited and then have to start over."

"What's a little while?" he asked.

She shrugged. "Three months?"

He sat back in his chair. "Sarah, I'll never make it that long."

She regarded him for a long moment. "I guess you won't, will you?"

"Do you feel all right, baby?"

She grinned. "I feel very excited. Very happy. Thank you, Cooper, my love. You're very efficient."

"I am, huh? Come on, let's go to bed. Just on the off chance I haven't knocked you up yet, this would be a backup plan."

Lou McCain had married on something of a whim. Once her nephew, Mac, had taken a wife, the woman he'd been in love with for years, Lou knew she was not quite so essential to his household. She'd spent ten years living with him and helping him raise his children, but now Gina was in residence. And everyone knew, one woman to a household was a rule worth paying attention to. So she gave in to Joe's pleas to say I do. And she did.

Joe lived in a nice bedroom community between Thunder Point and Coquille in a house just right for a couple. It wasn't fancy, but it was perfect with a master bedroom large enough to keep them from tripping over each other. It was a little on the masculine side with leather furniture, dark wood and bold colors like rusty red, dark blue and army-green. He offered her a free hand with decorating, but she liked that it looked perfect for him. Lou took over the second bathroom down the hall—she pointed out that she was too "mature" to be sharing bathroom space. Plus, they were on slightly different schedules—four days a week Joe would go to work at 2:00 p.m. and get home at midnight, sometimes later. And Lou worked five days a week in the Thunder Point middle school from 8:00 a.m.

to 3:00 p.m. Joe was usually sleeping in while she was getting ready for work.

But the best part? He loved to cook. When they had their three evenings a week together, he was in the kitchen. Lou was capable of getting something on the table, but she'd just spent a decade working full-time, chasing kids, feeding her hulking nephew and his family. It had been the same dozen or so dinners for as long as she could remember, and she took every shortcut she could get away with, from spaghetti sauce in the jar to frozen pizzas.

She continued to spend a great deal of time in Thunder Point, helping Mac and Gina with the kids' activities. She wouldn't miss a high school football game for anything. And there were also her girlfriends, who she was enjoying even more lately because they envied her.

She met Carrie and Ray Anne for a glass of wine before meeting Mac, Gina and the kids at the game. They sat at the bar in Cliffhanger's and Carrie asked her, "What's the best part about marriage so far?"

"That none of the things I worried about are happening."

"Like?" she pushed.

"I thought there might be big adjustments. I'm edging toward sixty-two and have never been married—I've never even lived with a man. I might've shared a house with Mac and the kids, but I had my own space and no one dared invade it. I thought Joe might get under my skin, being around a lot. I thought I might annoy him...."

"I can see that," Ray Anne said a little spitefully.

Lou flashed her a small smile. They'd spent many years as rivals and now were dueling friends. "He adores me," Lou said.

Ray Anne leaned an elbow on the bar and put her head in her hand. "Why can't I have some stud sneak into my bed around midnight?"

Lou put her hand over Ray Anne's and frankly, she didn't understand it herself. Ray Anne was perpetually sexy with her boobs, tight skirts, jeans and heels. But she said, "Because you have sinned and you must repent." Then she grinned at Ray Anne. "Now who's going to the game with me?"

"I'll go till halftime," Carrie said. Mornings in the deli came early for Carrie—she rarely stayed out late.

"I can stay for the game," Ray Anne said. "And for your information, I'm not sure I've sinned enough. Are we ready?"

As usual, most of Thunder Point turned out for the game and while the marching band played on the field, the women found their usual spot, reserved by Mac and Gina, Cooper and Sarah, Austin and Devon and Mercy. The stands were teeming with fans and their girls, Eve and Ashley, were down on the field with the other cheerleaders, warming up the crowd.

"I think it's time for us to have a sky box," Lou said.

"Put it on your Christmas wish list," Mac advised.

But what Lou was thinking was that she had everything she'd ever imagined wanting. She pulled Dee Dee, Mac's youngest, close, hugging her and asked her if she was warm enough. Then she joined her group in cheering as the team ran onto the field and the game began. No one enjoyed high school football more than this town. Two hours later, celebrating a nice big win, Lou was saying good-night to friends and family and driving toward Coquille to a little house on Bayberry Road.

She walked into the kitchen through the garage. He'd left the light under the microwave on for her and she would leave it on for him. She took a deep breath and felt that amazing sense of being where she was supposed to be. After all the years either on her own or with Mac's family, she was really home.

Lou had certain rituals. She put on her pajamas, texted Joe to say she was home, sat on the bed with the TV on and a book in her lap. When she was at Mac's she hid in her room in the evenings to get a break from kids. After teaching all day and dealing with nieces and a nephew after school till almost bedtime, she needed a little time to herself. Now she shared the space with Joe.

Her light was off by eleven-thirty and she dozed, but at twelve-thirty she heard him come into the bedroom. He was quiet while getting out of his trooper uniform, but she stole a peek. Lou really thought he was too handsome for her, but he was persistent and convincing and here they were. He got down to nothing—forget pajamas or boxers. He liked sleeping nude.

He curled around her and she wiggled against him. He chuckled deeply.

"So, you are awake," he said. "Good." He gave her shoulder a tug and she was on her back.

"Lotta bad guys tonight?" she asked.

"Two idiots and a few dipshits. Uneventful." Then he kissed her. "Mmm. Perfect." He pushed against her. She could feel his grin against her lips. "Let's get you naked."

"I might need to sleep," she said.

"All right. Then sleep naked."

She touched his shoulder. "I'm kind of surprised by this," she said. "I was a little afraid we wouldn't work. I've never shared space with a lover. Never. I wondered if I'd get claustrophobic or maybe drive you crazy."

"You do drive me crazy. Who won tonight?"

"We did," she said, sliding off her pajamas. "We have tomorrow off."

"Do you have Aunt Lou duties?"

She shook her head. "Of course, it's always possible someone could call, looking for help with something."

"As long as they don't call before six," he said. He never complained about her familial obligations. With two grown children, he had his own to think about.

"As far as I can recall, you're the only person in my life who's been able to tolerate me before six."

He gave a shrug. "Because I love all of you. And I'm a damn lucky man."

Eric Gentry had a date with his new daughter, seventeen-year-old Ashley James. He hadn't known she existed until last spring when her mother sought him out in search of medical history from his side of the family. Oh, he'd been more than aware that Gina told him she was pregnant almost eighteen years ago, but his life had taken a bad turn at about that same time and being the young fool he had been, he'd never confirmed that she really had been pregnant or that she'd chosen to have the baby. He rationalized that if he'd been Gina, pregnant with such a loser's baby, he probably wouldn't have taken the chance.

But...Gina had brought their child to life and

raised her, and had done an amazing job with just the help of her mother. And he'd missed his daughter's entire childhood, but he could see very clearly that she'd probably turned out so well because he hadn't been involved. Seems it had taken him a lot longer to grow up than it had taken Gina.

He was due to pick up Ashley at noon at her new residence, the McCain household. Gina and Mac had married and combined families and Ashley seemed to be very happy. He'd offered to take her to lunch and a little shopping in Bandon. School had just started and he wanted to contribute a little something. Like school clothes. Gina was okay with that idea, except... "Don't throw a lot of money around, please," she had asked. "We've always lived on a tight budget and it works for us. I'd rather you be generous with your time than your big bucks."

First, he'd never had big bucks, so that wasn't going to be a problem. But he also hadn't had that much time, owning his own business. Then everything in his life started to change, and it felt like a chain reaction had begun. His relationship had fallen apart and he was on his own again. His auto body and restoration shop had grown successful and someone wanted to buy it—for an offer impossible to ignore. There was a small service station with potential that had been for sale for months in Thunder Point and he had come to look it over. For the second time.

But that family he had run from so many years ago lived here. He liked the idea that he could see more of Ashley; maybe watch her cheer a game or two, maybe be in the crowd when she graduated. But he wasn't sure Ashley, or Gina for that matter, had any interest in seeing more of *him*. Even though everyone had settled into their lives, having the biological father show up could really bring attention to the fact that Ashley had been born out of wedlock. And her father was an ex-con.

Eric went to the service station and had his Jeep SUV gassed up. He pulled over to the side of the station and went into the garage to have a chat with Norm Sileski who had owned and worked this station for about forty-five years. He had a couple of grown sons who didn't want it. It was far beneath Eric's standards—it was run-down, dirty, greasy, broken down and weathered. But it was the only game in town, had room on the lot to expand and Norm did most of the car repair in town. Eric suspected people got their gas other places when they could; he was a little high-priced. He'd looked over the P&L reports—Norm made a decent living.

And no one knew better than Eric how to turn a run-down dump like this into a first-rate business. He'd already done it once in Eugene. He'd expected to be there for the rest of his life. But then some rich guy who wanted a chain of body shops came along and...

"You need new pumps there, Norm," Eric said.

"Need new everything, Mr. Gentry," he said. "But I'm not putting another dime in this place to pretty it up. I'm headed for seventy years old. Fast." And then he grinned. "You buy this place, I'll turn a wrench for you part-time as long as I'm upright."

"You don't want to enjoy your retirement?"

"Yes, sir, I do. If Mrs. Sileski has her way, I'll be going on cruises and traveling to countries where I don't speak the language. Just gimme a wrench."

Eric laughed at him. He asked a few more questions—who were his employees, mechanics, cleanup crew; had he ever kept a tow truck at the station; who was his distributor? They chatted about the weather for a little while. Eric asked Norm if he'd lived in Thunder Point his whole life and how he liked it. "Like it fine if you can take having everybody and their brother in your business all the time."

Hmm, Eric thought. That might be a downside, especially for someone like Ashley. And her mother.

He was a little early when he got to the McCain home to pick up Ashley. The place was alive with activity. Mac was rushing off with his son, Ryan. Eve McCain and her boyfriend were taking the youngest, Dee Dee, to her dance class, Gina was still at work. Everyone said hello, shook his hand and carried on. And Ashley was ready. "This is a typical Saturday," she said. "I usually have cheer practice, but we won last night's game and that bought us a day off."

"Hungry?" he asked.

"I'm starving, but I never shop after food. Can you make it another couple of hours? Two at the latest?"

He thought he might faint by then. Of course if he had his hands in an engine or was in the paint bay or hammering out a classic car bumper, he could forget to eat. But, trying to play the good father, he was going *shopping*.

"No problem," he said. "Just lead the way."

Eric hated shopping. He usually went about twice a year—once for a bunch of clothes, underwear and socks and the second time to buy Christmas presents. But there was something about shopping with the daughter he hadn't known he had that was a whole new experience, and it was energizing. She tried on everything; she was very particular. And as if she was spending her own money, she was painfully frugal. She turned away many items even after he said he could well afford them. Her choices were mostly sale items. In the end she had a very full shopping bag for a grand total of $247.68. Most girls her age would have taken advantage of an opportunity like this. After all, he owed her.

"Shoes?" he asked.

"I'm good."

"Lunch?"

She laughed. "Starving. There's a Red Robin around the corner."

They got a booth and wasted no time in ordering. And while they waited for food, Eric asked about school and about Frank, two things he asked about whenever he talked to her. When he'd first learned of Ashley and first met her she'd been going through a painful teenage broken heart— her serious boyfriend had gone off to college and found himself a new girl, throwing Ashley into a very vulnerable depression. That was, in fact, the reason Gina came looking for him. She'd been so worried about Ashley she thought it made sense to find out if things like depression ran in Eric's family.

And then in one of those fateful episodes no one can plan or even guess, one of the people to help her pull out of it was Crawford Downy's younger brother, Frank.

"Frank is good," she said. "He already has scholarship offers. He calls himself a nerd, but he's not really. Well, yes, I guess he is. But he's so interesting and so cute I forget about that. Besides, he's the nicest person in the world. And to think I wouldn't even really know him if Downy hadn't dumped me."

"What's that like? Dating an ex's brother?" he asked.

"Sometimes awkward. Thank God Downy went back to State. We see him around town when he's home for a visit and Frank swears Downy doesn't give him a hard time. I bet Frank would swear that even if it weren't true—he's so protective. I think Frank is going to go to MIT. I've lived in Thunder Point my whole life and not too many people I know scored that kind of education just based on brains. We've turned out some decent athletes, but nothing like what Frank's doing."

"And what about you?" Eric asked.

"Same," she said with a shrug. "I'm going to go to community college in Coquille for at least a year, maybe two. I'm just not quite ready to move away. Almost, though. I haven't decided where I want to go to school after that, but I can't wait to visit Frank on the East Coast. Something there might get my interest."

"Do you think you'll come back to Thunder Point after college?" he asked.

"I have no idea," she said with a laugh. "I have no idea what to study! I took one of those tests to show you what you're most interested in and have the best aptitude for and guess what it came up with? Coroner!"

He whistled. "Talk about job security. Always a need for coroners, unfortunately."

"Yeah, I don't think so. Although I do like to watch TV shows like *Rizzoli & Isles.*"

"Maybe you're just interested in science. Maybe you'll be a doctor."

"I think I could," she said. "But every time I think about twelve years or so of college and residency, I think—gimme a break."

He just laughed and right then their burgers arrived. "I didn't even finish high school."

"Yes, you did," she said. And then she did what so many females did—she rearranged her sandwich, moving the lettuce, tomatoes around, making it all neat and then cutting it in half. "And you have a little college."

He'd gotten his GED in prison. He'd taken a few more courses, mainly to pass the time, never having any idea he'd one day own his own business. "And Frank?"

She took a dainty bite of her burger, wiped her mouth, swallowed. "I think Frank might run the world someday. He'll be like the head of NASA or something. If he had the slightest interest in politics, he'd be the president. You just have no idea...."

He smiled at her. He'd met Frank. Nice kid, very cordial and respectful. But Eric hadn't been as dazzled by his big brain as Ashley apparently was. Then again, Frank hadn't really been showcasing his brain. He'd been paddleboarding. And Eric had been studying his physique and the way he looked at Ashley. Frank really cared about his daughter. It was a very odd feeling.

"And what's going on in the car business?" she asked.

"Day to day," he said. "There has been an interesting development. Some guy wants to buy my business. He's been in contact several times over the past year. I've been ignoring him."

"No kidding? That's very cool."

"Yeah, I guess it is. My lack of interest just makes him want it more. I'm kind of proud of that—that some guy with money is impressed with the shop. With the help of some friends, I built it from nothing."

"But you'd never sell it."

He gave a shrug. "Part of me thinks that would be crazy, starting over now after all the work I put in. Another part says, take the money and run. I could do it again. In fact I've been looking around to see if there's anything out there."

She got a panicked look on her face. She swallowed. "Would you be farther away?"

"Well, funny you should ask," he said. He hadn't meant to bring the subject up like this, but he told himself he'd learn a lot just from Ashley's expression. "There's a possibility in Thunder Point."

Her eyes sparkled, it was unmistakable. "Seriously?"

"Nothing I can confirm—I haven't even decided it makes sense to sell the shop. But Thunder Point...the question is, is that little town big enough for both of us?"

"What do you mean?"

"Ashley, it's one thing for me to spend a couple of hours there every so often. It would be another matter to have me there all the time. It would probably raise questions about our history. About your birth. It could be uncomfortable for you."

She smiled at him. "Eric, everyone in town knows my mom wasn't married when I was born. I've introduced you as my biological father even though I think you'll always be Eric to me."

"You could be teased or criticized for having a father who served time in prison...."

"Well, I haven't mentioned that to hardly anyone, just my best friend, who is now my stepsister. And I'm sure my mom told Mac. I don't know if anyone else knows, but I don't really care what anyone says about that. It's not on me, Eric. But I can understand if it bothers you."

"Look, I gave up trying to conceal my past a long time ago. I sure don't brag about it, but if it comes out I don't deny it. But your mom, Ashley. She's in a new marriage.... Having an old boyfriend around..."

"I don't think it matters anymore. But maybe you should talk to her. If you moved here, would your girlfriend come? Is it Cara? Is that her name?"

"Hmm. That ended. A couple of months back."

"Ended? Oh, no, what happened?"

He actually smiled. "She's a web designer, remember? She threw me over for a computer geek."

"No way!"

"Way. She was pretty married to her computer and I was..." He rubbed a hand along the back of his neck a little self-consciously. "I've been putting in long hours. It's probably my fault. I could have been more attentive."

Ashley sat back. "You don't seem all that broken up about it."

"My pride was hurt. But I think our relationship ran its course and we both knew it. The truth is—I'm glad I didn't hurt anyone. I've hurt enough people in my life. Which brings us back to... Ashley, I don't want to put your mother on the spot. I don't want her to feel backed into a corner. She's a nice person—if I come right out and ask her if living in or near Thunder Point would be a problem for her, she'll probably tell me to do whatever I want to do. Even if it's not her first choice."

"You think you could stand living in a little town like Thunder Point?"

He gave a shrug. "It's a good little town, I remember that much. And I think I'd like running into you more often. But I'm not making any assumptions—we're friends. You can come to me with anything, but I'm not going to try to step in as a father figure. I'm not ever going to assume any authority over you. I promise."

"You're very funny, Eric. It's almost too late for anyone to have much authority over me. I'm real close to being out the door."

"Yes, I guess you are. So—want to toss this possibility out to your mom and Mac? Give them time to think about how they want to respond?"

"I could do that. But I like the idea, if it works out for you."

He felt a little funny. Kind of warm and fuzzy inside. He had never expected his life to take a turn like this, to have such a positive relationship with Ashley. He knew he didn't deserve it.

Sixteen

Laine had screwed up. The compound was shut up tighter than a tick these days. If the men were leaving and returning, she was unaware of it, and part of her job was to be aware of everything. Last night, in the middle of the night, Lorna had made her escape through the woods with two children— her two children. Jacob's two children.

Laine hadn't had contact with anyone on the outside for a couple of weeks. While they sold produce at their stand by the side of the road a farm woman stopped by in an old pickup truck. She was tired-looking, hump-backed, dressed in muddy jeans and worn boots. She was missing a couple of teeth and read from her list with a lisp— six apples, six pears, pint of blackberries, squash. In the lower left of this ragged slip of paper was written 9-13.

Laine knew there was no hope of getting either

Pilly or Charlotte to leave so she had confronted Lorna and given her the chance. And in the morning there was no one in the kitchen because that was Lorna's domain. Laine thought perhaps she should have gone with her, but there was one reason she just couldn't bring herself to flee—sweet little Liam. She hoped to somehow rescue him. If she could think of a way to take Charlotte's four-year-old as well, she would, but Liam was too little to fend for himself. And for that she paid a large price.

Jacob stormed into the house at six in the morning, his face red, his fists clenched. He looked so frightening she jumped back with a gasp. And she thought, *It's going down.*

"It's you," he said in a low, menacing growl. "It has to be you."

"No," she said. "Lorna's gone. She must have left on her own. Or one of the men, I think. Not me! If I'd known she was going, I would have gone with her."

Out of nowhere, his fist flew into her face, knocking her back about four feet. It was so sudden, so powerful, she was momentarily dazed. Had she guessed this might happen, she could have been better prepared, but everything they knew about Jacob was that while he could get very angry and abusive, he didn't seem to be violent.

He came at her again and she put up her arms in

defense and began to scream, which brought Pilly and Charlotte running. Jacob was delivering his first kick to her midsection when they came into the kitchen, and they ran to him, trying to pull him away, joining in the screaming. And while Laine had not really bonded with these two, the sight of her down on the floor, under assault by Jacob, must have brought them naturally to her side.

Jacob had slapped people around—he'd even been known to grab one of the women and give her a shake, but he was more inclined to rant and shout, bluster and stomp around, maybe throw something. Laine would not be here if he had a known violent streak. He was fully expected to try to fight back against the law, but this assault was shocking.

The man known as Sam came in the back door and stood in shock at what must have looked like a pile of women on the floor and an enraged Jacob. Right behind him came the man known as Joe. Between them they pulled him back and held him, but they said nothing. Jacob was rigid with rage and strained against the hold his men had on him.

Laine was so grateful that it was in character for her to cry. She was reduced to sobs; her mind buzzed from the blow. Pilly and Charlotte tried to help her sit up, but she was almost too dizzy.

"Jacob, what happened? Why are you doing this?" Pilly asked. "What did she do?"

"Lorna is gone. Lorna and the children! Someone is doing this—it has to be her. The only women left are you, Charlotte and Laine, and I *know* you two wouldn't betray me. I *know* it!" He shook off his two men and said, "Take her across the river and tie her. Then check the fence. The *entire* fence!" Then he stormed out of the house.

The two men exchanged looks and then, apparently resigned, went to Laine and lifted her to her feet.

"Please," she whimpered. "Please, no... I didn't do it. I wouldn't do that...."

"Come along now," Sam said. "Like a good girl."

How many Sams and Joes had worked for Jacob? she wondered. She looked beseechingly at Pilly and Charlotte who both looked shocked and scared. "Tell him I wouldn't do that," she begged. "Pilly, don't let him tie me up. He's going to hurt me."

Laine knew better than to struggle against these two big men even if there was a chance she could get away from them. It was safer to stay in character and play her part. But to her dismay this meant that if she had a chance to flee she'd have to take it and just hope that no harm came to the two remaining women and their children. Right then Laine vowed to herself that if she got out of this place, she'd run far and fast and never look back. This wasn't what she'd signed on for. This was supposed to be a simple fact-finding mission and when she had the information she needed, she was simply going to walk away from this compound. Then she found the guns, the pot, the danger to the children...

They tied her to a kitchen chair in Jacob's house, her hands behind her back and her ankles bound to the chair legs. Then she heard the men talking with Jacob, telling him they were going to secure the perimeter and she thought, that sounded like police talk. But these men were not police. She heard one of them tell Jacob not to do any more damage. And then they left.

Every nerve in her body was on high alert and her heart was hammering so hard she trembled, but took comfort in the fact that this would be a normal reaction and would not raise suspicion. She watched the clock on Jacob's oven and it ticked by slowly. She could hear him talking on the phone but she couldn't hear what he was saying. Who could he be communicating with? she wondered. He'd led them all to believe his entire world was inside the fence; that he neither wanted nor needed anything else.

Around ten in the morning she heard a knock at his door, heard him get up and open it and heard Pilly talking to him. Her voice was faint and trembling, but Laine thought she could make out a bit of what she was saying. "Don't do this, Jacob, you're scaring us. Let me take her back to the house and we'll watch her. Please, Jacob, I'll do whatever you need, but don't hold her prisoner."

And then Jacob could be heard, and there was no mistaking his words. "She's not going anywhere until I get to the bottom of this! I think it's her and she's ruining everything!"

There was a bit more pleading then the door closed again, presumably on Pilly's departure. At almost two, the men were back and she distinctly heard three voices in addition to Jacob's. And she could hear their words, which were remarkably calm.

"The breach of our security has gone too far and has involved too many people. Too many have left and they're talking—I'd bet anything."

"It's time to shut it down."

"No! I'm not giving it up!" Jacob shouted.

"We'll never get another shipment out of here and I'm not going to jail! It's time to follow the original plan. Burn it and leave it."

"No! We fight back!"

"Jacob, they're bigger than we are, and too many people have left. We can't rely on their silence. They're going to sell us out—these women. Burn it, and while they're dealing with the mess and the torch, we'll take what we can out the back way. We'll pick up a couple of cars and get out."

"I'm not giving it up until they're here with a warrant. Then we can torch it!"

"I'm telling you, I've seen this before. If you think the town constable is coming with a warrant, you're delusional. They'll come with a small army. And no one's getting away unless we get out before they try to get in. Leave the girls and their babies behind, take the cash on hand and let's move."

Laine cursed under her breath because that was as much of a detailed conversation as she'd ever heard among the men. And she had to pee like a racehorse.

They continued to argue, except that Jacob's men didn't try to get tough with him. They calmly advised him, and they were articulate. Very well-spoken drug dealers. These were businessmen. Jacob was half-loony, a self-aggrandizing fool. But the people around him, the women and the men, appeared to be intelligent and in control.

How had he managed that?

"I'm not for taking more chances. We always said we were exiting this property before it got hot. When a dozen people take off, it's hot."

"We have a little more time," Jacob said.

They're going to run, Laine thought. And her greatest fear was that Jacob could be willing to die for it. She'd been here for months and his anger had been steadily escalating. He didn't like the size of his tribe getting smaller.

Finally the talk stopped and the door to Jacob's house closed. She used her small, pitiful voice. "Jacob?" she called softly. "Jacob?"

He stood in the kitchen doorway. He crossed his arms over his chest. One side of his mouth lifted in a half smile. "Something?"

"I have to… I need to use the bathroom."

"Finally dependent on me, are you? And if I say no?"

"I'm afraid I might… I could have an accident."

"If you piss on my floor, I'll beat you. And you already look like bloody hell."

Oh, he was getting dangerous. "I just want to use a bathroom, Jacob. Please."

"I'll think it over." Then he turned and left her. And she put her mind in a Zen state that allowed her not to lose control. She would not invite another beating.

Devon's next-door neighbor, Mrs. Bledsoe, was very sweet and thoughtful and not only frequently brought a half-dozen cookies over for Mercy, but a couple of times she invited Mercy over to help make them. The only family she had in the area was a twenty-eight-year-old grandson who checked on her regularly even though he had to drive from Coquille to do so. And because Mrs. Bledsoe was more than happy to watch Mercy for a little while, Devon got back into running. Well, it was more like jogging, but she did like to sprint up the hill to her house. And it felt so damn good.

Rawley wasn't big on time off from work, but he loved it when Devon called his cell phone and asked him if he'd like to come to dinner at her little house. The one thing she couldn't seem to break him of was bringing little gifts. Sometimes it was something inexpensive for Mercy or some item for Devon's kitchen. Although he was deadpan if not grumbly when he came to dinner, she could tell he was delighted. And while she was neither a good cook nor extravagant at the grocery, she did try to serve things she thought he'd like. A small roast, red potatoes and green beans like the ones he'd gotten her at the Farmers' Market. Or a meatloaf, mashed potatoes and sliced tomatoes. And, she remembered a dish of Lorna's—sausage, squash, onion, peppers and spinach. Mercy wouldn't eat the sausage dish but Rawley seemed to enjoy it. Or maybe he was just happy to be asked.

"Rawley, you should come to a football game with us sometime," she said.

"Can't. Cooper has to go on account of Landon. And I keep the bar open."

"Does anyone show up out there when there's a football game in town?"

"Sometimes someone comes in off the bay. But not often. I just ain't big on a lot of people."

"It's really fun," she said.

"I bought me a DVR," he said. "I learned how to record shows and I record the sports. If you ever want to see some game..."

"I might join you sometime. But I have a confession to make. I spend some time in front of Spencer's TV because...well, I have a boyfriend."

And Rawley showed her a wide expanse of dentures. "Like no one knows? Chickadee, we all know you have a boyfriend. He nice to you?"

"He's wonderful to me," she said. "I can't believe how much my life works right now."

She felt that Spencer was made for her. She fought the feeling of greediness, because it would feel so good to be able to go places with him other than just Thunder Point, but that was impossible until something changed in the investigation of Jacob's Fellowship. And to her embarrassment, she secretly wished they could become more official, like maybe a couple with some sort of future plans.

She acknowledged that was probably not the best idea in the world. They'd both just come out of difficult situations. Patience was definitely required.

But in addition to her sweet neighbor Mrs. Bledsoe, her good friend Rawley, her wondrous lover, Spencer, Devon now had girlfriends. She often went to the diner for an afternoon break because she would sometimes see Sarah and Gina, sometimes Lou and Ray Anne and Carrie. They laughed together, shared secrets, told each other things they swore secrecy on and, her favorite, exchanged town gossip.

Now when people came in the clinic, they usually said, "Hey, Devon, how's it going?" When she went to the football games, as she made her way down the front of the bleachers to her spot with the McCains and the Coopers, people waved and sometimes yelled, "Hi, Devon, hi, Mercy!" If she crossed the street to the diner, it wasn't unusual for a passing motorist to toot his horn and give a smile and wave. And when she ran down her street, down the hill to the marina and across the beach, almost everyone she passed raised a hand in hello. And once she heard someone say, "The coach's girl."

She couldn't remember being this happy, ever. She had friends, family, love, work.

And then she screwed it up.

She was at Spencer's—a pretty typical Saturday night. They played Candy Land with the kids followed by a bowl of ice cream. Then Mercy was tucked into Spencer's bed while Austin headed for his room to watch a movie. Spencer put on a movie for them. Devon reclined on the couch and Spencer reclined on Devon. They cuddled up for the movie. After about an hour, Devon asked, "Spencer, do you think we'll last?"

"I hope so," he said. "Since I can't even think about giving you up."

"Really?"

"Really," he said, kissing her neck and pulling her closer. "I think we give it a little more time then maybe talk about the future? Hmm? If you feel the same way?"

"That would be like a dream come true. But I have to ask something else. If you answer no, that's completely acceptable."

"Shoot," he said.

"Well, I have almost everything I've ever wanted. When The Fellowship is finally shut down and there's no more possible problems from Jacob, it will be like I've been completely reborn. I can't remember being happier and a lot of that is because of you. I love you so much."

"Was there a question in there?" he asked.

"Yes, there is. If we're still together and something should happen to me, will you take Mercy?"

"What could happen to you?" he asked.

"Nothing will happen to me," she said with a laugh. "But there's no one. Well, there's Rawley, who I'm sure wouldn't hesitate and Mercy loves him. I love him. But he's a sixty-three-year-old man who I'm sure would find taking on a child full-time to be a huge challenge. And I don't think that would be the best situation for Mercy, no mat-

ter how much we love him. But you're a wonderful parent…"

He was silent and she waited. The arms that
held her relaxed a little bit. It was a long time before she said, "Uh-oh. I crossed the line, didn't I?
I asked too much, too soon.…"

He pulled her near again. "Of course not. Of
course I would do that."

"Listen, if you want me to back off this question until…well, you know, until later. When we're
more sure of each other."

"No," he said. "I'm sure."

She pulled away a bit and looked at him. "You
know, I'd make the same promise about Austin, but
Cooper and Sarah might object. He's set, should
something happen to you."

"It's all right, Devon. You're right to ask—you
have to watch out for her. Yes, is the answer. Of
course I'll take care of Mercy. Don't worry about
it again."

But that night, after the movie, rather than trying to wheedle her into staying longer, he carried
Mercy to her car and, for the first time, didn't
follow her home. "I shouldn't leave Austin alone.
And you have your phone. If you're worried about
anything or have a problem, call me. I'll lock the
front door and run down the block to help you."

"I'll be fine," she said. "I'm sorry, Spencer. I

think I upset you. I asked too much of you. It's not your obligation."

He kissed her lightly on the lips and said, "Don't be silly. You have to think about things like that. We'll talk more about this later."

"Okay," she said.

But she could feel the instant distance between them. And when she called him the next morning he said, "I might be coming down with something. I have a headache and I'm all plugged up. I'm going to take Austin out to Cooper's and get some rest."

"Okay. Feel better. I'll be here all day."

Spencer didn't sleep. His mind was spinning all night and by morning he had a blistering headache. And all this because Devon had asked him to be Mercy's guardian should something happen to her while they were a couple? It was a logical request. And Mercy was cute as could be; well-behaved and smart. In fact, if he and Bridget had had a second child, he would have loved a daughter like Mercy.

But they hadn't. Instead Bridget had left him widowed.

He walked with Austin to the beach, got him set up with his fishing pole at the end of the dock, grabbed a cup of coffee and went to the deck to keep an eye on him, make sure he didn't try diving off the dock. He sat on the deck and just watched the sea. And thought about things.

Less than two weeks after arriving in Thunder Point, three months after burying his wife, Spencer had been called to Missouri because his father had passed. It was far from unexpected. His parents had been in the same nursing home, his father suffering from the effects of a massive stroke that should've killed him but left him completely incapacitated instead. His mother, suffering from advanced Alzheimer's and several heart attacks, survived him, but not for long. The last time he took Austin to visit his parents, over a year ago, his mother didn't recognize either one of them.

But he took his mother in a wheelchair to his father's burial. There were a few people there from the nursing home, but all their friends and family were gone. And his mother had been on another planet the whole time, gazing off at nothing, making weird little movements with hands that were crippled with arthritis. She had absolutely no idea what was going on.

The nursing supervisor from the nursing home said, "Spencer, you've had a very hard year. Let me be completely honest—your mother isn't going to be with us much longer. In fact, some of us were surprised that your father predeceased her. All the arrangements have been made for her—you made sure of that quite a while ago. Say goodbye to her now. It will be a matter of weeks at the very most. Just take care of your young son. It's time to get on with your life."

The call had come a few weeks later. Spencer silently grieved, but he didn't mention it to anyone except Austin, to whom he said, "Grandma passed away peacefully. She's with Grandpa now and I believe they're dancing. When I was a boy, I remember, they loved to dance."

And Austin who was sometimes a thirty-year-old in a ten-year-old body, asked, "Did she have a happy life?"

And he nodded with a smile. "Until the past few years, after Grandpa had a stroke and Grandma's Alzheimer's got the better of her, they were very happy. They laughed a lot. They had fun. They were thrilled when you were born and visited a lot when you were small. But then..."

"I know. Then she went around the bend. And Grandpa stroked out."

Exactly correct, Spencer thought. His father had been eighty-six, his mother seventy-nine when they passed. Not bad, considering Bridget hadn't even made it to forty.

After talking about it with Austin, Spencer mentioned it to Cooper, in case Austin ever brought it up with him. And he had said to Cooper at the time, "Let's not get all emotional about it—I expected it a year ago. I'm relieved. Another chapter of suffering closed."

Cooper, who many consider a little hard-edged, said, "But, man, buddy, you've had a real load this year. I'm sorry. Really sorry."

He hadn't thought about it much after that. He was relieved.

He hadn't cried about it. He wasn't the crying type anyway. He'd let it all go and embraced his new life, his new town, his team—God, what a team! And there had been that woman, Devon. Despite all adversity, what a fighter she was! She was so alive and, man, had he needed all that life. Especially in the ashes of his buried grief.

And then she'd said, "If something should happen to me..."

Devon thought it was the request that he be responsible for Mercy that had thrown him, but that wasn't even close. The minute Devon had said that, something roared to life inside him—probably all that grief he hadn't let see the light of day. And like an arrow through the heart he thought, *I can't do it again! I can't bury one more person I love! I don't have any more in me!* Jesus, if he were a country-and-western song all he'd need is a broken-down pickup and a dead dog and he'd get an award.

Cooper came outside a couple of times, sat with him a minute, talked about his new house a little, though it was still just cement and dirt. Cooper asked him what was wrong and needing him to go away, he said, "Could be flu. It's been running through the school. I'm achy and my head is pounding."

He sat there, licking his wounds and feeling sorry for himself for at least a couple of hours when he saw her walking across the beach. She held something in her hands and she was almost to the base of the stairs before he could see it was a covered pot that she held. She stood at the bottom of the stairs, looked up at him, then began the climb. When she got to the top she sat down, put the pot in the middle of the table and asked, "How are you feeling?"

"Plugged up," he said. It wasn't a complete lie, since he was starting to understand that he was emotionally plugged up. Devon had scared him and he had freaked out.

"Have you taken anything?"

"Advil," he lied. "I probably need a decongestant. What's that?"

"I made you chicken soup. By now I'm sure it's not hot, but Rawley will be glad to warm it up for you. Spencer, I'm sorry."

He took a deep breath. He leaned forward. "No, *I'm* sorry. Your question—it took me by surprise, but the real surprise was in my head. And I've been thinking about it a lot. I want to say two things, two important things. First, whether we're a couple or not, I will take responsibility for Mercy. I will be sure she's safe and cared for and loved, no matter what. I promise. I give you my word, and my word is good. And the second thing—when you asked me that, it really hit me just how serious our relationship is and how fast it became serious. Devon, I love you, I can't help it. But I just buried my wife last spring. I buried my parents last summer. I need a few days to think about things, to be sure I'm not just desperate for some stability, for an answer to some of the aches and pains the past couple of years have given me. I don't want to rush into anything. I don't want to rush you. I just want to think about this. For a split second, I felt ambushed."

She flinched as if she'd been slapped. "But I tried to discourage you!"

"You did. I didn't realize I might be moving too fast. My feelings haven't changed. Give me a little time."

She tapped the pot. "This isn't going to cure what you've got."

"I know."

"Here's what I'm going to do," she said. "I'm going home. Don't call me unless you think you know what you want. Because I'm doing this exactly one time." Then she stood, ran down the stairs and across the beach.

He watched her go and asked himself if he was

just some kind of fool or a man being smart. It was reasonable, wasn't it? They'd met in June. It was September. A few months. When she was out of sight, he sighed and turned his head.

Cooper stood in the doorway from the bar. His arms were crossed over his chest and his heavy eyebrows were furrowed. "What the fuck was that?" he asked.

"If you're going to eavesdrop, at least pay attention," Spencer said.

"I was paying attention! You brought your grumpy self out here, claiming to have the start of the flu, but what you were having was idiocy. You've been sniffing after that pretty little thing for months! Did you really just cut her loose and tell her you needed *space?*"

"Cooper, I'm warning you—stay out of this. We'll sort it out in a couple of days...."

"When men say they need to think, that they need space, women know what they mean. When I was a teenager or idiot guy in my twenties, I thought I was getting one over on them, but they always knew—it was an excuse because I couldn't make a commitment. You're such a jackass."

"Fuck you! I'm committed all over the place! I was with Bridget every day while she was dying! I'll be Austin's father till he's old and gray even though he's got your DNA! I took care of my parents the best I could! I'm a teacher, a coach, a friend! I don't take this shit lightly!"

"Was one more commitment, the one that actually feels the best, just too much for little you?" Cooper asked. "Because she's already got a heap of worries and struggles and I think you probably just broke the hell out of her heart."

"I'll fix that up," he said sulkily. "But right now I think I'm getting the flu!"

"Flu of the brain, that's what. If you don't run after her right now and beg for another chance, you're not getting any sympathy from me when you're too late."

"I don't need your sympathy. I also don't need your advice. It's not like you're that slick with women!"

"Listen, Spencer," he said, pulling out a chair and sitting at the table with him. "I understand you might be a little gun-shy—what you went through with Bridget, that would be rough. But Devon's a good kid and she's been through a lot, too. Maybe you'd be better off working on holding each other up than taking a break to think things over."

"Cut it," he said, drawing a finger across his throat.

"All right, then, if that's the way you want it, do it your way. Just trying to share the wealth of my experience. You could be alone a long time. Just trying to be useful, bud."

"You wanna be useful? How about a beer? And some silence."

"Whatever," Cooper said, going into the bar. But he didn't bring back a beer.

When Devon got home, Mercy was still napping. Mrs. Bledsoe was sitting on Devon's couch, reading one of her novels. She slowly stood as Devon came in the house. "How is he feeling?"

"He's feeling like the ass he is," Devon said.

"Oh, dear," Mrs. Bledsoe said. "You've been crying."

"Wasted tears," she said. "It's probably my fault. I probably pushed him into a serious relationship. I didn't mean to, but I think I did. Because he asked me to give him some time to think about this. About us."

"Oh," she said, smiling. "Don't worry too much about that, lovey. Men have an enduring reputation for things like that."

"Asking for think time?"

"No. For being stupid." She shook her head sadly. "I don't know what it is. Men do things like that regularly. Take these silly time-outs. Like it erases all the important things on their minds. Haven't you noticed?"

Well, no, she hadn't. Because when had she had a man? There had been a couple of boyfriends when she was young and then there was Jacob, who didn't count at all because he was not a steady guy: he was a benevolent despot. Spencer was nearly her first. The first guy to love and want her exclusively.

"I had a husband, a son, a grandson and I eat up these romance novels. Everyone knows men can't stand to be confronted with their feelings. They'd rather wrestle alligators."

"Maybe I should read more of those," Devon said.

"I have a few recommendations and a ton of books if you ever want to borrow a few."

"Maybe I will," Devon said. "I think I'm going to have a little free time all of a sudden."

Seventeen

Ashley cornered her mother in the kitchen. "Can I talk to you and Mac tonight? For a couple of minutes? Just you two?"

"Of course. Is anything wrong?"

"Not at all. I have something to run by you. It's not really for the whole family."

"You've got me on pins now," Gina said.

"Is Mac here tonight? He's not working?" When Gina shook her head, Ashley said, "See you here right after dinner? When the kids have scattered?"

"Perfect."

Before the dishes were even done, Mac and Gina sat expectantly at the kitchen table. Eve had gone to their room to talk to Landon on the phone while the younger kids were in the basement with the piano, computer and TV. Ashley looked at her mom and new stepdad and laughed. "I really didn't mean to alarm you. I wanted to talk to you about Eric."

"What is it, honey?" Gina asked.

"I went shopping with him, you know. And we had lunch. And he was telling me that someone has been after him to sell his body shop. At first he just said it wasn't for sale, but then he started thinking about it and wondered if just maybe he shouldn't do it. I guess the offer is pretty good, but I don't have any idea what that means. But... he said he's been looking around at other things, other opportunities, if he did decide to sell. He said it's almost an offer he can't refuse. I told him I hoped it didn't mean he was moving even farther away and he said there was a potential thing in Thunder Point, but he was worried about it— he asked me if Thunder Point was big enough for the two of us. Everyone would take one look at us and know—he's my father."

"Oh, jeez," Gina said. "How do you feel about that?"

"I'm okay with it," she said with a shrug. "I've introduced him as my biological father to people we've met. It doesn't bother me a bit. In fact, I'm kind of proud that he wanted to meet me once he found out about me. But then the conversation went to you guys. He doesn't want to put it to you directly—he doesn't want to blindside you. He said it might make you two uncomfortable. You know, dredging up the past, which was kind of a scandalous past for you. Mom, I know you didn't have it easy when you were this teenage mother with the missing boyfriend. Then, he reminded me, add to that the fact he went to prison. Holy crap, huh? I mean, that isn't a big deal for me—I didn't go to prison! And he's pretty embarrassed about it, but he said he's never tried to hide it. He said it wouldn't work to try to hide it—it would always be found out eventually, so he admits it and that's all there is to it." She shrugged. "He turned his life around. It's a good thing."

All Gina said was, "Thunder Point?"

"Yeah. Well, here's what he said. He said if he approached you with the possibility—and it's still just a possibility, he hasn't accepted the offer on his body shop or anything—but he said you're the kind of person that would tell him to just do the thing that worked best for him. You'd just be nice about it. That's why he asked me to tell you and Mac about this, give you time to talk about it, give him an answer that really fits what you feel and not just the nice answer. Because he promises no matter what he does next, he'll see me now and then, just like he does now. He doesn't want you to feel uncomfortable if he lives nearby. So, could you guys talk it over? Really talk it over? Decide how you really feel about the idea? And then I'll tell him. Okay?"

"You mean to say he'd turn down a good move to this town if it made me uncomfortable?"

"Mom, I know he's sorry about the past, about the loser he used to be. He said you're in a new marriage now and wants to make sure you don't feel, you know, embarrassed by him."

Gina looked at Mac. "That's kind of sweet."

Mac frowned. "It's kind of sweet as long as he doesn't have feelings for you."

Ashley laughed. "Do you think he'd dare? Actually I think he has feelings for me. And while we were driving home, he admitted he's scared to death of Grandma."

"He probably should be," Gina said.

"So, don't answer the question. Talk about it. Be sure. Because you could be stuck with the answer."

"And, Ash? This would make you happy?"

"I'd be okay. But, Mom, I'm almost out of here. Another year or two, I'm on my way to college and then—whatever comes next. I don't know if I'll live in Thunder Point the rest of my life. I know I'll visit a lot if you're here, but where Eric lives isn't that big a deal. We'll stay in touch. This has a lot more to do with you and Mac."

Devon was on the quiet side at the clinic. And to make matters worse, it wasn't very busy—just young mothers with small children who weren't in school and one woman who stayed home from work with a terrible sore throat and fever. Scott fixed her right up with a strong antibiotic and did a throat culture for possible strep.

And of course he noticed Devon's mood, though she tried to act bright and happy. "I sense trouble in paradise," he said.

"Maybe I'm coming down with the flu," she said, borrowing Spencer's excuse.

"That's okay, Devon. You don't have to talk about what it really is."

And she said, "Thanks. I can't at the moment."

She was being completely honest. She couldn't talk about it without tears threatening. She was trying so hard not to hope and pray he'd call to say he'd been a fool who overreacted. She wanted to be as over him as he apparently was over her. She was failing in her mission, but suspected Spencer was succeeding in his—she didn't see him. At all.

She finally dragged herself over to the diner for a coffee break and found Gina in her usual place behind the counter. There was a trio of elderly ladies in a booth, gossiping and laughing up a storm. A lone man sat down at the end of the counter, finishing up either a late breakfast or early lunch.

"Well, hey," Gina said. "Where have you been?"

"Just working," she said.

Gina automatically poured her a cup of coffee. "What did you and Spencer do over the weekend?"

Well, she thought. *Word usually travels much*

faster. She wondered if Spencer was keeping this little issue they had to himself. "Well, let's see," she said, sipping her coffee. "We had a raucous game of Candy Land with the kids on Saturday night...then a bowl of ice cream..."

Gina laughed. "Isn't being a single mother dating a single father romantic?"

"And then I think we broke up."

Shock showed all over Gina's face. "Are you kidding me?"

Devon shook her head. "I think it was something I did. I think I screwed up."

She could tell Gina was momentarily speechless. "What could you have done?"

"I asked him for something, and I didn't think it through very well. I should have waited. It was too soon, but at the time it felt safe enough. I reminded him that I have no family, just Rawley, and he's not really family. So I asked if we're a couple and something happens to me, would he watch over Mercy. Take her on. Take her in. And it was like he closed the blinds right at that moment. Pulled down the shades. Closed the door. He said he thought he was sick, but that was an excuse to avoid me. I tracked him down at Cooper's on Sunday and he leveled with me—he isn't interested in getting that serious. I haven't heard from him since."

Gina poured herself a cup of coffee, shaking her head. "Oh, brother."

"He doesn't really want more family. He's in a different place. His singleness is not so single as mine—he's got Cooper and Sarah to look after Austin. He said he'd take on Mercy if something happened to me, but he needs some time to think about us. He's been thinking for a few days, so I'm done. I'm adjusting to that idea." She sat back and pasted a fake smile on her face. "I'm all right on my own."

"Maybe a little time is really all he needs?" Gina ventured.

Devon sighed. "Yeah. Well, I spent a few days fantasizing he'd call saying he just panicked…but the call didn't come. And tempting as he is, I really don't want a guy who feels like he's all in and then he suddenly freezes up like that."

"Maybe it has something to do with his late wife?" Gina suggested.

"Oh, definitely. He mentioned that, but we've talked about her before, about what a huge life lesson that was for him. He seemed so stable, so right with the world, you know? But he's got secrets—did you know his parents both died last summer?"

"I knew about his dad. He left Austin with Cooper and went back east to see him buried. But I didn't realize…"

"I think Spencer has stuff to work out. And I

know I have stuff to work out. I think maybe this is for the best, much as it hurts. We shouldn't be working stuff out on each other."

"I can't argue with that," Gina said, sipping her coffee. "I'm just so sorry. And surprised. Not only do you seem like one of the least troubled people I know, so did Spencer. I don't know him well, but I know him."

"We don't always advertise our baggage. You know?"

"I know. Someday we'll have a glass of wine and I'll tell you how well I know about that."

"I guess everyone has their stuff," Devon said. "You know, I look at all my new friends and they all look like they have everything in life figured out and sometimes I feel like the only person with a past to put in perspective. Sometimes I pray one day I can be like everyone else."

"There is no everyone else, Devon. Life is complicated and difficult for everyone. Absolutely everyone. And you shouldn't feel alone. You're just like the rest of us—hard stuff to work through so you can have a stable, productive, happy life. There's no reason you can't. If you ever start to feel like the struggle is bigger than you are, there's help. I have the name of an excellent counselor."

"Really? Because that was suggested to me, but I'm not sure I can afford one."

"She has a sliding scale based on income. My

insurance helped, but I would've had trouble paying her fees if it hadn't. If you ever want her name, if only to find out what the fee might be, just let me know."

"Is she a friend of yours?" Devon asked.

"No, sweetheart. She was my daughter's counselor. She got us through a very rough patch. Counseling works."

Devon gave the idea of counseling some thought through the afternoon. She might look into that, but for now she was determined to get on with her life. She picked up Mercy from Gabriella and took her home. Once there she asked Mrs. Bledsoe if she could keep an eye on her for a little while so she could get a little exercise. While it was still light, a run on the beach would solve some immediate problems, like feeling sorry for herself. And if she saw him or he saw her, she would just run in the other direction.

"A half hour? Maybe forty-five minutes at the most?" she asked Mrs. Bledsoe. "She had a snack and I'll give her dinner when I'm back."

She was about twelve minutes into her run when the adrenaline kicked in and she was reminded that what had just happened with Spencer was probably normal. It was probably the kind of complication "regular" people go through when forming relationships, but she'd gotten a little off the track because of her unusual circumstances. People who lived in the real world, people who weren't so alone and screwed up probably examined and reexamined their relationships constantly.

Spencer was not in evidence on the beach. She didn't see him on the deck, either. She ran across the beach as far as the dock, then back across and up the hill, past Spencer's house to her own.

And in front of her house was the deputy sheriff's car!

She sprinted to her door and burst inside. Mrs. Bledsoe, looking so small sitting on her secondhand sofa next to Mac, was weeping into a tissue.

"What?" she shouted. "What is it?"

Mrs. Bledsoe struggled for control. "He took her," she said. "He said he was her father and he took her."

Devon looked at Mac. "Jacob?" she asked. "Was it him?"

"Sounds like it was. I've notified the sheriff and the FBI."

Looking back at Mrs. Bledsoe, she demanded, "What did he look like?"

"I don't know," the poor woman faltered. "Tall. Dark hair. A little gray, but not much. Strong. He told me not to try to fight him or I'd get hurt. He said this was a dangerous world and he was taking Mercy to a safe place. Oh, my dear, I was so afraid of him!"

"And what was he driving?" Devon demanded.

"I don't know. It was blue. It was a truck," she stammered.

"What else did he say, Mrs. Bledsoe?" Devon said, getting right in her face. The older woman backed up, clearly frightened by Devon. "What did he say? *Exactly!*"

"That Mercy was his daughter. He said, 'Come here, Mercy,' and she went to him. He picked her up—she wasn't afraid of him. He said, 'No one takes my child from me,' and that if I tried to stop him I'd get hurt. I had to go home to call the police, but I came right back here. I couldn't stop him, please believe me."

"How long ago?" she asked.

"Half hour, maybe. Not long after you left. I called Mac right away," she said. "I'm sorry. I'm so sorry!"

Devon grabbed her truck keys off the kitchen counter and ran for the door.

"Devon!" Mac barked. "You should stay here! Where are you going?"

She glared at him. "I'm going to get her."

"Devon! Don't!"

But she was out the door and in the truck so fast no one could have possibly stopped her. She drove immediately across the beach, parked and ran up the stairs, through the bar and into the kitchen.

There were people on the deck and inside, but she took no notice of them.

"Rawley! Jacob found out where I live and he took Mercy! About a half hour ago. Mrs. Bledsoe was watching her. I have to go get her. I have to have... Rawley, I need a wire cutter to cut through the fence. And I need... Do you have a weapon? Any kind of weapon?"

He grabbed her by the upper arms and gave her a little shake. "Shh! Do you think he took her back there?"

"He hated to leave. I never saw him leave the compound alone. Where else would he take her?"

"I'll go get her," Rawley said. "Can you tell me where to go once I get into the camp?"

She nodded and said, "I'll go with you. We'll go together. I'll show you."

"No, you shouldn't go, you should—"

"She's mine! She's my little girl! I'm going to get her and I don't care if he makes me stay, I won't leave her there with him! I'm going!"

"And I'm going," a voice said from behind her. She whirled to see Spencer standing there. "We'll go together. I'll go with Rawley to the inside. We'll get her."

"You ever done this before?" Rawley asked him.

"Done this?" Spencer asked stupidly.

"Snuck into a village or a prisoner camp to get someone out?"

Spencer was clearly stuck for an answer. With something that sounded almost like a laugh, he asked, "Have *you?*"

"Unfortunately. Been a while, thank Jesus. Get Cooper. Right now."

Spencer blinked a couple of times, then did as he was told. When Cooper followed Spencer into the kitchen he was muttering, "What the hell...?"

"I need to get in your closet," Rawley said. "I need a black or dark green jacket or dark-colored sweatshirt with sleeves. Camouflage would be good, but you probably don't have that. Devon needs something real dark from Sarah's closet—just a jacket'll do it. She'll be okay in those tennis shoes—she's not walking far. We'll be going through the woods and can't be seen."

"What the hell?" Cooper said again.

"Mercy's father came for her. He took her back to that commune and we're going to go get her," Rawley said. "He's likely dangerous."

"The police were called," Devon said. "I told Mac I was going to go get her. Jacob has some men who work for him and they have rifles. They always said it was for hunting and to keep us safe, but I always wondered about the protection part."

"We'll have to look out for them, too," Rawley said. "Coop, I gotta have a little help here. There's no time to waste. Best chance is gettin' right on him, surprise him."

"Hell," Cooper said. "I'll be right back." He took the stairs two at a time, rummaged around in his closet, in his trunk, under his bed. He was back in the kitchen with his arms full of clothes plus one very large handgun. He threw the clothes and gun on the counter and pulled one dark brown hoodie over his head.

"Wait a minute," Spencer said. "You have to stay here for Austin."

"Sarah will take care of Austin and I have to go to make sure you don't get shot."

"What's this old guy gonna do to get her back?" Spencer wanted to know.

"This old guy served three tours in Vietnam as a Green Beret and stands a better chance of pulling this off than you or I," Cooper said.

Rawley was pulling on a navy blue shirt, buttoning it up to his neck and around his wrists. "I'd have a better chance if you two dipshits would stay right here. If four are going, we're going to have problems...."

"I'm going," Devon said. "I can tell you every detail of the buildings inside the fence."

"I'm going," Spencer said, picking up a pair of boots and a jacket.

"I'm going," Cooper said.

Rawley sighed and shook his head. "We'll have

to take your extended cab," he said to Cooper. He headed for the door. He looked back over his shoulder. "We on coffee break here?" And then he was out the door, leaving them to follow.

Devon followed first, still pulling on a jacket she'd pulled out of the pile. She found Rawley digging around in the tool storage bin in the bed of his old truck. He removed a rifle and a very large, very intimidating knife in a leather holster of some kind. She didn't gasp but she did say, "If I had known you had these things, I would've been afraid to stay with you."

"Always locked up tight, chickadee. Wouldn't leave nothing like this around a child. You sit in back with me—tell me the lay of the land while Cooper drives."

"All right." She touched his arm. "Rawley, I'll get her back, won't I?"

"You think I'd do this for the fun of it? You wanna help? Do what I say to do and don't argue. What I sure the hell don't need right now is the Keystone Kops following me around the jungle."

"Rawley, it's a forest."

"It is what it is. Cooper!" he shouted.

The man came scrambling out of the bar, Spencer behind him carrying a jacket and pair of Cooper's boots. Once Cooper was behind the wheel Rawley said, "Get us over to Highway 5

and head south. Be quiet and listen to Devon—
she's the only intel we got."

Spencer sat in the front beside Cooper and listened to Rawley question Devon; he listened to
Devon answer. She had told him a great deal about
her experience in this commune, but he'd never really created a visual before now. He never really
put himself in her position until tonight.

"What are the buildings in the front, by the
gate?" Rawley asked.

"A long driveway, a long yard, a very big house,
kind of an old country farmhouse, almost like an
inn—two stories with a wraparound porch. A barn
and south of the barn, a chicken coop. Between
the barn and house, a large dirt patch, a place we
played, a place the men parked those big SUVs.
Behind the barn is a corral. Pastures and our produce gardens back up to the river."

"Fence around all that land?"

"No, just around the compound—they let the
stock out of the compound and there is just normal
pasture fencing. They don't worry about the cows
or horses getting away. There aren't that many
animals. It's the people who are fenced in who
are at risk."

"How far to the river from the gate?"

"At least a half mile. Almost a mile. There's a
bridge—the men would drive their SUVs across

the bridge because over there was Jacob's house, right between two big barns. They're not barns— that's where Jacob was growing marijuana."

"Is there any other road inside except for that front road?"

"I don't think so, but I don't know. We never went over there. Jacob would take women to his house one at a time. I think there are only four women left there—Lorna, Laine, Pilly and Charlotte. And four children. When I got there four years ago or so, there were eighteen women and six men and a bunch of kids. In the past couple of years, people started leaving and Jacob started getting strange. Angry and paranoid and weird. I think he knew law enforcement suspected him of stuff."

"How did you get out?"

"There was a hole in the fence behind the chicken coop and Laine told me to carry Mercy and to run down the road—there was a truck waiting to give me a ride over the mountain. She arranged everything at a Farmers' Market."

"Why didn't people just walk away at that market?" Rawley asked. "That market's a busy place."

"Because, Rawley—the kids were home, inside the fence."

"Where do the men keep the guns?"

"With them, I think. There's a bunkhouse back

by the marijuana barns. There were never guns in our house."

Spencer listened as she described the property, a beautiful big farm on a lovely river in a valley where food and shelter and friendship was plentiful... And where they were surreptitiously guarded by men with guns, men who were there to serve the master, the man who took them one at a time to his house for sex and liked to say they were all one big happy family.

"I think we were part of Jacob's fantasy or delusion," she told Rawley. "He wanted to be the grand pooh-bah, the big daddy, the king of his little kingdom, served by women, loved by his many children. He hardly ever left the farm. The men came and went pretty freely, but Jacob only left occasionally. He liked his animals, his gardens, his family. He liked to walk across the bridge to the house, sit at the head of the table with one of the children on his knee, ask us about our day, then lecture a little or talk about himself or maybe rant against the government. He wrote volumes on his beliefs, his philosophies and believed his writings would one day be legendary. There were times it seemed so lovely. Then there were times it seemed so sick and demented. One thing—once you were there, there was no leaving. And they didn't let people inside. He used the excuse that we were a private religious order. But there wasn't much religion going on there. Reese, the oldest of us, called it a tribe. A militant tribe."

Rawley asked the same questions over and over again. Devon answered, and her answers were consistent. Spencer memorized her answers, as he assumed Cooper was doing.

Spencer was beginning to understand what she had been through in a way he hadn't before, even though she'd told him about her experience. This was completely different and for the first time he was impacted by how trapped she must have felt and how much courage it must have taken for her to flee. And, to his shame, he realized how much trust she must have churned up to be able to trust someone like him.

Had he really done what he'd done? Chased her, seduced her and then rejected her because of sudden terror that he'd somehow be hurt again? He felt the fool and he wanted to stop everything right now so he could explain, beg her to understand and forgive him, to tell her he was really not that kind of wimp. If they got Mercy and got through this, he would never let her down again.

Ahead were the flashing lights of a patrol car.

"Do not turn around," Rawley said sharply. "Pull up to the copper. Ask him why the road is closed. Tell him you're just taking a shortcut to Canyonville where your folks have a farm. Let the copper turn you around. You turn yourself around they'll be after you that fast."

And Cooper did just that, pulled right up to the officer and put down his window. "What's happening? Accident?"

"Where you headed, sir?"

"My folks have a spread near Canyonville. I been taking this shortcut for years. Can I get through?"

"Road's closed, I'm afraid." He peered into the car. "I better have a look at your driver's license and registration."

"You bet," Cooper said, fishing for those things in the glove box and his back pocket.

The patrolman shone a flashlight on those items while he asked, "What takes you to your folks just now?"

"Hunting, what else? We get there tonight, start up first light."

He looked into the backseat. "You hunt, little lady?"

Devon laughed. "Please. I cook!"

"I like that," he said. Another patrol car pulled up behind them. "Get outta here," he said. "Road's closed."

Then Cooper took his turn and headed back in the opposite direction.

"Now what?" Devon asked.

"Now we go upstream and head down the river. I hope you swim."

"Like a beaver," she said. "If they find out what we're doing, will we be in trouble?" she asked Rawley.

He laughed. "Trouble? I reckon we'll prolly go straight to jail."

Eighteen

Laine spent a couple of days at Jacob's house, in and out of her bonds. Jacob gave her water and he brought her back a small plate of food from the house now and then. It was hard to stay in character as a meek and submissive female while he kept her tied, and when he did talk to her he ranted angrily about how he *knew* she had betrayed him, had betrayed them all.

Of course he didn't know the truth. She hadn't confessed to a thing.

Laine slept upright in the straight-back kitchen chair, testing her binding, trying to scoot to the counter to see if she could reach into a kitchen drawer to get something that would cut her ropes. When he came home from the big house after dinner to find she had moved, he gave her a black eye and split lip and then lectured her for an hour on his plan for his Fellowship and the conspirators who would strip them of their bounty, leave them homeless and poor. Everyone who wasn't with them was against them.

And then he came back after what she presumed was his dinner at the house, except he had Mercy with him. She gasped when she saw him and said, "Is Devon back?"

"I'm finished with Devon, but this is my daughter and she stays with me. If I untie you and take you to the house with the other women, will you stay? Or will you just run?"

Her mind raced. What had he done with Devon? Had he hurt her, perhaps killed her to kidnap this child? Because, as she knew, her former friend Devon would not have given up Mercy, not at the point of a knife. "Why would I run?" she asked him. "You'll just catch me and bring me back. I'll take Mercy to the house, see she's fed and put to bed and I'll—"

He laughed at her. He grinned and said, "I wouldn't put that kind of pressure on you." He untied her and said, "Come with us, Sister Laine. We'll take you to the house—you can help the women with the children. I'll keep Mercy with me."

"I'll take care of her, Jacob. I'm sure you have too much to do to take care of her. She needs to be with the children."

"I guess you really do think I'm an idiot. Stand up."

She stood from the chair and turned to face him. "Mercy, I want you to sit at the table here until I get back. Don't move, don't leave the table for any reason or I will be very angry with you. Do you understand?" The child looked up at him fearfully and nodded. Laine noted that the children were not ordinarily afraid of Jacob, but perhaps whatever act he had committed to gain the custody of this child had filled her with fear. And then he said to Laine, "Let's go."

He held the door for her and she preceded him out of the house, walking toward the bridge. She was almost there when he said, "Sister Laine, you really don't have anything I want anymore. Why don't you just leave now?"

She slowly turned toward him. "How am I to leave? The gate is locked."

He gave her a patient smile. "Then I suppose you should find a way. You've found other ways. Maybe you left a hole in the fence somewhere. If you can get out, you can run down the road—the police have blocked the road. You can just run to them—they'll take you in."

"Jacob, why don't you just ask them what they want? It can't be anything so terrible. You always took good care of your family, you always—"

"They'll take all of this if I let them in," he said, gesturing around. "And I won't leave a single thing for them to take! And when they take me down, they'll be forced to show the world my work. Good work. Thousands of pages of brilliant work inspired by my beliefs."

And suddenly she feared the worst. If he didn't escape, he would be on a suicide mission. She had known for months it was possible he was a thundering lunatic and might do something desperate, but she wasn't sure what…or how. "Jacob, where are the men?" she asked suspiciously.

"Yes, where are the men? Well," he said, turning his head right and left as if looking for them. "Where are they?" he asked facetiously. "Not with me. And if they're not with me, then they're against me." And with that he left her there and went back toward his house.

So this would be it, she thought. It was going down. She ran for the house and burst into the kitchen where Charlotte and Pilly were cooking. Liam was in his high chair and four-year-old Abe was sitting at the long table. The room looked strangely forlorn, one small boy sitting at a table that could comfortably seat twenty to twenty-four. Jacob's dynasty; Jacob's legacy, down to two women, two small children and one undercover FBI agent. She was panting. Charlotte and Pilly looked at her in shock. It could have been their surprise at seeing her or maybe surprise at the condition of her face. "Jacob kidnapped Mercy. I don't know what he might've done to Devon. He's keeping Mercy at his house. He's talking crazy. He says the police have blocked the road and he's not giving up his home, this home. He's talking about his legacy if they take him down. You have to get the kids out of here."

Charlotte put a hand over her mouth but Pilly looked enraged. "I won't leave Jacob," she said. "He needs me!"

"Needs you?" Laine said. "Did he even tell you he had Mercy? Do you even know what he's planning? Pilly, I'm afraid for you and Liam!"

"I'll leave if he tells me to go," she said indignantly. "But he won't!" And leaving the pan she was stirring on the fire, she stormed out of the kitchen through the back door, headed for Jacob's house across the river.

Laine looked at Charlotte. "Take the children, Charlotte. I'll show you the way out—follow the road to the police. Jacob said they're blocking the road."

"What are you going to do?"

"I'm going to try to get Mercy out of his house. I don't know how, but I'm going to try. If Pilly won't take Liam, if she risks her life and her son's to stand by Jacob in his craziest hour, we have to get the kids out of here." She pulled Liam out of his high chair. "Charlotte, if you don't do this, bad things are going to happen. Now come with me. Come!"

Laine didn't have wire cutters or tools or weapons, but even though she felt dangerously alone in here, she did have partners. She would walk along the fence with Charlotte from the front of the fence line to the river, kicking and shaking the fence as she went, and she would undoubtedly find a break in the fence for an emergency getaway.

"How do you know this?" Charlotte asked her.

And Laine gave the standard response. "Because I was going to go, but Jacob held me captive in his house and I couldn't leave!"

They left the house from the front door so neither Jacob nor Pilly would see them if they were coming. They were just beginning their trek along the fence, partially concealed by the trees and bushes, when there was a smell. A pungent and thick smell. Laine knew what it was. "Holy mother of God," she said, holding Liam against her and running along the fence. "Hurry! He's burning everything down!"

They were almost to the river before Laine found a break in the fence. She held it open for Charlotte and handed Liam to her. "Go through the woods and pasture to the road. He's burning the warehouses and he'll probably burn everything and if you're here, you're in terrible danger. Take the baby, hang on to Abe. Just go!"

"What will you do? Will you be safe?"

"I'm going to try to get Mercy. Don't worry

about me right now, just go quickly. And when you get to the police, tell them who's left here!"

"Jacob will send the men after us!"

"Charlotte," she said gravely. "The men are gone."

Rawley told Cooper where to park in a small stand of trees near the river. He lit out at a pretty fast clip along the riverbank. He had his knife strapped to his waist and anchored to his thigh and he carried a rifle.

"Rawley, how far?" Devon asked.

"I'm not sure, chickadee. Just stay on my tail and don't slip. If I have to fish you out, it costs time."

"The odometer said it was six miles," she pointed out.

"By road. The river is a straight shot." Then he stopped, listened, sniffed the air. Everyone came to a standstill behind him—first Devon, then Spencer, then Cooper.

"What is it?" Devon asked.

"Might be burning green cannabis," he said. Then he put his head down and said, "Step it up. This just keeps getting worse." And he began to jog along the riverbank.

Laine could see that a fire had been started inside one of the warehouses; smoke was pouring out through cracks in the roof and doors. Any minute the thing would combust and the outer shell would go up in flames. The whole forest could be at risk, but certainly Jacob's house, the bunkhouse and the other warehouse.

Laine ran past the burning warehouse to the bunkhouse and tried the door, only to find it locked. She assumed weapons must be stored inside, but she couldn't get in. She reared back and gave the door a furious kick, but it didn't budge. There was only an old blue pickup near the bunkhouse and now she could see one lone black SUV parked behind Jacob's house. The rear hatch was open and it looked as if Jacob might be loading up his belongings.

And between them, an ax sitting beside a stack of firewood.

She picked up the ax and ran toward the house. She softly opened the front door to the house and heard voices within, slightly muffled but she thought she could make out at least some of the words—"No, take that box while I fill this suitcase."

"What about that?"

"I'll take care of that. Hurry—there won't be much time now."

"Where will we go?"

"Doesn't matter, just that we leave before they get here."

It was Pilly and Jacob, with no sound from Mercy. Ax in hand, she followed the sounds and peeked into a room to find the two of them in the back of the house, a room she'd never seen before. It appeared to be Jacob's office. She dared to peek in the door and what she saw was surreal—Jacob and Pilly were loading boxes full of stacks of papers—it looked suspiciously like manuscripts. His brilliant opus; his manifesto. And from an open safe he was stacking what had to be tens of thousands of dollars in bills into suitcases.

But of course. If he'd been selling his "medicinal herbs" he was operating a completely cash business. He wouldn't have had the luxury of making deposits into a bank—his illegal operation would be exposed. Law enforcement always followed the money in search for clues and suspects.

She crept through the house, beginning with the kitchen where she had last seen Mercy sitting at the table, but she wasn't there. She looked in the living room, in the bedroom, searched in vain for a cellar door, but the child was not there. Laine felt a rising panic. She had some theories about Jacob but in reality she wasn't sure how sick or crazy he was. Would he keep Mercy as some kind of hostage? Would he just kill her out of spite? And what of Pilly? Was she that bonded with Jacob that she'd leave her baby behind in a compound in flames just to be with him?

When all else had failed, she went to the doorway of the office where the frantic packing up was happening and stood there, ax hefted in two hands.

"Where is she?" Laine asked in her most threatening voice.

Pilly gasped, but Jacob turned toward her with a controlled expression on his face. He was composed. And then it happened so quickly, Laine never saw it coming. He picked up a gun from the top of his desk, a handgun that looked like a Smith & Wesson .40 caliber, turned it on her and fired. He hit her in the upper right chest with a force so powerful it blew her out of the doorway and knocked the ax out of her grip. Laine whirled around and backed up against the hallway wall, leaving a large smear of blood on the wall.

Willing herself not to fall, Laine hurried down the hall toward escape, leaving a trail of blood behind her.

"Jacob, go get her!" Pilly yelled.

"She's too late," he said. "She can't get out. She'll just die out there. Get this in the suitcase. Hurry. We have only minutes."

She's too late, Laine thought. And she ran from the house, around to the back where the SUV sat with its tailgate open. It was her intention to disable it—maybe she'd pull out a bunch of wires and close it down. She pulled open the driver's door to pop the hood and glancing into the backseat, there was Mercy, lying there on the seat, sleeping.

Laine had but one usable arm. She opened the rear door and pulled Mercy toward her with one hand, terrified that the worst might've befallen the little girl. "Come on, sunshine, come on," she cooed, jostling the little girl. And thank God, Mercy opened her eyes and sat up. "Come, angel, we have to hurry. Come with me now." Laine's shoulder was injured and bleeding profusely; she held that arm tight against her body and with the other, she scooped Mercy out of the SUV and lowered her to her feet. "You have to help me, angel. You have to run with me."

"Mama?" she asked, her voice laced with tears.

"I'm taking you to her right now. Come with me."

Jacob might not bother too much with Laine, feeling he'd done enough damage to slow her down, but he was going to be enraged when he saw that Mercy was gone. Knowing this, Laine pulled Mercy by the hand in the opposite direction from whence she came, around the front of the house and toward the bridge, but after she crossed it, she huddled in the darkness beneath it at the river's edge. The rushing water would muffle any sounds they made should Mercy start to cry.

"Not a sound," she cautioned Mercy. "We have to hide here now, long enough for him to leave and

then I can take you to your mama...." If she lasted
that long. She was growing weak and a little dizzy.
She shivered; the wet and night air were only making things worse. She tried to keep Mercy above
the water, dry as possible, but poor Mercy shook
with the cold. But little Mercy was so brave, burying her face in Laine's neck. It seemed a long time
before she heard him roar in outrage, screaming
Mercy's name. Then the SUV came to life, the
headlights shining.

Laine heard a couple of gunshots, and with
Jacob in the truck she wondered if they were under
attack. She consoled herself that if he tried to escape out of the front of the compound, law enforcement would surely stop him before he got far.
She waited tensely for the sound of that big SUV
to rattle across the bridge, but it didn't come. She
heard the engine, then heard it traveling away and
she took a peek and saw something unreal. He was
driving right down the river.... She shook her head
in confusion, standing up to peek over the bridge
and yes, he was driving down the river. There
must be some back road out of here, totally concealed and blocked by the forest. The right jacked-
up SUV could travel down the rocky river in the
shallow parts, then exit the river to a road that
Laine had never been aware of and she'd poked
around as much as possible.

He was going to get away.

Shaking almost too much to stand up, Laine pushed them to the shore beyond the bridge, pulling Mercy with her. "Come, little angel, we have to hurry away..." But she could barely move. She was on her knees, trying to stand. Mercy was on her feet and Laine tried to push up with her one good arm, but fell to her knees. Her only rational thought was, *Shit, I'm going to die from a damn bullet to the shoulder.* Mercy was crying and Laine was literally crawling. Even if she had to crawl to the break in the fence, she was going to get Mercy out of this compound and as close as possible to the police barricade.

And then she was aware of footfalls, heavy thuds, running toward her. She glanced up to see a man in a dark ball cap and dark shirt with dirt on his face running toward her. He was carrying a gun and she did what came naturally—she pulled Mercy down to the ground and covered her with her body. And there were more sounds of running coming at her.

As she was being lifted off Mercy, Laine struggled and fought, but it only caused her shoulder to scream in pain, matching the screaming that came from her throat. "No! No! Let the child be, leave her alone! No!"

"Easy there, young lady, easy—you're hurt," the man said.

And then a woman's voice cried, "Mercy!"

"Mama!"

Laine looked up through blurry vision and saw Devon standing over her. And then she passed out.

"We better move out of here fast," Rawley said. "I don't know what threat we got in here, so best slink around the back side of that house up there. One thing is for sure—we're gonna have us one big goddamn fire here pretty soon. We have to go out the fence and through the woods and to the road, see if we can meet up with that nice copper again." He pulled a large handheld bolt cutter off his belt and handed it to Cooper. "Stay to the shadows, Coop. Get us the hell out of here. This here girl is hurt."

"That's Laine," Devon said, holding her shivering daughter tightly against her. "She's the one who showed me the way to get out of here. Rawley, what if there are women and children in the house?"

Rawley seemed to consider this for a moment, then he transferred his burden into Spencer's arms. "Well, since I planned this circus, I guess I'll check the house." He picked up his rifle again. "Don't wait for me. Make tracks."

Spencer lifted the young woman in his arms, getting her solidly against him. "Devon," he said, "follow Cooper and try to be small as a shadow, in case there are snipers in here. I'm right behind you."

They marched off in a group toward the back of the house and before going any closer to the buildings, Cooper stopped and made fast work of the fence, pulling back the loose aluminum so they could slip through. First Devon climbed through, and then Spencer ducked and maneuvered through. The woman was light in his arms, but she was so pale she almost gleamed in the moonlight. Cooper was the last to get through. "What about Rawley?" Spencer asked.

Right then there was the unmistakable report from a rifle and everyone froze.

"I hope he didn't shoot anyone," Spencer muttered.

"He's not above it," Cooper said, pressing on. "He'll get out, don't worry," Cooper said. "That crafty old devil knows what he's doing. Follow me," he said. And Spencer doubted Cooper was a tracker, but he was the only one without a body in his arms, so he led them through the thick growth and trees. By the time they got through the woods and met the road, they also met Rawley.

"We heard a shot," Cooper said.

"Yeah, I blew the lock off the gate and opened it up. We need us a fire truck and ambulance," he said. He stripped off his shirt, draped it over Mercy and partly over Devon and asked, "She doin' okay there, Mama?"

"I think so. Scared and wet, but okay."

Laine stirred and groaned in Spencer's arms. He stopped walking, looked down at her. "We'll get you some help. Is there anyone left in the compound?" he asked.

She shook her head. "He got away," she whispered. "Mercy?"

"I've got her, Laine," Devon said. "We're getting out of here."

"I can walk," she said, wiggling a bit in Spencer's arms.

"You wouldn't make it two steps. Let's go."

"Stay behind me," Rawley said, handing off his rifle to Cooper. Then he took off at a jog down the road.

They half jogged, half power walked down the road for a good half hour—it was at least a mile, maybe closer to two. Rawley was ahead by a hundred yards and he approached the police vehicles with his arms high in the air. And suddenly the place lit up and was brought to life by a SWAT team, many police vehicles, Fire and Rescue and lots of guns pointed right at him.

"We got wounded," he yelled, and they charged him, guns drawn, securing him in handcuffs real fast.

Then they charged the rest of the party, same

drill. Except, they didn't cuff them all. They just took the weapons and brought them forward.

Things began to happen fast. Rawley told them the place seemed to be deserted but for this wounded woman and the child, but one of the warehouses was on fire and it smelled like burning green cannabis. Laine was taken to an ambulance, Mercy and Devon were taken to another while Cooper, Spencer and Rawley were held and locked into the back of police vehicles. From where they sat they could see SWAT move down the road in their armored vehicle with lots of armed men hanging on. They were followed by the fire department at a safe distance, waiting for an all-clear to go in and fight the fire. More vehicles appeared, a helicopter flew overhead and a spotlight was shone down on the area. Dogs were pulled out of police cars by their handlers and they jogged to the scene.

While there had been a couple of Trooper vehicles a couple of hours ago, now there was a small army. Floodlights were up, sirens wailed, radios chattered.

And Rawley said to Spencer and Cooper, "It's always better when they don't shoot back. I can't believe we got 'em out that easy."

Spencer and Cooper exchanged looks and said in unison, "Easy?"

He grinned, showing off his straight, white dentures. "You're just pups. Spoiled little pups."

* * *

Everyone in the rescue party was detained for questioning and because they were separated, Devon had no idea what had happened to Rawley, Spencer and Cooper. She was allowed to stay with Mercy and they were taken to the hospital together where Mercy was checked over by a pediatrician. It wasn't long before she was reunited with her friends from the FBI, including Emma Haynes. She explained everything that had happened and urged them to call Deputy McCain to verify. They didn't grill her like before—this time they asked her some questions, then let her join Mercy in a hospital room where she lay down with her.

In the morning Agent Haynes informed her that the fire had been stopped before it spread into the forest, but some buildings were destroyed. Jacob had tried to escape down a hidden back road that led out of the compound via the river, but when he reached a closed road and was met with armed police, there was an exchange of gunfire. He was killed.

And she cried. Sobbed against Emma Haynes's shoulder.

She wasn't sure if it was relief, that he could never threaten her or hold her captive again, or if there was something inside her that was a sense of loss.

Devon asked about the other women and children. Charlotte had rescued her son and little Liam, but Priscilla had stayed behind with Jacob. Her body was found in the house. Not even Laine could explain what had happened, but clearly Jacob shot her. Perhaps with Mercy rescued, he didn't need her anymore. Of all the people in The Fellowship, she was the only fatality besides Jacob. She was also the only one completely loyal to him.

Hours later Devon was told that Laine had come out of a successful surgery removing a bullet from her shoulder and repairing the damage as much as possible. She had been able to give most of her story so the authorities understood that none of them were a part of any conspiracy—they had merely gone on a mission to rescue Mercy. After many hours of statements and many dire warnings about taking such measures without the police, Devon was told that everyone had been released. Devon was asked if she'd be willing to go over her statements again, add information if she could, help them to wrap up the entire investigation.

"Yes, but I think you're going to have to come to Thunder Point with your fancy equipment and try not to disrupt my life too much. I'm the single mother of a child who has been through a lot and if I help you, you're going to have to help me a little."

Then Devon called Scott Grant and asked him if he'd come to pick her up and bring her and Mercy home.

Of course he wanted all the details, and he deserved them, but she was tired and almost limp with relief. She gave him the quick version and then told him that when she recovered, she'd tell him the whole story with all the little details. "Right now I just need a day of rest and some time alone with Mercy. Can I have a day off?"

He laughed and told her she could have whatever she wanted. "Spence went with you," Scott pointed out.

"Yes, because he's that kind of man. He's a good friend. A good neighbor. But that doesn't mean he's sorted out how he feels about me. And Mercy. That's a different story."

There was a football game the next night and Devon didn't go. She tried pretending she didn't even know about the game, but she was completely aware and wondered if he looked into the stands, noticing she wasn't there. And she wondered if it would matter to him.

She invited Rawley to come to her little duplex for Saturday night dinner. After they'd eaten and Mercy was occupied with one of her DVDs, they sat at the kitchen table over coffee and cookies and talked about their adventure. They exchanged information and filled in the blanks.

"The FBI has offered to get me some counseling," she told Rawley. "I'm thinking about taking them up on that."

"Might help," he said. "Now that's all a memory, you do what's right for you."

"And Mercy," she said.

"I ain't no expert, but if it's right for you, it's prolly right for her."

"I'll have to thank Cooper for his help."

"Aw, I think he had fun, truth be told," Rawley said.

"And Spencer."

"That boy's stronger than he looks," was all Rawley had to say. "Carried that woman at a jog for darn near two miles."

"He did," she said. And right up until he decided he wasn't ready to be serious, he had carried her a little bit, too.

Devon called Cooper to thank him for his help. It was no small thing, what he'd done. Not only could his life have been in danger, but then he had to suffer through at least twelve hours of questioning before he'd been allowed to go home. But being the kind of guy he was, he just said anyone would've stepped up just the same. "And if I hadn't gone with Rawley, I'd never have heard the end of it."

Nineteen

Spencer had dropped by the clinic the day after their rescue mission looking for Devon, and Scott had explained that she was relieved to have Mercy home and was exhausted, begging time off from work to try to rest and get her life back. He looked for her at the football game, of course, but was not entirely surprised she wasn't there.

He wanted to talk to her. Wanted more than talk, but he thought maybe she could use a little time. By the time Sunday rolled around, he could wait no longer. He made sure Austin was in Cooper's care then went to her house, but she wasn't there. He called her cell phone, but she didn't answer. He really didn't know what to do with himself, so like a smitten high school kid, he sat on her front step, waiting.

"Devon isn't home," Mrs. Bledsoe said when she saw him there.

"I know. I have to talk to her. I'll wait."

"Or you can walk down to the beach. The sun is out and she took that bag of beach shovels and pails that Mercy likes."

"Thanks, I'll do that."

He'd been to the bar, dropping off Austin, but he hadn't seen her on the beach. He decided to walk down the street past the marina and across the beach to find her. It was a little chilly although the sun was shining and there were only a few people on the beach. And Devon was on the part of the beach closest to the marina and farthest from the bar.

She must not have wanted him to see her from the bar. It filled him with dread.

She didn't look up until he was standing beside her. Mercy played in the sand a short distance away and she smiled at him. "Pencer," she said, and then went back to scooping sand.

Spencer dropped to the sand beside her.

"I've been meaning to call you to thank you," she said. "What you did, it was far and away the bravest thing in the world. Thank you."

"Devon, you were the brave one. You were ready to go alone."

She just shrugged. "When your child is at risk, you don't even think. You just do what you have to do."

"It's the same deal when it's the woman you

love," he said. "I went to the clinic to see you. Scott said you were taking a couple of days to try to recuperate."

"And think," she said. "I really needed to think. It's like a bad dream. A four-year bad dream. And it's finally really over. I don't have to be afraid to leave Thunder Point...don't have to be afraid of some bogeyman just around the corner."

"Listen," he said. "I've been wanting to talk to you. To explain..."

"Spencer, it's all right. I understand. After all you'd been through you weren't ready to get involved with some woman with a mysterious and bizarre past, with a child, with baggage. You don't have to explain."

He turned toward her. "If we hadn't been sidetracked by Mercy's abduction, this would be coming sooner. I realized immediately, I made a mistake."

"I know. It's all right. At least you caught it before it was too late."

"Devon, my mistake was that I almost lost you. I almost let you get away. The idiotic part is that I let you go *because* I was afraid of losing you. When you asked me to be responsible for Mercy, it hit me like a ton of bricks—if I let myself make a life with you and something happened, something completely unpredictable and catastrophic, like a car accident or...or cancer..." He stopped for a second. He reached for her hand. "It makes no sense at all, but I panicked. I thought—if something happens to her? How will I live? How many people can I lose before I go completely crazy? And you? Lose *you?* For just one split second I thought it would be easier not to have you at all than to face something like that. Again."

"I understand," she said. "I really do."

"Not yet, you don't. When you came to the bar to ask Rawley for a weapon so you could go after Mercy, I faced it head-on—there it was, that thing I feared the most, that your life could be in danger. And, Devon, I love you too much to let you go. I don't know if we'll have six weeks together or sixty years—it doesn't matter. All that matters is that I have you in my life, in my arms, for as long as we're lucky enough to get."

She stared at him, openmouthed.

He smiled at her. "Now is the part where you say you understand."

She turned toward him. "Spencer, think about what you're saying. You're not ready, you know you're not. This panic could rise again anytime. Don't get ahead of yourself here, because I don't want to love you and count on you and have you—"

He slid an arm around her waist and pulled her to him, holding her hard against his chest while he went after her mouth like a starving man. Her eyes flew open in surprise, but a moment later she was holding him, returning the kiss. He moaned in appreciation, wishing he would never have to release her. But eventually he did because there was talking to do. "I love you, Devon. I wasn't looking for it, I didn't expect it, but I love you. I was so busy worrying about my own fears, my own losses, I didn't really think about yours. You've been through so much, but you didn't even blink. You never panicked. You just faced it all head-on." He took a breath. "I don't know what life will throw at us, but I can't reel it back in. I'm in love with you. It's a done deal."

She just shook her head. "I don't know, Spencer. I do love you, but I'm afraid to get involved again. Maybe we should just give it some time."

"No time like the present," he said. "If you ever feel like you're in over your head or if you're having second thoughts, you tell me. I'm not going to hold you captive—I'm just going to love you as well as I can for as long as I can. I don't deserve it, but will you give me another chance? We were so good together."

"We were," she said, giving him a small smile.

"I want to marry you."

"Now wait a minute. I'm not sure I'm convinced enough to take that plunge."

"I just want to negotiate one plunge at a time—it's all up to you. Let's start with dinner and a game of Candy Land and after the kids are asleep..."

She couldn't help it, she laughed at him. But then she started to cry.

"Aw, baby, don't," he said, pulling her into his arms again. "Don't be afraid. I had a meltdown, that's all. You know I'm not really that guy—that afraid-of-commitment kind of guy. That was just an overreaction. I know how I feel, I really do."

"I'm a little too emotional to make a good decision about this."

"I scared you, that's all. I screwed up and made you think I'm fickle. That I don't know what I want or how I feel. That I scare easy. But I'm not any of those things. I'll prove it. Just let me try. Any time it doesn't feel right, all you have to do is say so, tell me what you want and you'll have it. I just want a chance. I can't walk away from you again."

"I want to," she said. "It made me so happy, loving you, being loved by you."

He wiped away her tears with the pad of his thumb. "Devon, I'd walk into hell for you, I love you that much. Let's take it one day at a time. Together. Can you trust me that much?"

She put her hand against his cheek. "Do you have any idea how special I felt with you? Curled up on the couch, just watching a movie? Hanging out with the kids? Watching you train or coach your team? Making love?"

"We'll have all that again, I promise. I'll be there for you, I swear."

"One day at a time? You'll let me relearn that I can count on you?"

"Absolutely. I won't rush you, but I'm ready."

She sniffed back her tears. "Okay, then. I'll give us a try."

He grabbed her and kissed her again, deeply, passionately, holding her against him so tightly he was surprised she didn't break.

There was a tapping on his shoulder and he broke away to stare into Mercy's beautiful blue eyes.

"Why you always kissing?" she asked.

"Because I love your mommy," he said.

"Oh," she said. And she turned and went back to her bucket and pail.

He chuckled. Then he looked at Devon and said, "The first thing we'll do is spend some quality time together. Then I'm taking you to a jewelry store so you can pick out a ring."

"Spencer," she said in warning.

"You don't have to wear it until you're ready, but I want you to have one. I want to spend my life with you. With you and Mercy and Austin."

"You're going to rush me," she said.

"Go easy on me, honey. I almost lost you."

"I almost lost you, too, Spencer," she whispered.

Eric got a call from Ashley—Gina wondered if he'd be willing to come to the house to have a chat with her and her husband. *Here it comes,* he thought. He didn't regret the way he played it out—giving them plenty of time to talk it over and give him an honest answer regarding his possible full-time presence in Thunder Point. It had been the right thing to do. He didn't expect her to be happy with such a decision. After all, it brought into focus so many regrettable things from her past. Not only had she gotten pregnant by some loser who'd abandoned her, but that loser had gone to prison. What woman in her right mind wanted regular reminders?

The service station in Thunder Point had been a good piece of property, one that he could easily renovate. It wasn't a rich town and he hadn't expected to turn a big profit on gas and repairs, however some of his customers had come from far away for his custom restoration work and if he added space and equipment to any property, many of them would follow him. Classic car restoration was not only good business, most of his customers collected cars—it wasn't usually a matter of one or two, but many. To that end, Eric had looked at many similar properties. He'd begun to like the idea of taking the investors' money and putting it into something new, some little gem he could grow into something good.

When he arrived in Gina's neighborhood at the edge of town, he felt an odd kind of happiness knowing that she'd settled herself so well. Life couldn't have been easy for her, living with her mother and raising their daughter alone. But now, while she was still young, she had a fine husband, a good home and many nonjudgmental friends in Thunder Point. It gave him a sense of comfort, if not relief, to know he hadn't completely destroyed her life. And she'd done an outstanding job with Ashley—she was as fine a young woman as any he'd ever met.

He had to park across the street and down the block. He walked to their house, up the walk and knocked on the door. Gina answered, smiling. "Hi, Eric. You're right on time."

"You said four o'clock. Listen, I hope you know I just want to be considerate of your feelings. Yours and Mac's."

"I know. That was thoughtful. And I want you to know, we discussed it at great length and you will have an honest response."

"Thanks, Gina. I understand, I really do. I know I asked a lot. Ashley doesn't really understand what it's like to have ghosts and hard memories."

"Oh, Eric," she said with a laugh. "Ashley understands that better than just about anyone."

"Right, I guess that's right," he said, remembering the rough spring she'd had, terrible breakup with a serious boyfriend, some cruel texting going on meant only to cause her hurt. "And I sure wouldn't want to cause her any more…"

"We're in the backyard, Eric. Follow me."

She turned and walked through the house. He passed by the kitchen and saw a couple of women who seemed to be preparing food in there. Then out the sliding doors onto the deck and there, in the backyard, mingling around a couple of barbecues and sitting at picnic tables were many teenagers and children and older couples.

"I'm interrupting something," he said.

Gina laughed. "No, Eric. You're definitely not."

Mac broke away from the grill, passing his spatula to a man beside him. He approached with his hand outstretched. "Welcome," he said. "Glad you could make it."

"What's going on?" Eric asked, immediately uncomfortable.

Gina put a hand on his arm. "The answer was easy," Gina said. "If you find a good business in this town and this is a place you'd like to settle, we'd be happy to welcome you to town. So we thought we'd introduce you to some of our friends."

It was a good thing he wasn't a crying fool, he thought. Not only was this one of the last things he ever expected, it was one of the kindest things anyone had ever done for him. "I don't know what to say…."

"Well, say hello. I'll make some introductions.

Then you can tell me how you'd like your burger, not that I'm very great at getting it right," Mac said. "Most of these folks have been here forever, but there are a few newcomers. They can give you some tips on settling in."

"If you decide this is the right place for you," Gina said. "We just thought we'd find a way to let you know—it would make us happy to have a new business and responsible citizen come to town. This seemed like a good way to demonstrate that."

Good way to let him know? he thought. If these people had any lingering hope that he'd give up this opportunity, they were going to be disappointed.

He wanted to be a part of a community that behaved with compulsive kindness.

There were only two more football games left in the season and the Thunder Point team was going to regionals. It was an outstanding team; Spencer was very proud of them. But on this overcast late October Sunday afternoon he stood on the beach with Cooper and Devon. They were looking not at the bay but up at the hillside. Cooper's house was framed already—no doubt because Cooper was relentless and wanted that house done enough to move into before his new baby was born.

Cooper pointed at the hillside, designating lots as he had divided them. "I'll show you the plot map, but understandably we have the lot next to the bar. There are twelve more single family sites available. I'm leaving a large piece of land between the last home site and the edge of town—I won't sell it. It's a nice buffer zone. Now how big a hurry are you in?"

Spencer dropped an arm around Devon's shoulders. She now wore a shiny diamond engagement ring, and it really hadn't taken that much convincing. "We're not as desperate as you and Sarah are, obviously. We have plenty of space for now. My house in San Antonio closed and there's no lease on the house I'm in, as you no doubt know. Devon has four more months on her lease, but we can always work with that. Another month or two, she'll be ready to move in with me."

"But when's the wedding?" Cooper asked.

"We're still talking about that," Devon said. "There's no hurry. I'm still giving interviews to the FBI and I really want us to have some time to adjust. And maybe get married when we both feel we've recovered from some of the challenges of the past few years."

He squeezed her tighter. "I'm ready right now," Spencer said. "And I'm ready to build her a house by the sea. Right here. It appears we're going to have some excellent neighbors."

* * * * *